8- 2024

MURDER
AT VINLAND

Books by Alyssa Maxwell

Gilded Newport Mysteries
MURDER AT THE BREAKERS
MURDER AT MARBLE HOUSE
MURDER AT BEECHWOOD
MURDER AT ROUGH POINT
MURDER AT CHATEAU SUR MER
MURDER AT OCHRE COURT
MURDER AT CROSSWAYS
MURDER AT KINGSCOTE
MURDER AT WAKEHURST
MURDER AT BEACON ROCK
MURDER AT THE ELMS
MURDER AT VINLAND

Lady and Lady's Maid Mysteries
MURDER MOST MALICIOUS
A PINCH OF POISON
A DEVIOUS DEATH
A MURDEROUS MARRIAGE
A SILENT STABBING
A SINISTER SERVICE
A DEADLY ENDOWMENT
A FASHIONABLE FATALITY

Published by Kensington Publishing Corp.

MURDER
AT VINLAND

ALYSSA MAXWELL

KENSINGTON
PUBLISHING CORP.

www.kensingtonbooks.com

KENSINGTON BOOKS are published by

Kensington Publishing Corp.
900 Third Avenue
New York, NY 10022

All Kensington titles, imprints, and distributed lines are available at special quantity discounts for bulk purchases for sales promotion, premiums, fund-raising, educational, or institutional use. Special book excerpts or customized printings can also be created to fit specific needs. For details, write or phone the office of the Kensington Special Sales Manager: Attn. Special Sales Department, Kensington Publishing Corp., 900 Third Avenue, New York, NY 10022. Phone: 1-800-221-2647.

Library of Congress Card Catalogue Number: 2024936521

The K with book logo Reg. US Pat. & TM Off.

ISBN: 978-1-4967-3621-5
First Kensington Hardcover Edition: September 2024

ISBN: 978-1-4967-3622-2 (ebook)

10 9 8 7 6 5 4 3 2 1

Printed in the United States of America

To Paul and Sara, who have each been my rock and my haven these past two years, and always.

Acknowledgments

Many thanks to the Facebook group Newport Lost and Found and to Mike Franco, who manages the group. Their thorough examination of Newport in days past made it possible for me to see pictures of Vinland in its original form, before the renovation and expansion that began in 1907.

A huge thank-you to my editor, John Scognamiglio; Larissa Ackerman, senior communications manager; Evan Marshall, my agent; and Stephen Gardner, cover artist, all of whom have worked closely with me to ensure the success of this series.

Chapter 1

❦

Newport, Rhode Island, August 1901

Even flanked by the palaces that were Ochre Court and The Breakers, the red-sandstone mansion dominated the near horizon like a mythical castle. Framed by the Atlantic, the house spread its wings as if in invitation to the men who had inspired the building of it, men who had braved the perils of the sea in their open longboats to explore our shores a millennium ago. Rugged ashlar-block walls, precipitously pitched rooflines, and wide, peaked turrets stood as a testament to the courage and sheer audacity of those Viking seafarers who may or may not have touched the shores of Aquidneck Island centuries ago.

It was a hotly debated subject on our island.

As I drove my carriage past the gatehouse and onto the circular driveway, I recalled how the former owner, Catherine Lorillard Wolfe, had been inspired by the Old Stone Mill in Touro Park, which, many said, had been built by visiting Vikings. She had insisted Vinland be designed with these Norsemen in mind. But as I alighted from my carriage and handed the reins off to a waiting footman, I couldn't help noting that, while the architecture might have harkened back to the Norway of a thousand years ago, I very much doubted the average Viking's longhouse bore much resemblance, in length, breadth, or height, to this behemoth of a house.

A tide of ladies engulfed me as I made my way toward the wide stone archways of the porte cochere, the sounds of wind, birds, and ocean no competition for their upraised voices. There wasn't a man in sight, other than footmen and grooms. But on a Tuesday in Newport, that was to be expected. Most gentlemen of the Four Hundred traveled back to New York during the week to attend to business and dutifully returned to join their wives on the weekend.

Several ladies called my name, and I paused to exchange greetings. My aunt Alice Vanderbilt and her daughter, Gertrude Whitney, caught sight of me and hurried over, the crowd between us parting liked scattering leaves at their approach. Aunt Alice, as *The* Mrs. Vanderbilt, even in widowhood, had that effect on most people. It had been two years now since Uncle Cornelius had left us, and Aunt Alice had abandoned black crepe and veils in favor of gray silk with lavender trim and a lace-covered hat trimmed in satin. It was good to see her resuming her social schedule and philanthropic activities. They had been a love match, Cornelius and Alice, and had shared both a religious devotion and a passion for charitable causes.

More familiar faces came into view: a now-elderly Caroline Astor leaning on the arm of her daughter, Mrs. Carrie Wilson; a stately Mary Wilson Goelet; and, perhaps the most welcome sight of all, Mrs. Edith Wetmore, wife of U.S. Senator George Wetmore, and their daughter, Maude. We had begun our friendship on the shakiest of foundations, and Maude, in particular, had treated me with skepticism at best, suspicion at worst. But all that was in the past, and now we often collaborated on charitable endeavors.

We were funneling through Vinland's entrance when a voice I did not recognize called out, "Mrs. Andrews, what a delight to find you here."

Expecting to encounter a familiar face, I turned to find a complete stranger at my side. I wondered, at the same time I opened my mouth to reply, whether I should pretend to recognize this dark-haired woman of middle years, still slender but with a sturdiness that suggested she was no delicate society matron. A much younger woman accompanied her, someone about my own age. She was a plain, auburn-haired individual who also struck no chord in my memory.

Before I could force out a word, the elder of the pair widened her smile and broke out into laughter. "Yes, that's right, my dear, I know who you are. I'm afraid I do have an advantage over you. But not for long, I assure you."

Her companion said nothing, but merely watched us with solemn hazel eyes. Before any further words could pass between us, we were swept through Vinland's front door along with the others, into the dark-paneled hall adorned with moldings whose geometric designs I guessed to be Norwegian in origin. While the others proceeded along the corridor and through a wide doorway into the dining room, the three of us paused beside the staircase. Three tiers of stained-glass windows at the half landing sent a mosaic of colored light cascading down on us. I glanced up, making out the forms of Norse gods and goddesses immortalized in the glass.

The elder of the two women gave my hand a firm shake. "Mrs. Andrews, do forgive my having taken you off guard. I am Amity Carter. *Miss* Amity Carter." She emphasized this with a note of unmistakable pride. Her voice also conveyed that I should now understand everything. I did not. She gestured to her companion. "This is my niece, Zinnia Lewis. We are lately come from Florida."

Amity Carter. Should that name have meant something to me? It failed to, as did the name Zinnia Lewis. Once again, I felt at a great disadvantage.

"My dear, I own the property adjoining yours on Ocean Avenue. I thought you knew."

Once again, she had rendered me speechless. I shook my head. "But the records state the property is owned by one Cecil Briarton . . ."

"Yes, my uncle. My mother's brother. He passed away at the beginning of the summer and left the property to me. He died childless, you see, and he and I were quite close."

"I see," I replied rather stupidly, and blinked. Miss Lewis offered me an almost apologetic smile, but I barely noticed as my mind raced ahead. Cecil Briarton had never built on the parcel, indeed had shown little interest in it for as long as I could remember. How would this sudden development affect my husband's and my quest to purchase the property, where we wished to build a new home for ourselves? The house we currently lived in, Gull Manor, which I had owned for nearly a decade, would become a school for girls.

At least, that had been our plan. Would Amity Carter wish to retain the property, perhaps build a summer cottage for herself? Then a different question had me frowning in puzzlement. "How did you know me?"

Before replying, she turned to her niece. "Zinnia, be a dear. Go in and find our seats, and I'll be along in a moment."

"All right." Miss Lewis spared me another slight, ambiguous smile, reminding me of the pictures of the Mona Lisa I had seen in books. "Lovely to meet you, Mrs. Andrews."

"Likewise, I'm sure."

She scurried off, her simple straw sun hat paling beside the silk, taffeta, tulle, and jewel-adorned chapeaux of the other ladies streaming into the dining room. She seemed a plain little sparrow lost among a bevy of exotic birds.

But speaking of which, I suddenly realized something—or the lack of something. Apparently, the guests either had been asked not to wear hats decorated with feathers, or they had deduced for themselves that displaying the plumage of rare birds at a fundraising luncheon to benefit the Audubon Society would be in bad taste.

I turned back to find Miss Carter grinning at me, her own hat lined in gray-blue silk to match her ensemble. "My dear, it seems everyone in this town knows who you are. It's not every city in America that can boast a lady journalist." She tittered. "But the other day I happened to pass you on the street while driving with Miss Twombly in her carriage, and she pointed you out to me."

"I didn't know I caused such a stir." I joined her in a chuckle. "You must have been on Spring Street?"

"Yes, Zinnia and I are staying at an inn on one of the side streets nearby." She told me the name of the place, and I disclosed the location of the *Messenger*, the newspaper owned and operated by my husband and myself. I burned to continue speaking with her, to discuss the property and what her intentions might be, but the settling of the commotion in the dining room signaled that we should hurry to find our seats. The program would soon begin.

Just inside the doorway, we passed along the receiving line, headed by Vinland's current owner, Mrs. Hamilton Vanderbilt Twombly, sister of Cornelius Vanderbilt and technically a distant cousin of my own. However, unlike the close relationship I had shared with Uncle Cornelius while he graced this world, and still shared with his wife, Alice, and their several children, Florence Twombly and I were virtual strangers. Hence, when I greeted her, I said, "Mrs. Twombly, thank you for inviting me. It's a pleasure to be here."

"You're quite welcome, my dear. But . . ." She leaned in, and I noted that her oval face, with its large eyes and prominent nose, retained a European-like charm even as she neared sixty. "I will remind you, Mrs. Andrews, that you are here as a guest, and while I will certainly understand mention of today's event in your newspaper—it is, after all, a good cause and we wish to gain as much support as possible—I admonish you to be discreet and not to report on intimate details about the house or my guests."

"Of course, ma'am." I struggled to keep my features steady, to betray nothing of my inner thoughts. But, like a child, I felt tempted to hold out my hands to show her I held no pencil or notebook. "You needn't worry."

"Needn't I?" She cast me a sideways glance and dismissed me with a blink before turning to the next guest in line. This happened to be Miss Carter.

"Amity, darling, I'm so glad you could come." Mrs. Twombly embraced this woman newly come from Florida, and I wondered how they knew each other. I searched my memory for prominent families named Carter, thought of a few, but couldn't place an Amity in any of them.

Miss Carter returned to my side, and the two of us wended our way through Vinland's dining room. Whatever large table usually dominated the space had been replaced by about a dozen round tables, each seating ten. Sprays of lilies and roses adorned the center of each table, artfully arranged but low enough to allow everyone to see their luncheon mates across the table. The ocean and a cloud-studded sky framed the view outside expansive windows.

At every place setting, a tented placard embossed in silver gilt bore the name of each guest, and throughout the room, footmen holding similarly embossed charts were assisting ladies to their seats. Where had I been placed among the crush? Halfway across the room, a lace-mitted hand went up, and I spied Miss Lewis's simple hat.

"I believe you're over there," I said to Miss Carter, pointing.

"Ah, yes, there she is." My companion craned her neck. "Is that an open seat beside her? Do come and see. I'd love for you to sit with us."

I wanted that, too, but as I set out with Miss Carter, a hail came from the opposite direction, closer to the podium that stood in front of the unlit fireplace, which was filled with long-stemmed roses. My cousin Gertrude waved at me. She was easy to spot in any crowd, being so much taller than the average woman. Rather than retake her seat, she started toward me at a brisk pace.

"Emmaline, come along," she admonished when she reached me. Then she noticed Miss Carter beside me. "Forgive me, Emmaline, do introduce your friend." I did, and once pleasantries had been exchanged, Gertrude said, "Please do excuse us, Miss Carter. Perhaps we might speak later. Come, Emmaline, Mother is waiting, and there is someone at our table who is anxious to meet you."

"But . . ."

Miss Carter patted my arm. "We'll talk soon enough, Mrs. Andrews."

I swallowed back a sigh. Whomever my cousin wished me to meet, I doubted my time would be more productive than if I sat beside Miss Carter. But Gertrude would not be deterred. She linked her arm through mine and drew me away.

"Wait till you see who it is." My typically composed cousin was nearly breathless with excitement. "We're lucky enough to be at the table of honor, and this person in particular—well, it's such a thrill to be seated with her. And what a coup for your newspaper. It was entirely Mother's doing that you're with us. Otherwise, Aunt Florence might have seated you somewhere in the back."

This last didn't surprise me. But the fact that Gertrude referred to the *Messenger* without shuddering or curling her lip made a significant statement and piqued my curiosity. However much my Vanderbilt cousins held me in their esteem, none of them understood my inclination to work. Never mind that for most of my adult life, working had been necessary to put food on the table for my little household. That I continued in my employment as a news reporter even though I'd come into an inheritance a year ago *and* married a wealthy man utterly baffled them.

We hurried along, returning greetings as we went, until we approached a table positioned directly in front of the podium. Aunt Alice sat beside Mrs. Twombly and her daughter, Florence, or Flora, as we called her to differentiate between mother and daughter. Across from them sat the two Wetmore ladies. The woman beside them was unfamiliar to me.

No, on second thought, I *did* recognize her, from having seen her photograph in the newspapers. Now I fully understood Gertrude's excitement.

"Emmaline, there you are." Aunt Alice forewent tsking at me, but only just. "Whatever kept you?"

Mrs. Twombly conveyed her own annoyance with a twitch of a dark, delicate eyebrow. I smiled apologies, which in the latter case met with imperial indifference. I wondered about the two empty places that remained at the table. Who besides me dared to offend the formidable Florence Twombly in her own home?

Gertrude's enthusiasm was not to be thwarted. "Emmaline—that is, Mrs. Andrews—I'd like you to meet Mrs. Theodore Roosevelt, our esteemed Second Lady of the United

States. Mrs. Roosevelt, my cousin, Mrs. Derrick Andrews. Of the Providence Andrewses."

I nearly winced at my cousin's reference to my husband's hometown, but managed to maintain even shoulders and a steady expression. Dear Gertrude, attempting to increase my social worth through my husband's connections. But then, my connection to the Vanderbilts was a thready one, my being a descendent of the first Cornelius — the Commodore, as he had been called — through one of his daughters.

But whether Gertrude's tactic worked, or if Edith Roosevelt simply possessed impeccable manners, I couldn't say, for she glanced up from under the brim of an elaborate picture hat and smiled as if truly interested in me. She was not a beautiful woman, her face being rather too square, her mouth flattish and her lips thin, and the shape of her eyes unremarkable. Nonetheless, the directness of her gaze and the confidence in her bearing made her a handsome woman, a woman who commanded respect.

"It's a pleasure and an honor, ma'am," I said, and half-wondered if I should curtsey. I was saved from such a quandary by Aunt Alice bidding both Gertrude and me to take our seats. A footman came up behind us and held first Gertrude's chair and then mine.

After settling, I greeted the Wetmore ladies, and we exchanged brief inquiries about our respective families. It was no surprise that the wife and daughter of a United States senator would be seated with the Second Lady; they must know each other well.

"I understand you're a journalist, Mrs. Andrews," Mrs. Roosevelt noted as a footman filled our glasses with citrusy Roman punch. "A noble profession, one our great democracy could not survive without."

"Indeed," Aunt Alice put in. "So rightly put."

Beside her, Mrs. Twombly harrumphed. I almost did too, as I happened to know Aunt Alice felt no love for the press. Both ladies would undoubtedly have disapproved of my wish to tell Mrs. Roosevelt that had I been able to, I would have voted for the present administration. However, when my gaze happened to connect with young Maude Wetmore's, I saw an admiration in her eyes, directed toward Mrs. Roosevelt, that suggested that if she could, she would have voted for that lady herself in a presidential election.

Imagine.

Two women hurried to the table, apologies on their lips. One appeared to be about Aunt Alice's age; the other, closer to the younger ladies at the table, myself included.

"We're so sorry to be late," the elder said.

"We tried our best, truly, but the ferry from the mainland ran late today," the young one said. A footman instantly appeared beside them and held their chairs for them.

"Ladies, this is Mrs. Harriet Hemenway, founder of the Massachusetts Audubon Society." Mrs. Roosevelt gestured to the elder woman, who nodded generally to all of us while attempting to rein in her rapid breathing. Mrs. Roosevelt then indicated the younger of our new arrivals. "And this is Miss Jeanine Pierpont, who is attempting to establish a society here in Rhode Island."

"Lovely to meet you all. Thank you so very much, Mrs. Twombly, for agreeing to host us." Miss Pierpont carried a youthful spark accompanied by a gleam of mischief in her wide-set blue eyes. "Call me Jennie, please."

"That's rather familiar at a first meeting, isn't it?" Mrs. Twombly sniffed and raised her glass of sparkling citrus punch to her lips. Beside her, her daughter, Flora, compressed her own lips in an effort not to grin.

Mrs. Twombly was even less appreciative of what happened next. Mrs. Roosevelt held up a hand toward me and addressed the newcomers. "Ladies, this is Mrs. Andrews, the reporter we've heard about."

That was all she said, but Jennie Pierpont's expression became immediately animated, even more so than a moment ago. "Delighted to meet you, Mrs. Andrews. I'm hoping you and I might talk afterward. Perhaps your newspaper might be of help in raising local awareness about the Audubon Society's role in protecting our native birds."

"Yes, of course. I'd be happy to discuss it with you. May I ask if you're related to John Pierpont Morgan?" I had had the privilege of making that man's acquaintance a year ago. It had been during a particularly trying time involving his cousin, Edwin Morgan, and the house he had built, called Beacon Rock, overlooking Newport Harbor.

"I am, but in a rather roundabout way," she replied. "Much as you are related to Mrs. Vanderbilt and Mrs. Twombly."

Aunt Alice cleared her throat loudly. I gathered she didn't like the direction my conversation with Jennie Pierpont had taken. One of Aunt Alice's quirks was that she often liked to pretend I was more closely related to her branch of the family than I was. I didn't hold it against her; in fact, I found it endearing that she preferred to think of me almost as a daughter rather than a distant cousin. Bluntly, she asked, "Emmaline, who was that woman you entered the dining room with?"

"That is Miss Amity Carter."

"Carter? Amity?" She drew her eyebrows together. "I don't believe I know her."

"I do," Mrs. Twombly put in. "She's a very old friend of mine. We attended finishing school together. Miss Porter's in Connecticut. She and her family had a falling out some years ago over her refusing to marry."

"Refusing to marry?" Aunt Alice looked as though this

were the highest of crimes. She turned back to me. "Emmaline, what interest could you possibly have in this individual?"

"Aunt Alice, you needn't worry. She owns the property next to Gull Manor, which Derrick and I wish to purchase."

"To do what with?" She sought Gertrude's eye, as if her daughter knew the answer to this question. Gertrude shrugged as I endeavored to satisfy Aunt Alice's curiosity.

"We wish to build a new house for ourselves and establish Gull Manor as a school for girls."

"Oh!" Her eyebrows went up, her eyes alight. "Yes, Newport could use a private finishing school for refined young ladies. Like Miss Porter's in Connecticut."

"Well, my plans are for it to be more than that. Much more."

Her frown returned. "You mean you wish to fill girls' brains with stuff and nonsense?"

"Aunt Alice . . ."

I got no further. At that moment, a small army of footmen began winding their way among the tables, each bearing a large silver platter held high in one hand, until he reached his destination and began serving the guests. The luncheon portion of the event had arrived, and I knew we could look forward to several lavish courses consisting mostly of meats and vegetables shipped here from Florham, the Twomblys' sprawling farm in New Jersey. As the rattle of china, the clink of crystal and porcelain, and the high-toned chorus of ladies' voices filled the room, conversation turned to the usual matters of upcoming weddings, debutante balls, summer soirees, and the latest fashions from Paris.

Such talk usually bored me, but it distracted Aunt Alice from the topic of my planned school, for which I was grateful. While I looked forward to the speeches that would be given following lunch, for now I busied myself with making mental notes of society's interests and concerns. It had become a habit several years ago, when I'd begun my journalistic career as a society columnist for another local newspaper, the *Newport Observer*. Nowadays, I reported on real news—politics, crime, economic matters, both local and farther afield, but my observations today would not go to waste. Although Mrs. Twombly had forbidden me my reporting tools, I possessed a long and accurate memory. I would relay many of these details to the society columnist currently employed by the *Messenger*, a young man who enjoyed the job with the enthusiasm I had lacked.

But that didn't prevent my attention from wandering from time to time, and as I studied the dining room, my gaze rose toward the ceiling. A gasp of appreciation broke from my lips. Circling the walls just below the ceiling was a wraparound frieze that appeared to tell a continuous story. As with the stained-glass windows on the staircase, these colorful and spectacular paintings depicted figures in medieval garb outside Nordic castles and on Viking ships, and other particulars out of both history and myth. As I scanned the scenes, my gaze lighted on a familiar sight: the Newport Tower in Touro Park, also called the Old Stone Mill, silhouetted against a sunset-streaked sky. Catharine Lorillard Wolfe had certainly taken Newport's legendary Viking heritage to heart in designing her summer cottage, creating a visual tribute to those adventurous tales.

Finally, the plates were cleared. With a somber expression, Mrs. Twombly came to her feet and went to the podium. She rapped on its surface twice for attention and was rewarded with a silence that spread instantly through the room.

She briefly thanked the guests for attending, urged everyone to open their purses and checkbooks to such a worthy cause, and introduced Mrs. Roosevelt. Thunderous applause brought a congenial flush to the Second Lady's cheeks as she rose. She talked about her and her husband's great appreciation for the bounteous natural beauty to be found in this country, and of her gratitude to people like Harriet Hemenway and Jennie Pierpont for their tireless efforts to ensure that future generations would reap the benefits of our natural world.

She ended by introducing Harriet Hemenway. The applause was rather less fervent, merely polite, making it obvious that many in attendance had never heard of her or her Audubon Society of Massachusetts. She soon remedied that, explaining the delicate balance of nature, the importance of every species on earth in maintaining that balance, and describing the vital role our nation's birds played in protecting the environment.

"Through the art of John James Audubon and his quest to make a pictural record of every native species of bird in America, awareness of one of our greatest national resources was born. Decades later, naturalist and explorer George Bird Grinnell carried on with Audubon's important work by continuing to document bird species and establishing the first Audubon Society. Today, we are furthering the cause of both men by creating Audubon Societies across these United States."

As Mrs. Roosevelt had done, Mrs. Hemenway ended her speech by introducing her successor, Jennie Pierpont. Like a schoolgirl, Jennie hopped up from her seat and very nearly skipped to the podium. Her buoyancy brought a smile to my face, and I decided I must make the effort to know her better. Rather than repeat Harriet Hemenway's treatise on the environment, Jennie outlined her efforts thus far to emulate the Massachusetts Audubon Society by creating one here in Rhode Island. She spoke of needing funds to establish a central group that would be headquartered in Providence, as well as local chapters around the state. One goal, she told us, was to organize squads of bird-watchers whose job it would be to catalog local birds and record the numbers of their populations.

Although for the most part I paid close attention to her plan, my gaze swept the room. I knew from experience how quickly the attention of the Four Hundred could roam. Many appeared rapt, but I also saw, here and there, the rolling of eyes and the raising of hands to hide yawns. At the next table, two older doyennes who were regular summer residents, Lottie Robinson and Ada Norris, eyed each other askance while avoiding looking directly at Jennie. I wondered what they found objectionable about today's topic, or were they merely bored? I hoped Jennie wouldn't notice and conclude that Newporters were rude by nature.

As I watched, Lottie Robinson sighed, but then instantly cheered. "I see they're about to serve dessert."

Footmen had entered the dining room, once more bearing silver platters. These held crystal stemware filled with something that looked fruity, creamy, and luscious. Other footmen carried silver coffee carafes and teapots. It didn't take long for attention to wither away from Jennie Pierpont and home in on the anticipated delicacies. Dismay that she was quickly losing her audience crept across her features. She sped her words to finish before all was lost.

"I therefore beseech you, ladies, to open your hearts and your checkbooks to this most worthy cause before it is too late. Before we come to regret our carelessness with the beautiful creatures entrusted to our keeping by God. Thank you."

Applause rang through the dining room. Had Jennie won them over? Would they not only make generous donations, but join the Rhode Island Audubon Society at well? Or were they applauding the arrival of the fruit trifles, now being set before each delighted guest?

"Good grief, Harriet," Jennie whispered to her neighbor

when she resumed her seat. "I believe it was a mistake to come here. Most of them didn't seem to care a whit."

Her voice, hardly a whisper, carried to the nearest tables, evidenced by several contrite expressions.

"Don't worry, Jennie, you did splendidly," Mrs. Hemenway assured the younger woman.

"You were positively an inspiration," Mrs. Roosevelt generously offered.

"You were, Jennie." As I spoke, a footman set a trifle before me. "I believe you made more of an impact than you think. If some of them appeared uncaring or disrespectful, I believe it was out of their own embarrassment for not understanding, until today, the consequences of their fashion choices."

With a puzzled look, Mrs. Wetmore set down her spoon. "Whatever do you mean, Emma?"

Before I could answer, Aunt Alice hissed at me from between her teeth. "Emmaline, that is quite enough, thank you."

Gertrude cleared her throat and turned her attention across the table. "My cousin is correct, Miss Pierpont—"

"Please, do call me Jennie."

Gertrude blinked and hesitated. Like her mother and Mrs. Twombly, my cousin found such familiarity among newly made acquaintances quite unacceptable. Without using Jennie's first or last name, she said, "You and Mrs. Hemenway have opened my eyes. I intend to join your organization, and at such time as there is a chapter in New York, I shall join that one, too."

Maude Wetmore nodded vigorously. "The same goes for me as well, Miss Pierpont—uh, Jennie, if I may. You are right, birds are lovely creatures and should be protected. Isn't that so, Flora?"

Her spoon buried in trifle, Flora Twombly looked up. "Indeed, yes. Most definitely."

"There, you see?" Mrs. Hemenway patted Jennie's forearm with motherly affection, while Mrs. Roosevelt looked on with approval. "Our cause shall prevail."

As soon as the dessert course ended, the ladies in the room began to mingle and open their handbags to donate to the future Rhode Island Audubon Society. I wondered how many of them truly had been persuaded of the importance of such an endeavor, or were some merely saving face by contributing? With an inner shrug, I excused myself to my tablemates and hurried to find Miss Carter and her niece.

"I'm glad you haven't left yet," I said as I reached them. "I wished to invite you to my home tomorrow so we might discuss the property—your property—if that's agreeable to you, Miss Carter." I held my breath, hoping she didn't demur.

"It most certainly is, Mrs. Andrews. Your home is Gull Manor, isn't it?"

"It is."

"Then name a time, and Zinnia and I shall see you tomorrow."

We settled on nine o'clock the next morning. Then I handed a check for my donation to Jennie Pierpont, took my leave of Edith Roosevelt and the others, and left Vinland with a gleeful sense of optimism.

That feeling would not last long.

Chapter 2

At eight o'clock the next morning, Derrick drove our carriage into town to pick up Miss Carter and Miss Lewis. By a little past nine they, Derrick, and I were picking our way along the rocky shoreline of Miss Carter's property. A swirling fog had settled over the coastline, merging sea and land into a study in muted gray that even the sun couldn't burn off. My dog, a mixed brown and white spaniel named Patch, bounded ahead of us, sometimes disappearing into the shrouded landscape and suddenly reappearing like an apparition. The mist dampened our skin, but Miss Carter had waved off my suggestion that we return to Gull Manor and come out again later.

"I walk every morning, no matter the weather," she said stoutly, and Miss Lewis confirmed this with a nod and a crooked smile. Miss Carter took large steps as she counted off the yards from one side of the property to the other, her hems trailing haphazardly in the wet grass. Miss Lewis, meanwhile, held her skirts aloft and surveyed the area from a convenient hillock. Whenever Patch circled to her side, she reached down to pet him.

Derrick and I followed slightly behind Miss Carter, allowing her to explore, measure, and take stock of her inherited land. Would she decide she couldn't part with it? I couldn't imagine selling such a parcel, but then, having grown up on Aquidneck Island, I couldn't imagine a more beautiful place on earth, even on such a somber morning as this.

"I wish I knew what she was thinking," I whispered to Derrick, as we walked arm in arm at a respectful distance behind Miss Carter. "Her expression gives no hints."

"She said she wished to sell," he reminded me and patted my hand where it rested in the crook of his elbow. "We've no reason to believe she'll change her mind."

"Then why is she being so meticulous?"

He gave a half shrug. "It's sensible to know exactly what one is parting with."

"I suppose." But I loathed this waiting, this wondering. Over the years, from when I'd first come to live at Gull Manor with my aunt Sadie, and later, after I'd inherited the house from her, I'd given this neighboring property little thought other than its being the vacant lot next door, which eventually, someday, would be built upon. It wasn't until a month ago, when Derrick had proposed purchasing the land, building a new home, and using Gull Manor as a school—such an exciting prospect—that a sense of urgency to own the lot had filled me. And once I set my sights on a goal, letting go of it became a near impossibility.

Over my shoulder, I glimpsed Miss Lewis standing on her vantage point and slowly turning to take in her surroundings. Unlike me, she showed infinite patience with her aunt's musing and measuring, as if she were content to remain here all morning enjoying the views.

I turned back to Derrick. "I'm going to see if the niece knows what Miss Carter intends to do."

He chuckled in reply and allowed me to slip my arm free.

Miss Lewis didn't appear to notice my approach. She faced the ocean, the fingers of her right hand curling as if to grasp something. She looked entranced—even, I thought, enchanted. Oh, dear, was she thinking she might like to live here? Was that the advice she would give her aunt?

"Miss Lewis, what do you think of our coastline?" I asked as a precursor to what I truly wished to know.

"It's spectacular. The light in the clouds, and on the waves—it's sublime. So silvery and luminous. I grew up in Pennsylvania and never saw the ocean until I joined my aunt in Florida. The ocean there, and the coastline, is entirely different. Brighter—so much brighter. Oh, I realize it's a foggy day here, but in Florida, there are many shades of blue and green in the waves. Here, there is a deepness of hue, in spite of the mist, or perhaps because of it, and a kind of solemnity to the waves and rocks that touches one's soul." Finally, she turned toward me and curled her lips in a rapturous smile.

My eyes had widened at her surprising assessment. "Goodness," was all I could think to say. Not that I didn't agree with her. But I hadn't expected such a philosophical view from a first-time visitor.

She glanced away and back, and then laughed. "I am sorry, Mrs. Andrews. You'll have to forgive me, but I look at all nature with an artist's eye. I dabble in watercolors and oils, and I sometimes forget myself."

"I suspect you do more than dabble, Miss Lewis, to have such insight into the landscape."

"You must think I'm ridiculous."

"Not at all. My father is an artist, so I do understand. You also show an uncanny appreciation for the environment. Is that why you and your aunt attended the luncheon yesterday?"

"Did you not know? We're both members of the Florida

Audubon Society and have been since its founding a year ago."

"I didn't know. How fortuitous your visit coincided with yesterday's luncheon."

"Indeed, yes. Aunt Amity is a naturalist and an author who writes about our Florida environment." Miss Lewis hopped down from the hillock, plucking damp strands of hair from her cheek. "I suppose I get my appreciation of such matters from her, but my main interest is in capturing my surroundings on canvas."

"This explains quite a lot, and no, I didn't know about your aunt's occupation. I'm delighted to hear about it. I'm always pleased to learn of other women engaging in professional endeavors." I paused a moment, then decided to satisfy my curiosity. "I understand she attended finishing school with Mrs. Twombly."

"Yes, and Mrs. Twombly has read some of Aunt Amity's books."

Obviously, Amity Carter hailed from society, or she could not have been educated at the same institution as a Vanderbilt. Yet her name continued to elude me, suggesting that Miss Carter had removed herself from that society a good number of years ago. I wished to satisfy my curiosity about her, but it was far too personal a matter to ask about.

"I'd never met Mrs. Twombly before," Miss Lewis confided. "Tell me, does she frighten everyone?"

That drew a laugh from me. Based on our short conversation so far, I revised my opinion of Miss Lewis from yesterday. Then, I had believed her shy and rather uninteresting, I'm ashamed to say. Now I saw that she not only possessed keen artistic perception, but a sense of humor as well.

"She is certainly a woman of the old school. Very nineteenth century in her views and tastes, like so many of the doyennes of the Four Hundred. But don't let her frighten you. She's made of flesh and blood, just like the rest of us."

She held my gaze for a long moment, then asked, "You speak of the Four Hundred with a note of censure. Are you not of them? I'd heard you're a Vanderbilt."

"I am related to the Vanderbilt family, but, as Jennie Pierpont would put it, in a roundabout way. I was raised here in Newport in a modest home. My parents are currently living in France, among other artists. My husband comes from wealth, but he and I are working newspaper people, as I'm sure you know."

She suddenly beamed at me. "I'm glad of it, Mrs. Andrews. Although Aunt Amity hails from one of the Philadelphia Main Line families, neither she nor I are what one would consider wealthy." She had referred to Pennsylvania's version of the Four Hundred, railroad investors who made vast fortunes and built their mansions along that state's main railroad line. "I was feeling rather out of my element here, until now."

I regarded her, then had an idea. Before I could voice it, Miss Carter and Derrick came walking toward us. "Your delightful husband has filled me in on your plans for the property, Mrs. Andrews, and I must say, I highly approve. I believe this is a situation in which we can all win. You shall have your new home and your school, and I shall have a tidy income, once the money is invested properly, for Zinnia and me to live quite comfortably."

My heart leapt with joy, but I drew a breath in an effort to appear calm. "Your niece has told me you're an author, Miss Carter. And a naturalist."

"Has Zinnia been singing my praises again?" She bestowed a fond look on her niece. "Yes, both are true. If the two of you have never been to Florida, please do accept my invitation to visit us in Palm Beach. You'll want to come in the winter months, of course. I shall introduce you to the marvels and curiosities of our subtropical environment. It's quite different from anywhere else in this country, with a beauty all its own. And, oh, the birds! They are quite spectacular."

Derrick and I exchanged glances. I nodded eagerly, and he said, "We would love to take you up on that offer, Miss Carter. Thank you."

"Why don't we go to the house, have some tea, and discuss the sale," I suggested, and the four of us started back across the damp terrain. "Patch, come," I called over my shoulder, and he came prancing to us with a chorus of happy yips.

Since we had all breakfasted before our outing, upon returning to Gull Manor we adjourned to the parlor while Katie, my maid-of-all-work, prepared tea. Nanny had greeted us at the door, but immediately the telephone beneath our staircase had set to jangling, and she had shuffled over to answer it. Now, her voice drifted into the parlor, raising my curiosity.

"You don't say . . . How odd. No, she seems fine to me, but I'll ask her. We have guests this morning who were also at the luncheon. No, they seem perfectly all right . . ."

I listened for the click of the mouthpiece settling onto its cradle and then heard Nanny's footsteps in the hallway. I called out to her, and she entered the parlor with her hands clasped at her waist and a solemn look that suggested unfortunate news. "Nanny, what is it?"

She replied with a question of her own. "Are all of you feeling all right?"

Derrick and I exchanged a glance, as did Miss Carter and Miss Lewis. "Whatever do you mean?" I asked her.

"That was Agnes Singleton," she said, and for the benefit of our guests added, "the housekeeper at The Breakers."

There were few servants along Bellevue Avenue whom Nanny didn't know; they kept track of one another and all the news at the grand cottages, often learning of illnesses, crimes, and even financial disasters before anyone else in town. It was a network of information that had proved invaluable to me countless times. "It seems one of the ladies who attended Mrs. Twombly's luncheon has taken quite ill with what appears to be food poisoning."

"Oh, goodness." Miss Carter pressed a hand to her bosom. "Zinnia, do you feel unwell?"

"Why, no, not at all." Miss Lewis's gaze darted to me. "Mrs. Andrews?"

Derrick reached across the small space between our easy chairs. "Yes, Emma, are you quite well?"

"Fit as a fiddle." I frowned as a vague sense of alarm prodded. I had felt somewhat under the weather earlier this morning when I'd first awakened. But it had passed quickly, and I'd been fine ever since. Then I did a mental count. "There were quite a lot of ladies there. Around one hundred and twenty. It goes without saying that we were served from different cuts of meat, different batches of shrimp and capon, so not all of us would have consumed the tainted food. Who is ill?"

Nanny crossed to the sofa and perched on its overstuffed arm, beside Miss Lewis. "Charlotte Robinson. Was she at your table?"

"No, although she sat nearby." A burst of fear brought me to my feet. "What about Aunt Alice and Gertrude? And Mrs. Roosevelt? Are any of them ill?"

"No, they're fine," Nanny replied without hesitation. "Agnes said her two ladies were right as rain this morning, and the Second Lady hasn't reported any ill effects either. She's been staying at Vinland, too, but she's leaving today."

"Too?" I sank back onto my chair. "Who else is staying there?"

"Why, Mrs. Robinson," Nanny said.

I cocked my head. "Doesn't she have her own house on Narragansett Avenue?"

"She sold it after her daughter married," Nanny said with a touch of know-it-all pride. I noticed our guests following the conversation with intent looks on their faces. "The couple has moved to Maryland, so Mrs. Robinson intends to relocate near them and isn't planning to spend a lot of time in Newport anymore."

I couldn't suppress a wry grin. "You certainly do keep informed, don't you, Nanny?"

She grinned back, looking like a Cheshire cat. "It was a bit of a scandal, Miss Robinson marrying that young man. Chester Herbert is his name. He'd been previously engaged, but . . ." Nanny cast a sideways glance at the two ladies on the sofa and compressed her lips. "Here I am carrying on. You must think me a wretched gossip." They started to protest, but Nanny lifted her bulk from the arm of the sofa. Katie strode in with the tea tray, and once she set it on the sofa table, Nanny moved to follow her out of the parlor. "I'll let you four discuss the property next door. Call if you need anything."

Miss Carter and Miss Lewis looked disappointed, and I guessed they would have liked to hear more about the scandal concerning Mrs. Robinson's daughter. I, for one, intended to ply Nanny with questions at the first opportunity.

Before Miss Carter and Miss Lewis departed, intending to return to their inn near Spring Street, I offered them a room at Gull Manor. Seeing how relieved Miss Carter was at the prospect of selling the property next door, I realized money might be tight for the pair, as it was for so many single ladies.

While Derrick was bringing our carriage around, I proposed they collect their things and return that very afternoon.

"My dear Mrs. Andrews, we couldn't," she said, holding up her palms.

"Of course you could. That is, if you don't mind sharing. But our guest room has a large bed, and I daresay the two of you would be quite comfortable."

"Well . . . we're sharing now." Miss Carter questioned her niece with a look.

Miss Lewis first raised her eyebrows, then gave a little nod. "I could paint the ocean, especially in the morning, when the sun is rising." Her face took on a rapt expression. Her gaze shifted to me, and she added, "I have a travel easel that folds up into a carrying case that also holds my paints and brushes. It allows me to paint anywhere."

"Perfect," I said, with a clap of my hands. Patch rubbed against Miss Carter's skirts, conveying his concurrence as well. "You must join us here, then. The morning light on clear days is exquisite. I can't wait for you to see, Miss Lewis. And being on the south end of the island as we are, we also see the last of the sun's rays on the water as well."

Still, Miss Carter hesitated. "But what about Mrs. O'Neal? We'd make more work for her, doubling the amount of cooking she'd need to do."

"Nanny has Katie to help her, and besides, she need only add more to what she's already preparing." I moved closer to the woman and lowered my voice, as if to impart a special secret. "And her cooking is quite a treat, I can promise you that. Do say you'll stay."

Miss Carter once again consulted silently with her niece, whose expression had turned to one of entreaty. Miss Carter nodded. "Thank you, Mrs. Andrews. Yes, we will stay, and be ever so beholden to you."

That notion I waved away. "Not at all." Carriage wheels

could be heard coming around the house. "Here is my husband. I think we can all squeeze in together. He and I must get ourselves to the *Messenger* this morning. When it's time to come home, we'll swing by and collect you. Oh, I think we should bring along an extra carriage for your luggage. We'll hire one in town."

"We haven't much," Miss Lewis said. "But who will drive the second carriage?"

"I will, of course."

That brought a grin to Miss Lewis's face. Derrick jumped down and assisted each of us up onto the leather seat. On the way into town, I announced my intention of stopping in at Vinland that evening to inquire after Mrs. Robinson.

Derrick and I kept busy attending to usual matters at the *Messenger*—he with issues of management and finances, me with local articles and those sent over the wires from the Associated Press. I also typed up the social and fashion details I remembered from the luncheon for Ethan, and then drafted my own article about the Audubon Society and Jennie Pierpont's goal of establishing a chapter in our state. I still needed to interview her privately. Vinland had been too noisy yesterday, Jennie too involved in taking donations, and Mrs. Twombly too disapproving of my profession, for us to have conducted the interview there.

Just before lunchtime, Derrick came down the hallway to my small office near the rear of the building. Detective Jesse Whyte of the Newport Police strode in behind him, his derby in his hands and his reddish hair tousled by the wind.

"I was just informed by Dr. Kennison that Mrs. Robinson doesn't look to be suffering from food poisoning." Before Derrick or I could ask what the doctor did think, Jesse went on. "It looks more like some kind of toxin."

Derrick, who had perched on the edge of my desk, as was

his habit, came quickly to his feet. "You mean someone tried to poison the poor woman?"

"I didn't say that." Jesse and I had known each other as long as I could remember, both of us having lived in the Point section of Newport before I moved to Gull Manor. We never stood on formality, and in recent years, he had come to rely not only on my connections to members of the Four Hundred, but also on the insights I shared with him about both our summer residents and our year-round locals. "It could be some kind of household chemical, most likely used in cleaning, that somehow got into something she ate."

"Has anyone else at the luncheon taken ill?" I asked. "What about the Second Lady? I heard she was of sound health, but—"

"Apparently she was also staying at Vinland," Jesse said. I nodded, and Jesse confirmed what Nanny had told me. "She's gone on to Providence and from there to Boston, apparently. As far as we know, she hasn't reported having any illness."

"Thank goodness for that." I allowed a sigh of relief to escape my lips.

"Mrs. Robinson might have ingested the toxin this morning at breakfast." Jesse began to pace back and forth in my small office, one I typically shared with our society columnist.

"Ethan is out on assignment," Derrick said. "As soon as he returns, we'll ask him if he's heard about anyone else falling ill in the past twenty-four hours." He turned to me. "Where is he now?"

"The polo grounds, and after the match, I believe he'll be covering the picnic at Chateau-sur-Mer." I consulted the watch pinned to my shirtwaist. "In fact, that's probably where everyone is by now."

"Good, then he'll be in a position to notice any unusual absences." To Jesse, Derrick said, "So what's next?"

"We've sent a pair of bluecoats to Vinland to ask questions and poke around the kitchen. I'm going out there soon."

I narrowed my eyes at Jesse. "If you're so certain this was accidental, why are you going?"

He gave a soft laugh. "Because this is Mrs. Twombly, and we have to be certain."

Derrick widened his stance and faced Jesse down. "Are you about to involve my wife in a potentially criminal matter again?"

Jesse held out his hands, palms up. "Didn't I just say we believe it was an accident?" Before either I or Derrick could respond, Jesse's arms fell to his sides, and he assumed a sheepish expression. "But yes. Emma, if I might ask you to accompany me to Vinland . . ."

"Of course," I said without hesitation, before Derrick could object.

He did anyway. "Then maybe you should think about hiring her on instead of endangering her with no compensation."

"Derrick . . ." I murmured.

"I only need her to help smooth things with Mrs. Twombly. You know how your sort can be, especially the ladies." Jesse referred to Derrick's family being, essentially, members of the Four Hundred, even though they hailed from Providence. His father's New England newspaper fortune and his business interests tied to New York more than qualified him for membership in that particular club of America's elite.

Derrick gave a loud "Ahem." He didn't appreciate the reference and had no qualms about letting Jesse know it. They had engaged in an ongoing rivalry ever since they had met several years ago—mostly to do with me. And while time had alleviated the cause of their contention, they seemed often to revert to it out of habit. I believed they enjoyed it.

Men.

I came around my desk and grasped Derrick's hands. "Don't worry so. I've helped Jesse before and have come out all right in the end. And you know I can move about these cottages and talk to their owners in ways he cannot."

His mouth tightened. His eyes held mine in a kind of supplication. Then the hard line of his jaw relaxed, and he sighed. Then nodded. My long-suffering husband knew me too well to try to stop me from doing something I deemed important.

I smiled up at him. "We'll make short work of this, I promise."

He laughed, a sound that held more cynicism than humor. Jesse and I left shortly after, climbing into his police buggy and heading over to Ochre Point.

When we arrived at Vinland, Mrs. Twombly herself let us in the front door. She appeared visibly shaken, her usual poise having failed her.

"Thank you for coming, Detective," she said in a tremulous voice. "Your officers are already here. I believe they're looking through the kitchen and pantries."

"Yes, thank you. I'll join them there, if you'll point the way." He removed his derby and tipped his head. "How is Mrs. Robinson?"

"The same. I simply cannot understand it." Mrs. Twombly turned her attention to me. "Mrs. Andrews, I didn't expect you, although perhaps I should have." A raised eyebrow both censured and accepted the reason for my presence.

"I hope you don't mind." We kissed the air beside each other's cheeks, more like casual acquaintances than family.

"I do wish to check in on Mrs. Robinson. And then I can assist Detective Whyte in interviewing the female staff."

She nodded, closing the door softly behind us. When she turned back around, she said, "You might find it rather upsetting, seeing Lottie."

"Upsetting?" I exchanged a glance with Jesse.

"In what way, ma'am?" he asked.

"I suppose you should see for yourself." A shudder skidded across her shoulders. "But be prepared. It's quite unsettling."

She led us down the long hall and to the staircase. The stained-glass windows at the half landing washed us in myriad colors until we made the turn and continued up. Here, another long hall mimicked the one below it. We walked partway down, where we came to a closed door. Mrs. Twombly knocked softly.

A woman in nurse's garb opened the door. "Yes?"

"Miss Webber, this is Detective Whyte and Emmaline Andrews. They've come to see Mrs. Robinson."

"She's sleeping at the moment." Still, the nurse opened the door wider and stood aside to let us enter. I knew her face, youthful and fair, with small but keen eyes and a prettily bowed mouth. My good friend, Hannah Hanson, was a nurse at the Newport Hospital, and I had met Miss Webber through her. We nodded our acknowledgment of each other.

"Come," she said, and beckoned us to follow her to the side of the bed. Charlotte Robinson lay on her back in the middle of the mattress, her head and shoulders supported by downy pillows, the satin comforter tucked beneath her chin. Her hair lay in salt-and-pepper whisps about her head, and her eyes were sunken and surrounded by blue shadows in a face as white as tissue paper. But it was her mouth my gaze adhered to, the raw and peeling flesh surrounding her lips, and the lips themselves, split in several places and looking as though they would bleed at the slightest touch.

"Yes, you see now," Mrs. Twombly said.

"Yet they don't see," Miss Webber said cryptically. "Not really. Inside—her tongue, the roof of her mouth, her throat—all burned as if she'd swallowed fire. One can only guess at the damage to her stomach."

Beside me, Jesse hissed a breath between his teeth. A wave of fear and nausea swept over me. I tamped it down, and asked, "Will she live?"

Nurse Webber exhaled. "Only God knows, Mrs. Andrews."

Chapter 3

"When is the doctor coming back?" Jesse walked slowly around the bed, staring down at the patient, as if to view Mrs. Robinson's wounds from all angles.

The nurse consulted the clock on the clothespress. "Soon, I should think. He left orders for me to telephone the hospital if there was any change. But there hasn't been. He administered a dose of morphia before he left, and that's kept her sleeping ever since." She sighed. "She couldn't stand the pain, otherwise."

"Good heavens." I touched my fingertips to my lips. "What could have done this?"

Miss Webber—her first name suddenly came to me, Renata—leaned over the bed and touched a hand to Mrs. Robinson's forehead. "I don't know. Doctor Kennison isn't sure either. He's thinking perhaps it could be bleach or lye, but neither of us has ever seen anything this severe before. It's most perplexing."

I looked at Jesse. "Both are found in kitchens."

"Along with other strong chemicals. Carbolic acid, ammonia, rat poison—"

"Rat poison wouldn't do that." I pointed to Mrs. Robinson's inflamed lips. "Although I suppose ammonia and carbolic acid could. But how could she have ingested it?" I suspected an answer: It wouldn't be the first time carbolic acid, a common cleaner, was confused with baking soda in a kitchen.

"Did Dr. Kennison administer syrup of ipecac and activated charcoal?" Jesse asked the nurse.

"Yes, both. And while those might help flush out and neutralize the toxin, I'm afraid there's no undoing the damage already done to her internally."

"So her chances . . . ?" I left off saying the worst, but Miss Webber completed my thought.

"Aren't good, I'm sorry to say."

Jesse glanced around the room. "Where was she found, and by whom?"

"I found her, Detective." Mrs. Twombly clearly didn't wish to relive the initial shock of discovering her friend in such a state. "She was here in the room. There." She pointed to a spot right in front of one of the ocean-facing windows.

"What time was that, ma'am?"

"Just after nine. We had breakfasted early with Mrs. Roosevelt before she left. Then Lottie—Mrs. Robinson—came back upstairs. We had discussed possibly going to Bailey's Beach around midmorning, and I knocked on her door to see if she still wished to go. When she didn't answer, I opened the door . . . and saw her." Her gaze lighted on the wan face propped against the pillows, on those raw lips that resembled a tattered red flower. "That's when I telephoned the doctor."

Jesse had pulled out a small notebook and took down the details. "Did she say anything to you?"

"No, nothing. She was unconscious."

"All right. Thank you, ma'am. I'd better get down to the

kitchen and see what my men have found so far." Jesse nodded to Mrs. Twombly and left the room.

"What I found strangest of all," Mrs. Twombly said, after the door to the room closed, "is that she seems to have ingested so much. One would think that, at the first burning touch or the first rancid taste, she would have realized her mistake." She appealed to the nurse. "But that doesn't appear to be the case, does it?"

"No, and I can't understand it either, because what you say is true." Miss Webber adjusted the kerchief securing her hair away from her face. "Nature provides us with natural deterrents when it comes to toxic substances; they are pungent and repulsive to the taste. At least in most cases."

Most cases. What did that leave us with? I thought of certain flowers and plants, such as poison ivy and poison sumac. Then, a possibility came to mind: lily-of-the-valley. Those tiny, bell-like flowers carried a lovely, sweet scent, but were poisonous if consumed. They could even cause blisters on the skin.

I asked Mrs. Twombly, "Do you grow lily-of-the-valley on the property?"

"Yes, as a matter of fact, we do. Along one side of the box hedge surrounding the rose garden." Her brows drew together. "Could it be that? But why would Lottie eat the flowers?"

A good question. She wouldn't, unless someone had either ground them up and put them into something she ate or Lottie Robinson was not in her right mind. Aloud, I suggested the former.

Mrs. Twombly looked aghast. "Do you mean to say this was intentional? That someone . . ." She gave a quick shake of her head. "Why would anyone want to harm Lottie Robinson, a widow who lives quietly and modestly?"

I don't know that I would have termed Mrs. Robinson's

lifestyle modest. Although the house she had owned on Narragansett Avenue was no palazzo, chateau, or Gothic Revival mansion, it had nonetheless been elegant and large, and had undoubtedly earned a princely sum when she sold it.

Then Nanny's words from earlier sprang to mind, something about a scandal involving the marriage between Mrs. Robinson's daughter and son-in-law.

"I'm not saying it was definitely intentional, Mrs. Twombly. I'm only suggesting it's a possibility that must be considered." But I intended to quiz Nanny as soon as I got home. Again, I scanned the room, looking for a tray or a pot of tea. I saw neither. "Did you all eat the same breakfast?"

"Essentially, yes. I don't believe Lottie had anything other than fruit and toast, and all three of us partook of that. I've felt no ill effects."

I went to the dresser and studied the items inhabiting its surface. Nothing appeared out of the ordinary. A few magazines were stacked at one end, topped by a newspaper. I read the date and saw that it was today's *Newport Daily News.* A porcelain vase contained several pink roses amid a spray of white lilies. Beside it sat a jewelry box, a folded scarf, and a pair of silk gloves. And my own purse, which I'd placed there when I'd entered the room.

I drifted to her dressing table. Again, only what one would expect littered the leather-covered top: a brush and comb set, a cut-crystal perfume bottle with atomizer, a hand mirror, etc. The perfume bottle recaptured my attention. I lifted it and sniffed, then gave a careful squeeze of the rubber bulb. A mixed floral scent formed a cloud in front of me before dispersing into the air. I detected nothing unusual.

Turning back to Mrs. Twombly, I said, "Since you had all eaten downstairs, Mrs. Robinson would have had no reason to order anything sent up from the kitchen, true?"

"Lottie was not an overeater, I assure you. She always eats

sparingly until luncheon, especially if she's having lunch later at the home of a friend. She always says she doesn't wish to offend her hostess by turning down offered treats."

"Treats . . ." I went to the bedside table and opened the drawer. No secret cache of sweets greeted me. Frowning, I let my gaze roam the room again, avoiding looking directly at the patient. The nurse had retreated to a chair in the corner, pretending she wasn't listening to every word spoken by Mrs. Twombly and me. I addressed her directly. "Miss Webber, when you first came into the room, did you see anything Mrs. Robinson might have consumed?"

She shot me an offended look. "If I had, I would have told the doctor immediately."

"Forgive me, I thought it necessary to ask." I walked to the spot where Mrs. Twombly had indicated she'd found Mrs. Robinson. "Was she sprawled here? Or had she collapsed in a heap?"

Behind me, Mrs. Twombly huffed. "I can hardly see why that should matter."

I looked at her over my shoulder. "Everything matters, as Detective Whyte will tell you."

She exhaled audibly through her nose. "I suppose one might say she collapsed in a heap. She was not stretched out, nor on her back. She was on her side and curled up."

"Then, whatever happened to her, happened here, or very near to here." I walked the couple of feet to the window. Its low sill was about even with my knees, and its soaring height nearly reached the ceiling. Heavy damask drapes swooped on either side and formed a valance along the top, while sheer lawn curtains undulated in the breeze blowing through the raised sash. Then something caught my eye. "What's this?"

Behind one of the sheer curtains, a cardboard box sat on the sill, its gold-foil lid partly askew. Rather than reach down and lift it, I sank to my knees and moved the curtain out of the way. I could partially see inside to what looked like a few petit fours, each iced in a vivid color. I glanced around for Mrs. Twombly.

"Look at this. Had you seen it before?"

She bent low and peered over my shoulder. "Why, no, I hadn't. I wonder where she got them?"

I didn't wish to touch anything—not after seeing what had happened to Mrs. Robinson. I had removed my gloves, and now, seeing that Miss Webber had vacated her chair to see what we were looking at, I asked her to bring me my purse. "It's on the dresser. Please."

When she brought it to me, I opened it and extracted my gloves. Only after they were securely on my hands did I touch the lid of the box. There were three petit fours nestled in tissue paper, not enough to fill the box. How many had she eaten? Then I noticed a short length of gold twine attached to a calling card. Carefully, I lifted and turned the card enough to be able to read the words across its front.

I dropped the card and pressed my hand to my mouth.

"What is it?" Mrs. Twombly's hand came down on my shoulder, her fingers curling as if to hold me in place. "What does it say?"

"It says"—I drew a breath—"*To my dear Mrs. Robinson, with my compliments. Yours, Edith Roosevelt.*"

Leaving the box of petit fours exactly where I'd found it, Mrs. Twombly and I returned downstairs and sent a footman to find Jesse. We waited for him in the drawing room. Like most of the main rooms, this one lay at the back of the house, overlooking a covered piazza and, beyond that, the rear lawn and the ocean. It also adjoined the dining room. All traces of yesterday's luncheon had vanished, and the round tables had been replaced by the usual dining table.

Picturing the room as it had been, I tried to remember who'd sat where, and with whom. I remembered that Lottie Robinson had been seated at a table next to my own. Who had shared the table with her? It wasn't difficult to recall. Its placement so close to the podium meant that those seated there were noteworthy guests, and, one by one, faces appeared in my mind's eye: Mamie Fish; Tessie Oelrichs; May Goelet; an aging Mrs. Astor and her daughter, Carrie; and several others of their rank and wealth. There had been no one there whom I would have considered capable of such an act of violence against another human being, much less one of their own.

The sound of footsteps in the hall broke off my speculations, and I turned to see Jesse hovering in the doorway. He looked hurried, his brow creased with concern and his mouth tight with impatience. "Mrs. Twombly, you sent for me?"

"Yes, please come in, Detective." She gestured toward one of the chairs that faced the sofa on which she sat, her back flawlessly straight and her hands folded primly in her lap. "We—that is to say, Mrs. Andrews—has made a startling discovery upstairs."

Jesse took a seat, and so did I. "And what would that be?" he asked. Traces of impatience lingered in his bearing, in the tapping of his toe against the Persian carpet. I got right to the point.

"There is a box of petit fours upstairs on one of the windowsills in Mrs. Robinson's room. The window she collapsed in front of. And there is a note attached."

"How on earth was it missed earlier?" Jesse swiped angrily at strands of hair that had fallen over his brow.

"It's behind a curtain, hardly where one would expect to find a box of baked goods." Mrs. Twombly's tone mimicked a calm state of mind. But just as I recognized Jesse's impatience, I spotted the evidence of Mrs. Twombly's agitation: her rapid blinking and the ridge of trepidation between her eyes. The tightness in how she clutched her hands.

"Did you touch anything?" Jesse demanded.

"Only the cover of the box, enough to see inside," I said, "and I moved the card to be able to read it."

"You shouldn't have touched either." His greenish eyes sparked with censure. "You know that, Emma." He started to rise. "I'd better have it collected and brought down to the station, see if these petit fours contain anything harmful."

"It looks as though she might have eaten several," I told him. "And there's more." I held out a hand, as if to hold him in his chair.

He sank back against its cushion. "What?"

"The card. It was signed from Mrs. Roosevelt." As I made this pronouncement, Mrs. Twombly shook her head at the impossibility of it. I agreed. The thought of Edith Roosevelt having had a hand in what happened to Lottie Robinson was ludicrous.

"The Second Lady?" Jesse stared at me in incredulity.

"Do you know of another Mrs. Roosevelt who lately stayed at my home, Detective?" Mrs. Twombly shook her head again, this time in derision.

"No, I don't." Jesse's shoulders sank. "It's not possible . . ."

"Of course, it's not possible," my relative snapped.

Jesse went on as if she hadn't spoken. "Or if Mrs. Roosevelt did leave the box for Mrs. Robinson, then it can't contain anything harmful. Her illness must have been caused by something else."

"You won't know until the petit fours are tested," I reminded him. "It's possible that whoever gave that box to Mrs. Robinson used Mrs. Roosevelt's name as a ruse, so Mrs. Robinson would have no reason to suspect anything untoward."

"They did get on quite well together while they were both here," Mrs. Twombly commented. "However, Mrs. Roosevelt didn't leave me a box of petit fours. Which doesn't make sense since I was her hostess."

He nodded slowly. "If Mrs. Roosevelt didn't hand Mrs. Robinson that box herself, we need to find out how it was delivered, and by whom."

Mrs. Twombly cleared her throat. "Did your men find anything in the kitchen?"

"They found plenty, ma'am." Jesse shrugged. "But nothing that isn't found in any kitchen. We'll take samples and have them compared in a laboratory with any substances found in the cakes."

Mrs. Twombly wrinkled her brow. "How will you be able to tell?"

"There are chemical tests that allow for the identification of certain substances."

"And what if this isn't a certain substance?" she persisted.

Jesse blew out a breath. "Then we'll have a problem. But if not Mrs. Roosevelt, who might have taken the box to Mrs. Robinson's room?"

"A maid?" I looked to Mrs. Twombly for confirmation.

"If it had been delivered to the house along with other deliveries and today's post, it would have been taken up by one of the upstairs chambermaids."

"Then we'll have to speak with the chambermaids," Jesse said. "Can you have them assembled for me, ma'am? How many are there?"

"There are three." Reluctance entered her gaze for an instant, then faded. "I'll have my housekeeper tell them to report to the servants' hall. Will that do?"

"As long as the rest of the staff know not to enter the room until I'm through," Jesse replied with a nod. "And I'll need a copy of the guest list from the luncheon."

The reluctance crept back into Mrs. Twombly's features. "Yes, all right."

"I'd appreciate it if that were ready for me by the time I leave." Jesse patted the arms of his chair decisively and pushed to his feet. "Emma? Will you accompany me?"

In reply, I stood as well, and the two of us trekked through the house until we came to the door tucked beneath the staircase, which opened onto the servants' domain.

Jesse visibly relaxed once we'd left the formal part of the house. He walked and spoke with more authority than when dealing with Mrs. Twombly and didn't wait to be invited into a room. Apparently, Mrs. Twombly must have alerted the housekeeper to our imminent arrival on the in-house telephone. The woman led us into the servants' hall, a large room at the end of the corridor, opposite the kitchen.

"Please be seated. I'll send in the first girl presently." The woman didn't offer us any refreshment; Mrs. Twombly obviously hadn't told her to.

"You'll need someone to check the flower beds," I said to Jesse. "Specifically, the ones with lily-of-the-valley."

He nodded absently, though I knew he'd heard me and would attend to the matter later, even if he didn't think lily-of-the-valley a likely culprit. To be truthful, neither did I. Not with the kinds of burns we saw around Mrs. Robinson's mouth.

He drummed his fingertips on the table. Sharing his restlessness, I abandoned my chair and strolled into the half-round bay that formed part of the south turret at the front of the house. But whereas the upper portions of the turret drew the daylight inside through tall windows, the casements here were narrow, and a high stone wall formed a small courtyard outside, blocking most of the view and the light—while also shielding arriving guests from the servants' activities within.

From the kitchen and pantries came the sounds of prepara-tions—the clanking of pots, the clinking of porcelain, and the impatient intonations of a man I assumed to be the French chef.

A knock sounded on the jamb of the open doorway. "Sir? Mrs. Delgato says you're wantin' to see me?"

I turned to see a slip of a girl in her late teens perhaps, wearing the starched apron and cap of a chambermaid. Jesse came to his feet and politely beckoned her in. On the way here, he and I had acknowledged that whoever had delivered the package to Mrs. Robinson's room likely had no idea of its contents.

"Please, come sit down," Jesse said and pulled out a chair for the girl. Her eyes widened and adhered to Jesse's face as she approached the table.

"Thank you, sir," she said with a note of disbelief. When Jesse scooted the chair in for her, she craned her neck to look up at him, and then followed him with her gaze as he rounded the table to retake his own seat. I couldn't help smiling at the adoration I saw blossoming in her eyes, though it was a bittersweet sentiment that I felt. Poor thing, to be so taken with the simple act of a man holding her chair for her.

"I'm Detective Whyte," he said, "and this is Mrs. An-drews. She's here for your comfort, miss, and to assist me."

Her eyes, golden brown, widened even more. "Have I done anything wrong, sir?" Her gaze darted to me. "Am I in some sort of trouble?"

"No, you needn't worry," I assured her. "Would you tell us your name, please?"

"First and last," Jesse clarified.

"Marian Rush." Her bottom lip disappeared between her teeth. She waited.

"Are you from Ireland?" Jesse asked. I, too, heard the

faint lilt in her voice, but it was not nearly as pronounced as most of the Irish maids I'd encountered.

"I am, sir, but I've been here since I was twelve years old. My da says I sound like a regular Yankee..." Her lips pressed tightly together for an instant. "I'm sorry, sir. You probably don't wish to know about that."

"That's all right, Marian." It was Jesse's turn to smile a reassurance. "Can you please tell us if you delivered any packages this morning to Mrs. Robinson's room? She's a guest of your mistress. You know who I mean, yes?"

"Yes, sir. The nice lady who has been staying here these past few days. She gave me a tip and asked that I always be the maid that takes care of her room. Said I remind her of a maid she had years ago, who left her when she got married."

Jesse shot me a glance. It appeared we had gotten lucky on our first try in identifying who might have delivered the petit fours.

"The package," Jesse reminded her. "Did you deliver one this morning?"

She thought a moment. "Why, yes, I did, sir. A small one, with a ribbon. I took it up with her newspaper, fresh flowers, and her laundered linens, while Mrs. Robinson was downstairs at breakfast." Then she frowned. "Is anything wrong, sir?" Her nervous gaze darted to me again.

"Marian, Mrs. Robinson is very ill," I said. "You mustn't return to her room again until Mrs. Delgato says you may."

"Ill? But she was fine this morning. I saw her as she was going downstairs." She gave a little gasp. "Oh, but I didn't talk to her or anything. I wouldn't be so forward."

"It was sudden," I explained. "And we're trying to find out what happened. Now, this package...do you know where it came from?"

"It was brought in with the other deliveries this morning.

Probably with the post. I suppose it must have come from a shop." She shrugged. "That's all I know."

I nodded. Of course, that would be all she knew. The morning deliveries were typically brought in and separated according to whether they were intended for the kitchen or other service areas, or for the family in the main part of the house. I asked, "Who admits the deliverymen? Is there someone in particular in charge of that?"

"That would be Mr. Simmons. He's the butler."

Jesse and I conferred silently, and he said, "That will be all, Marian. Thank you."

"I can go?" She looked both hopeful and relieved.

"You may go." He stood as she did, once again impressing her with his gentlemanly behavior. Once she'd gone, he turned to me. "I'll need to speak with this Mr. Simmons, but I'm doubting we'll learn much more. I'd say whoever sent the petit fours did so cleverly, slipping them in with a host of other items. Possibly even hiring someone else to do it."

"I agree." I rose from my chair. "But at some point along the line, someone has to know where the box originated."

"That will mean checking with all the bakeries in town." He made a tsking sound. "That will take time."

"Why make Lottie Robinson ill, though?" I mused aloud. "So ill she might die?"

"Which begs the question whether they're hoping she does die, or if this was supposed to be some kind of warning." Jesse leaned with a hand propped on the table. "Seems if someone truly wanted her dead, she would be dead right now."

"A botched attempt," I suggested.

He shrugged. "What could that woman possibly have done to anyone to warrant this kind of deed?"

The question sparked my memory. "We need to speak with Nanny."

"Mrs. O'Neal?" Jesse looked taken aback. "What can she have to do with any of this?"

"Just this morning, she mentioned a scandal involving Mrs. Robinson's daughter." My heart beat faster. "Nanny always knows everything about everyone in this town. She just might have the answers to our questions."

Chapter 4

While Jesse instructed his men to check the flower beds for signs the tiny, bell-like blossoms had been torn from their stems, I made my way back upstairs to Mrs. Robinson's bedroom. The nurse had moved her chair to the bedside. She was leaning over her patient and holding her hand. Mrs. Robinson, by all appearances, slept on.

"Has she awakened at all?" I asked in a whisper after closing the door as quietly as I could.

Miss Webber shook her head. "Not a peep. She stirred a couple of times, groaned a bit, but her eyes stayed closed."

I drifted to the other side of the bed and gazed down at her. The sight of her pale cheeks and raw lips made my heart ache. Yes, Nanny had said there had been a scandal connected to her daughter's marriage, but at the same time, that marriage and the promise of future grandchildren must have been a joyful prospect for Lottie Robinson. Would she live to see their futures? Would she hold her daughter's children, take them on walks, slip them little treats, teach them games? I said a quick prayer that she would.

Mrs. Twombly came in a few minutes later and told me Jesse was waiting for me in the hall downstairs. She made me promise to keep her informed if the police learned anything.

Although the plan had been for Jesse to drive me back into town once we had finished at Vinland, he wished to talk to Nanny immediately. I used the telephone in the housekeeper's parlor to call Derrick at the *Messenger* before Jesse and I took our leave. We drove down Bellevue to where it turned sharply near the southern edge of the island, became Coggeshall, and then turned again onto winding, hilly Ocean Avenue. Three beaches alternating with rocky shoreline lined the road to our left, and to our right stood the mansions of some of Newport's summer denizens who eschewed Bellevue Avenue for the more spectacular views to be found here: The Rocks, owned by the Clews family; Beachmound, owned by Benjamin Thaw; and Crossways, summer home to Mamie and Stuyvesant Fish. The farther we went, the fewer homes there were, just the rugged landscape, the boulders crouching in the waves, and the endless, heaving ocean.

The sun was out, and Gull Manor presented a much more welcoming aspect than it had this morning in the mist. Enticing aromas from the kitchen filled the front hall, making my stomach rumble. "You'll stay for dinner," I said to Jesse, rather than asked.

He made the customary noises of declining the offer, of not wishing to impose, but in the end, he accepted with enthusiasm. Especially once Nanny had shuffled out from the kitchen and added her entreaties to mine.

"You wouldn't want to insult me now, would you, Detective?"

"Heaven forbid, Mrs. O'Neal."

"Nanny," I said, as I kissed her cheek in greeting, "you're just the person we wished to speak with."

"Me?" She pressed a hand to her bosom in surprise, while her eyes sparkled with curiosity. "In that case, you two go into the parlor while I make tea and something to go with it."

After Nanny left us, the sound of carriage wheels crunched along the drive. The front door opened, and Derrick led our two new houseguests inside. Jesse and I stood to greet them. I made the introductions.

"Jesse, this is Miss Amity Carter and Miss Zinnia Lewis. They're here from Florida. Ladies, Detective Jesse Whyte of the Newport Police Department."

"My goodness," Amity Carter exclaimed. "While it is a pleasure to make your acquaintance, Detective, I surely hope no one here is under suspicion of a crime."

"Certainly not, Miss Carter. No one here is under suspicion, but I have come in relation to what does appear to have been a crime."

With an outstretched arm, Derrick drew the ladies farther into the room. "Let's all have a seat. Then I'm sure Detective Whyte will explain everything."

While the ladies made themselves comfortable on the sofa, Derrick and I stole the opportunity for a quick kiss. Then I took one of the armchairs across the low table from them, while Jesse took the other. Derrick went into the dining room and carried in a chair for himself.

"Now then," he said, when we were all assembled, "does this have to do with the guest at Vinland who took ill this morning?"

"It does," Jesse said. "And from all appearances, it wasn't an accident." His brows drew inward. "Carter. Lewis. Those names are familiar." Reaching into his coat pocket, he drew out the list of Mrs. Twombly's luncheon guests, unfolded the paper, and scanned the names. "Ah. You were both in attendance at Vinland yesterday. Perhaps you can be of help, then."

"We were there, sir." Miss Lewis stole a glance at her aunt. "And we heard all about the poor woman earlier today. But I'm afraid we can't tell you much. We weren't seated at the same table as . . . Oh, now, what was her name?"

"Mrs. Charlotte Robinson," I told her. "Better known as Lottie to her friends."

"Was she at at all improved when you left her?" Derrick's dark gaze held mine; it was full of questions. Concerns. A wish that I didn't have to become involved, yet with the full knowledge that I would.

"No, she wasn't." I sighed and then suppressed a shudder at the memory of those tattered lips, blood-red against the pallor of her skin. "She's very ill. I've seen food poisoning before, but nothing like this."

Miss Carter played with a fold in her skirt. "Do you know what did this to her, Detective?"

Footsteps, softly scuffing against the floorboards in the hall, announced Nanny's return. "Do I hear more voices?" She poked her head around the doorway, then disappeared back into the hall and called out, "Katie, put more water in the kettle and set out three extra cups." Then she came into the room.

Jesse immediately hopped up from his chair. "Sit here, Mrs. O'Neal."

She didn't argue, but took his hand as she came around the easy chair and settled in. "Now then, you said you had something you wished to talk to me about."

"We do, Nanny, something you can explain for Jesse," I said. "And since the rest of us heard a bit about it this morning, there's no reason we all can't stay. It's about Lottie Robinson's daughter."

Nanny pursed her lips and assumed an innocent expression. "I don't like to gossip."

I bit back a laugh. So did Derrick. Jesse bit his bottom lip to keep from smiling. He had remained standing, leaning with one elbow against the mantelpiece. "Don't think of it as gossip, Mrs. O'Neal," he said with a flourish of his hand. "You'd be providing me with information about this case. Now, Emma tells me there was some sort of scandal to do with the marriage of Mrs. Robinson's daughter. Can you explain what it was?"

Nanny's eyes glittered behind her half-moon glasses. While it was true that Nanny didn't enjoy gossip when it hurt other people, she did enjoy being in the know and being able to supply information few others had access to. She crossed her ankles and leaned a little forward. "Apparently, Mrs. Robinson's son-in-law—"

"Chester Herbert," I said, remembering the name she had mentioned that morning.

"That's right. Well, he had already been engaged prior to his attachment to Charla Robinson." In an aside, she added, "The young lady is named for her mother, Charlotte. Anyway, while the first engagement hadn't been formally announced yet, family members on both sides were well aware the pair had an understanding, as were the servants in each household."

"And that's how you found out about it," I guessed.

Nanny compressed her lips and nodded. "And then Mr. Herbert simply broke it off with the other young lady and married Charla Robinson. It was a most ungentlemanly act."

"Who was he engaged to?" Jesse began to reach inside his coat pocket, then let his hand fall. I realized he had been about to retrieve his notebook and pencil to take notes, then thought better of it. Perhaps he thought it might distract Nanny from her story.

"A young lady whose name you will recognize." Nanny gazed at me, then Jesse, and then Derrick. "Miss Sybil Van Horn."

"Sybil Van Horn?" Jesse once more consulted his list. "Miss Van Horn and Mrs. Van Horn were both at the luncheon."

"Why, I believe we met them." Miss Lewis turned to her aunt. "Didn't we speak with them, Aunt Amity? After the luncheon, while everyone mingled before leaving." She turned back to Jesse. "They weren't at our table either, but being a pair much like my aunt and myself—you know, a mature lady accompanied by a younger one—we naturally found ourselves drawn toward one another."

"Yes, I remember them," Miss Carter said, a look of concentration on her face. "They were quite lovely and, coincidently, Mrs. Van Horn said they'd been to Florida only last winter. Stayed at The Breakers hotel. Funny how close they were to Zinnia and me, though we didn't meet them at the time. But yesterday they seemed in a hurry to leave. I believe . . . well, I don't like to speculate . . . but I had the distinct impression they didn't wish to make a donation. Or perhaps were not able to. They were quite well dressed and appeared well-to-do, but looks can be deceiving."

"I believe I can explain about that." I shifted when Patch came up beside me, placing his front paws beside my legs on the cushion of my chair. I stroked the fur on his neck while I spoke. "It was in all the newspapers, so I'm not divulging anything that isn't public knowledge." I paused, thinking back to events I had read about over the Associated Press wires last summer. I had included an article in the *Messenger* concerning the basic facts, but not how it affected Mrs. and Miss Van Horn. "Mr. Van Horn was indicted on extortion charges and this autumn found guilty. He'd been stealing from the bank he co-owned with a partner and coercing lesser employees to cover for him through means of blackmail."

"Yes." Nanny let out a sigh. "Such a terrible ordeal for his wife and daughter. So humiliating. They were left quite in arrears, weren't they?"

"They were," I said. "They lost almost everything, not to mention the family's reputation. But I had no idea Sybil had been engaged or that the young man broke it off because of her father's crimes. Poor thing."

"What you also might not realize," Nanny said, "is that it was Mrs. Robinson who brought these matters to the attention of Mr. Herbert. She wanted him and his silver fortune for her daughter, and she used whatever means were available to have her way."

After dinner, while Derrick and our houseguests pored over a map of Aquidneck Island, I walked Jesse out to his carriage. Patch followed us out, trotting down the driveway in the gathering dusk and sniffing among the plants and hedges.

"Do you think Sybil Van Horn or her mother attempted to poison Lottie Robinson?" I asked him bluntly.

"I don't *think*, Emma." He stood in profile to me as he watched Patch suddenly take off after something he must have heard near the west side of the property. "I consider. I look at all the facts. And right now, given the facts, I am considering that Miss Van Horn might possibly have had a hand in Mrs. Robinson's illness."

"Because of her father, Sybil Van Horn's prospects are virtually nonexistent. Chester Herbert might have been her only chance for marriage." I touched his shoulder, seizing the whole of his attention. "I think you should consider Mrs. Van Horn as well."

"You're right. Perhaps even more so than the daughter, come to think of it. The avenging mother and all that. Not to mention they were both at the luncheon."

"Actually, I'm not sure why that should matter. Their resentment would have begun long before the luncheon." A gust of cool ocean air had me hugging my arms around me; I hadn't brought a shawl. "If one of the Van Horns decided to take revenge against Lottie Robinson, being at the luncheon shouldn't have mattered."

"Perhaps it mattered a great deal," he replied. "It provided an opportunity. The guilty party was able to use Mrs. Roosevelt's name as the sender of the package, ensuring that Mrs. Robinson would open it."

I nodded consensus to his point. "When are you going to speak with them?"

"Tomorrow, if possible. Do you know where they're staying?"

"Not at the house they used to own before Mr. Van Horn's troubles. They sold it for the funds. I suspect they're staying at one of the inns in town, much like Miss Carter and her niece were. I'd say with a friend, but they have significantly fewer of those these days. They're no longer received by most of the Four Hundred."

"Vipers." He swung his gaze to me. "Sorry. No offense."

"Why does everyone assume I'm one of them now?" I gazed up at the first twinkling stars in a purpling sky. "I'm not. If anything, Derrick is no longer one of them."

With a shrug, Jesse grinned at me. That rivalry he'd always shared with Derrick had apparently extended to me, but in the form of good-natured teasing. Then he sobered. "An inn. Even that's a lot of money for a pair of women with very little."

"I suppose Mrs. Van Horn is hoping it's worth it, that Sybil might attract a suitor before the summer is over. Mrs. Twombly might know where they're staying. I'll see if I can find out."

I returned to Vinland the following morning to find its owner sitting on the rear veranda, staring off into the horizon. The sun had risen well above the waterline, and the waves carried frothing hues of pink and orange. I began by inquiring after Lottie Robinson.

"The doctor says there's no discernable change," she said, without taking her eyes off the scene before her. She beckoned me to sit beside her. "He considered transferring her to the hospital, but he's afraid moving her would do more harm than good." She shrugged one shoulder. "I don't want that for her anyway." Finally, she looked over at me. "Is that why you came? To see how she is?"

"Yes, and no. I'm also wondering if you know where the Van Horns are staying."

"Anna Rose and Sybil? Why? Do you mean to pay a call on them?" Mrs. Twombly regarded me with an eager, hopeful gaze that initially puzzled me, until she explained. "They've been so lonely this past year. It is so unjust of society to turn their backs on them during their time of such need." The moisture welling in her eyes astounded me, until she tempered their effect on me. "Perhaps . . . I misjudged you, Mrs. Andrews."

Misjudged me? We barely knew each other. What could I possibly have done to earn her low opinion?

She must have seen the astonishment in my expression, for she quickly went on. "Forgive me, but you are a news reporter, and I've come to expect them all to have ulterior motives." She held the edge of the lace cap she wore against an updraft pouring over the cliffs at the base of the property. "I do my best to shield myself and my husband from undue scrutiny from the press. They tell lies, Mrs. Andrews, simply to sell newspapers. You cannot deny it." Finally, her features relaxed, and she took on an almost congenial air. "But perhaps, in your case, I am wrong to make such assumptions."

"I . . ." Good heavens, here I was under false pretenses, not to befriend the Van Horns, not to offer them kindness, but with the object of helping Jesse interrogate two suspects in a case involving poison. I began to wither beneath Mrs. Twombly's regard.

"Anna Rose and Sybil are staying on Carroll Avenue," she said. "It's not far from here, or from you, for that matter. Come inside, and I shall write down the address for you."

She led the way into the drawing room and from there across the long hall to a room at the front of the house. This space held a desk, a settee, and several comfortable chairs. There was also a deep bay window and an entrance onto another covered terrace that looked out over a circular garden at the side of the house. A fountain bubbled in the middle of a pool of fuchsia begonias.

Mrs. Twombly went to the desk and retrieved a notecard and a clothbound book from the top drawer. After flipping through it, she held the page with one finger and jotted something down on the card.

Straightening, she came around the desk and held out the card to me. "Here you are. Do give them my regards. I'd invite them here for a quiet lunch, but with Lottie upstairs . . ."

"Yes, I understand." I fingered the letters of Mrs. Twombly's name embossed on the front of the card. When I turned it over, I saw the address written in her neat hand. "I'll tell them you asked after them."

"Anna Rose and I go back a long way. To our childhoods on Staten Island. We used to hunt shells together on the beach, with our mamas or our nurses looking on. She was one of my dearest playmates, and later, we were bosom friends." She sighed, gazing out the window onto the front drive. "She doesn't deserve what happened to her."

I couldn't have felt worse about the errand that had brought me to Vinland. But it had been completed, and it was time for me to go. "Thank you for this. Should Mrs. Robinson awaken today, please tell her she's in our thoughts at Gull Manor."

She turned back to me and blinked. "Yes. Perhaps you and your husband will come for dinner some night . . ."

"We would love that," I said hastily, knowing she was only being polite. I backed toward the doorway as she went to the wall and pushed a button. An instant later, the butler appeared just outside the room. He saw me out, and I continued my carriage ride to town, my guilty conscience accompanying me along the way.

I delivered the address to Jesse and hoped he would visit the Van Horns without me.

"You'll come, won't you, Emma?" he said, as he set his derby on his head and prepared to leave the police station.

A wave of reluctance hit me. I held up my hands, my drawstring bag swinging from one wrist. "I do have other work to do. I should be at the *Messenger* by now . . ."

His eyes held mine. "It's hard enough interviewing ladies, but without another one present, it's downright excruciating."

"Excruciating? Really, Jesse, I hardly think so."

"It is. It makes me feel like a brute."

"Perhaps we have no reason to suspect the Van Horns," I found myself saying. "I'm sure they had nothing to do with Mrs. Robinson's illness."

He eyed me suspiciously. "What makes you say that?"

Because Mrs. Twombly would have it so. And because, I realized, I was perhaps just a little bit afraid of her. It was her upright bearing, I supposed, her black-and-white view of the world, her single-mindedness. The way she stood framed by all that Norse imagery, the gods and warriors depicted in the carvings and frescos and stained glass. Against all that, she stood out as formidably as a Viking out of myth. Zinnia Lewis had been honest when she'd asked me if everyone was afraid of her; I had been somewhat less than honest in my reply.

"Never mind," I said with a sigh. "Let's be off. The sooner this is done, the sooner I can be at the *Messenger.*"

I used the carriage ride, however, to ask him about the rest of the investigation so far. "Have you and your men been around to the bakeries yet?"

"A few. Good grief, I never realized how many there are in this town."

"And . . . ?"

"And asking if they had sold petit fours recently is like asking a bird if it's flown recently. The box they came in was plain—they all use them—and any identifying label had been torn off."

"I was afraid of that." I watched the wharves going by to my right, and the Newport Illuminating Company to my left, as we drove out of town on lower Thames Street. Industry gave way to residences and small shops. Finally, we veered onto Carroll Avenue, lined with newer if modest homes, their porches overlooking neat front yards.

Near Ruggles Avenue, the houses became sparser, bordered by a few small farms, and as we crossed the intersection, I said, "I'm afraid that even if you should happen to find the right bakery, they won't be able to identify the culprit. It can't be as easy as that."

"I agree," Jesse replied, with a sinking note in his voice. "It's very possible someone was hired to make the purchase and deliver the box."

I nodded and murmured, "It's what I would have done, had I been inclined to commit such a crime."

We found the house on Carroll Avenue a little past the intersection with Ruggles Avenue, in the interior of the island a couple of miles north of Gull Manor. It appeared to be a private home, not an inn, as there was no sign designating it as such. An attractive, middle-aged woman answered our knock, and a strong sensation of having done this exact thing before overcame me. But then, of course it did. How many times had I tracked someone down in the interest of investigating a crime? How many obliging and unsuspecting landladies had opened their door to me on the pretense that I had only come for a friendly visit?

Perhaps Derrick was right to wish I didn't become involved in every case that crossed Jesse's desk. No, not every case; only the dangerous ones. Soon, there wouldn't be a landlady or inn proprietor in Newport who didn't lock their door at my approach.

I sighed, wondering where this sudden reticence of mine had come from. I had never been reluctant to help Jesse before. I turned my attention back to the woman at the door. She informed us that Mrs. Van Horn wasn't in, but Miss Van Horn was. She showed us into the parlor, and then retreated down the first-floor hallway to the back of the house.

Moments later, Sybil Van Horn swept into the room. Her hands clasped at her waist, she stopped on the threshold with a look of surprise. "Mrs. Andrews, isn't it? What a lovely surprise." Her gaze found Jesse. "And . . . I'm sorry, I don't believe we've met."

He and I stood, and I said, "Miss Van Horn, this is Detective Jesse Whyte with the Newport Police."

"Oh. I see." Her complexion paled against the darkness of her hair, pulled back into a simple chignon, the kind a woman wore at home when she had no immediate plans to go out. No, I amended, for it was also the way a woman arranged her hair when she didn't wish to stand out, when she wished to blend in with her surroundings and draw no attention. Is that how she had learned to live these past months since her father's arrest? Her jewelry, too, was sparse, just a pair of small gold earrings, winking with pinpoints of light. A plain muslin day dress complemented the blue of her eyes. "What brings you here?"

"Please, Miss Van Horn, won't you sit with us?" Jesse held out a hand to beckon her into the room. She choose a delicate armchair with a petit-point design on its rounded back and seat.

Suddenly, her eyes went wide, and she jumped up from the chair as if it were lined in hot coals. "This isn't about Mother, is it? Has there been an accident?"

Jesse patted the air with his open palms. "No, Miss Van Horn, nothing like that. We"—he stole a glance at me— "that is, *I* need to ask you a few questions about Mrs. Charlotte Robinson. You do know her, yes?"

Miss Van Horn had begun lowering herself back into the chair, but the mention of Lottie Robinson brought her upright once more, her legs straightening like a pair of springs coiling back into place. "Yes, I know her. And quite frankly, Detective, I've no wish to talk about her. I wish she were dead."

She spun around and fled the room.

Chapter 5

I caught up to Miss Van Horn as she reached the threshold of her room. I glimpsed a bed and a modest sitting area before she whirled again to face me. "Mrs. Andrews, I'll thank you to leave me alone. As I said, I have no inclination to discuss that woman."

"I'm afraid you'll have to," I replied, as I caught my breath. I'd practically sprinted down the hallway after her. "Especially after what you said in Detective Whyte's hearing."

She eyed me blankly. "What on earth do you mean?"

"That you wished Mrs. Robinson was dead."

A scarlet tide engulfed her face. "Do you know what she did to me?"

"I do. And I understand your resentment toward her. But she's ill. Someone has attempted to poison her." I received another blank stare, and then a kind of horrified realization crept into her eyes. "And you think . . ."

"Please, come back to the parlor and speak with the detective."

She shook her head. "I don't want to. I had nothing to do with whatever ails Lottie Robinson. I swear it."

"If you don't, he'll have to use more official means of securing your cooperation." I held out my hand. "I'll be there, right beside you, if you like."

Her hand came up slowly. I watched it rise and move toward me, and I held my breath until it finally settled in my own. I closed my fingers around hers.

"I want my mother," she whispered.

I drew her at a slow pace back along the hallway. I didn't want to frighten her off. "When do you expect her?"

"I don't know . . . any time, I suppose."

When we entered the parlor, Jesse stood and made a little bow to Miss Van Horn, as if we were starting all over again. She ignored the gesture and strode past him to the settee. As I had promised, I sat beside her. That, too, she ignored, or appeared to, as she sat with a rod-straight spine and a level chin. Pride and self-preservation emanated in waves off her person.

I heard Jesse's release of breath as he resumed his seat opposite her. "Miss Van Horn, it seems you don't hold Mrs. Robinson in high regard."

"That's to put it mildly," she murmured. Then, louder, with greater assurance, she said, "Charlotte Robinson ruined my life. She destroyed what little reputation I had left and rendered me quite without prospects for the future." One eyebrow quirked. "Have you any notion what that means for a woman like me?"

Jesse swallowed, and I felt his discomfort acutely. "I'm sorry for your troubles, Miss Van Horn, truly. However, I need to know where you were yesterday morning. Where you were and what you did."

"Yesterday . . ." The bluntness of his question seemed to take her off guard, yet she appeared to seriously consider the question. "Today is Thursday. Yesterday, after rising and having a small breakfast here, Mother and I walked up to Spring Street and took the trolley into town. We went for a stroll once we arrived there." She tilted her head, and once again, pride oozed from her very pores. "We window-shopped along Bellevue Avenue, one of the few pleasures left to us. We sat in Touro Park for a few minutes."

"Did you stop in at any stores?"

"Didn't you just hear me, Detective? We window-shopped."

"Did you visit the post office, Miss Van Horn?" he asked next.

"No, Detective, we did not." She took on an impatient tone.

"How far down Bellevue Avenue did you stroll?"

Her composure suddenly slipping, she swiveled her head toward me. "What is all this? What difference how far down the avenue we went?" I slid my hand closer to hers where it rested on the sofa cushion, touching my fingertips to hers.

Jesse went on, maintaining his calm in the face of her agitation. "Did you walk as far as Narragansett Avenue and Ochre Point?"

She suddenly jumped up from the settee, knocking the embroidered pillow beside her to the floor. "No, we did not walk anywhere near Narragansett Avenue. We did not pass Ochre Point, and we certainly did not visit Vinland with the purpose of poisoning Mrs. Robinson."

From the hall came the sound of the front door opening, and then a voice called out, "Sybil, is that your voice I just heard?" Mrs. Van Horn turned into the room, a small package dangling on a string from one hand. "What on earth is going on here? Sybil, what is the meaning of this?"

Miss Van Horn hurried to her mother and threw her arms around her, but only for a moment. Then she pulled back and aimed an accusing finger at Jesse. "The detective is accusing me of attempted murder, Mother, or some such. I don't know. It's preposterous."

Mrs. Van Horn set her package down and grasped her daughter by the shoulders. "What can you mean? Whom did you attempt to murder?"

"Really, Mother, don't say it like that." At her mother's contrite look, Sybil Van Horn hurried to explain, "Charlotte Robinson. She's taken ill, apparently, and well . . . they're blaming me! They're saying I poisoned her."

"I said no such thing," Jesse spoke up and, overcoming his astonishment at Mrs. Van Horn's sudden arrival, remembered his manners and pushed to his feet. "I've come only to ask your daughter—and you as well, ma'am—a few questions."

"That's not precisely true, Mother," Miss Van Horn whispered quite audibly.

Mrs. Van Horn's outraged gaze homed in on me. "Could you do nothing to stop this, Mrs. Andrews?"

"She's helping him, Mother." Miss Van Horn tossed her hands in the air. "She threatened me, saying the detective would take official action if I refused to answer his questions."

"Well!" Anna Rose Van Horn injected more venom into that single word than the most venomous snake into its prey. "I will thank you both to leave this instant. My daughter and I have nothing to say to either of you."

"I'm afraid that's not possible, ma'am. Not yet." Jesse resumed his seat. I imagined he certainly did feel quite the brute by now. For that matter, I wasn't feeling much less of one. "If we could all calm down and remain seated, we can finish up this business, and Mrs. Andrews and I will be on our way."

I moved to a side chair to allow the Van Horns to sit together. This also gave me a better vantage point from which to observe their expressions and movements.

Jesse waited until the ladies had settled before asking, "What is the nature of your relationship with Mrs. Robinson?"

"We do not have a relationship with Mrs. Robinson, Detective." Mrs. Van Horn sniffed with disdain, while her daughter's jaw hardened as she gritted her teeth. "Oh, perhaps at one time we considered her an amiable acquaintance. That was, until she interfered in my daughter's engagement..." She compressed her lips.

Jesse nodded his understanding. "You needn't relate those details. We—"

"Already know all about it?" Mrs. Van Horn huffed. "Yes, it's common knowledge, isn't it? How my daughter and I have been humiliated this past year." She stared down at her feet, then back up with blazing eyes. "It's quite amusing, isn't it, Detective?"

"What I was about to say, Mrs. Van Horn"—Jesse appeared unfazed by her short diatribe—"is that we are only interested in any encounters either of you have had with Mrs. Robinson in recent weeks, and what the two of you did yesterday morning."

"Oh." Her posture relaxed ever so slightly. She reached for her daughter's hand. "No, we have not seen Mrs. Robinson, other than at Mrs. Twombly's luncheon the day before last. And that was from a distance. We left immediately after the speeches specifically so that we didn't run into her."

"And as I have already told you," her daughter added, "we were window-shopping yesterday morning. Isn't that right, Mother?"

Anna Rose Van Horn turned her head to regard her daughter. A pause stretched into awkwardness as some sort of communication passed between them. Then the woman turned back to Jesse. "As my daughter says, Detective. Window-shopping."

He let another pause expand before speaking. "Can anyone corroborate your claim?"

"Such as . . . who?" Mrs. Van Horn held out her hands. I noticed that, for the most part, her daughter seemed content to let her mother do most of the talking.

"Such as," I interjected, "did you run into anyone in town yesterday? A friend, a shopkeeper, someone who can attest to your being on Bellevue Avenue in the hours before noon." Surely, the pair still counted a few friends from among their former social circle, besides Mrs. Twombly. I waited for their reply, hoping very much they could name someone—anyone. The thought of their being so alone filled me with sadness.

Mother and daughter again traded silent communications. I could have sworn some knowledge or other passed between them, but I could not have said what. Finally, they both turned back to us with bland expressions.

"I'm afraid there is no one," Mrs. Van Horn said. "It was early, and there weren't many people about yet. Perhaps you'll be good enough to take our word for it, Detective." She raised her chin with a moue of wounded pride that reminded me uncannily of her daughter.

Jesse cast a glance at me. With a nod, we both came to our feet. "Mrs. Van Horn, Miss Van Horn, thank you for your time. If I have further questions, I'll be back." I noticed he didn't respond to Mrs. Van Horn's suggestion that he simply trust them.

Jesse went to the front door, but I didn't immediately follow. "Please understand that a woman has been attacked, and it's necessary to discover who is responsible. You might look at this as the detective's way of weeding out possible suspects until he arrives at the guilty party."

Miss Van Horn quirked that eyebrow of hers in a show of haughty curiosity. "Do you believe we're guilty, Mrs. Andrews?"

"No, Miss Van Horn." My answer, or, rather, the decisiveness of it, surprised me.

"Why not?" her mother asked.

The answer came to me. "Because it's too easy. Too convenient." But, inwardly, I shrugged at my logic. Perhaps it was merely hopeful thinking. This pair had been through so much. Could they not simply be left alone to recover?

"Well." I gathered myself to leave. "I'm sorry to have upset you so."

In reply, they both compressed their lips, shut their eyes in a long-suffering manner, and nodded.

"What were your impressions?" Jesse asked during our drive back into town. "Were they hiding something?"

I chuckled. "Everyone is hiding something at one time or another." But then I considered his question more seriously. "They were on edge, that much is certain. But whether it's because they're guilty of trying to murder Lottie Robinson, or they're simply afraid of what life might toss at them next, is unclear."

He turned onto Broadway, heading south. "I can't say I blame them."

"What did you think?"

He gave half a shrug. "Like you, I don't want to believe they're guilty. And their indignation is perfectly in keeping with the way the ladies of the Four Hundred tend to behave when they have to deal with something unpleasant. The notion of cooperation often doesn't occur to them, even when it might be in their best interests."

He was right about that.

On the sidewalk, near where Marlborough Street met

Broadway, a uniformed officer strode along on his beat. I recognized him at once by the bulk of his shoulders and his easygoing gait. I pointed. "There's Scotty."

He saw us, too, and waved. Not a friendly wave, but an urgent one. Jesse maneuvered the carriage to the side of the road. Scotty, or Officer Binsford, I should say, trotted over to us. Before he could get a word out, Jesse demanded to know what was wrong.

Scotty, a young man I had grown up with on the Point, nodded, his expression conceding that something was indeed wrong. He wasted no time with greetings, other than to tip his police helmet to me. "There's been another incident, sir, another woman falling ill just like the first one, that Mrs. Robinson."

"Who?" was Jesse's terse query.

"A Miss Ada Norris," Scotty replied. "An older lady. Spinster."

"A familiar name." Jesse turned to me. "Do you know her?"

"I do. She's a friend of Aunt Alice's, about her age as well. Never married, but her father left her well-to-do. No surviving brothers or sisters. She owns a lovely Queen Anne house on Rhode Island Avenue. Turret, gingerbread trim, wraparound porch—what one would expect of a wealthy spinster."

Jesse took a moment to take in this information. Then he addressed Scotty. "When was this?"

"We got word of it only about a quarter hour ago. Not only that, but there were two other cases of ladies receiving letters that burned their hands."

"What did these letters say?" From the carriage seat, I leaned down closer to Scotty to be heard over a passing streetcar. "And was there any indication where these tainted letters came from?"

"I don't know what was in the letters, and there were no

return addresses. But the package was signed from another of the speakers at Mrs. Twombly's luncheon. Considering the burns, it could be the same toxin as in Mrs. Robinson's petit fours."

"The letters were probably dropped in one of the collection boxes rather than mailed from the post office," I said. "Which will make them impossible to trace. Who supposedly sent the package to Miss Norris? Not Mrs. Roosevelt again, I hope."

Scotty shook his head and bit the corner of his lip as he thought. "Harriet . . ."

"Hemenway?" I finished for him.

"That's it."

I leaned back against the leather squabs of the carriage seat. "Except that it wasn't Harriet Hemenway. The very idea." I shook my head. "But clever of the sender to use another trusted name. Jesse, we need to alert this town before more women fall victim. The *Messenger* can send out an afternoon extra. And I'll make a few telephone calls to spread the word." I thought specifically of my own relatives, Aunt Alice and cousins Gertrude and Gladys. At least Aunt Alva and my cousin's wife, Grace, weren't in town at the moment.

Jesse nodded, even as he blew out a breath of frustration. "It could start something of a panic up and down Bellevue Avenue. But I suppose better that than allow unsuspecting women to open tainted mail." He shot a glance at Scotty. "No word on any men having the same experience?"

"Only ladies, sir."

"Who did Chief Rogers send over to Miss Norris's house?"

"Davies and Osbourn."

"All right. You'd best get on with your beat. I'm headed back to the station now." He turned to me. "Emma?"

I nodded my willingness to accompany him on yet another errand.

Scotty saluted us with a touch of two fingers at his helmet.

We stopped at the police station long enough for Jesse to read the report about Ada Norris, and for me to telephone over to the *Messenger* to let Derrick know we had another stop to make before Jesse returned me to the office. I gave him the details of the latest attacks, and he agreed to print the extra. He would also telephone over to The Breakers to warn my relatives.

Soon after, Jesse and I wound our way east through town to Rhode Island Avenue, to the home of Miss Norris. Along the way, Jesse divulged the content of the tainted letters. "They appear to be about the same, an invitation to a tea to be held at the Casino. Except that neither invitation had been signed."

"An invitation from no one," I mused. "Yet, like Mrs. Roosevelt and Mrs. Hemenway's names, an event to be held at the Casino inspires trust in the recipient, who would see no reason not to open it."

"Exactly." Jesse muttered something under his breath. I knew better than to ask him to repeat his words more loudly.

Ada Norris's housekeeper at first balked at letting us in, until she recognized Jesse. "Why, Detective Whyte. Jesse." She opened the door wider. "And this is Emma Cross, isn't it? My, what a lovely young lady you've grown into, dear."

"Thank you, Mrs. Rudd. It's very nice to see you, too." Althea Rudd had once worked at the house next door to my own on the Point. She had been a cook and maid-of-all-work in those days, and had always had extra cookies on hand for Brady and me, which she would pass to us over the fence separating our yards. "I didn't expect to see you here."

"Yes, I've been with Miss Norris now for several years. A good position." She said this with a worried note in her voice, and her fingers twisted in the edge of the light shawl she'd thrown over her shoulders. "Dear Miss Norris. She's quite poorly."

"That's why we've come, Mrs. Rudd." Jesse removed his derby as he stepped over the threshold. "I'll need to question you both, if you don't mind." Of course, he would question them whether they liked it or not, but his curtesy typically helped smooth the way with fellow Newporters. "That is, if Miss Norris is up to it."

"Come upstairs. She's awake. The doctor left only a few minutes ago. I'll take a peek in first and make sure it's all right." The interior of the house was mid-century in style, rather like Kingscote or Chateau-sur-Mer with their dark paneling, parquet floors, and furnishings in deep, rich tones. Mrs. Rudd led us up an imposing, curving staircase of carved, meticulously polished mahogany—so much so I was loath to touch my fingers to it. The half landing contained two gilded, silk-covered armchairs and a small inlaid table between them, set beneath a wide mullioned window. At the second floor, a rectangular central landing that looked down over the entry hall let onto several rooms. Mrs. Rudd went to the one directly opposite us and knocked softly.

"Come in," said a thready voice within.

Mrs. Rudd explained who we were and the reason for our visit. Miss Norris gestured with a curl of her fingers for us to come closer to the bed. She half sat up against a stack of pillows, her graying hair gathered beneath a white cotton mobcap. Though she appeared weak and pallid, she surveyed us with sharp eyes, albeit ones surrounded by taut crow's-feet.

"Detective, thank you for coming." Her voice trembled, a sure sign of her weakened condition. "I'm not sure what has happened to me, but the doctor believes the package I received from Mrs. Hemenway was tainted in some way."

"We don't believe that package actually came from Harriet Hemenway." Jesse brought the dressing-table chair to the side of the bed and sat. "Did he treat you for possible poisoning, ma'am?"

She made a face, her mouth turning down at the corners. "Tasted awful, but it helped, I believe. I do feel a smidgeon better. He seems to think I'll make a full recovery, thank goodness."

"That's heartening news, ma'am." He glanced around the room. "Where is this package?"

Mrs. Rudd stepped closer to the bed. "It's downstairs in the breakfast room. That's where Miss Norris was when it arrived. I took it to her there. The other police officers are examining it now."

"How stupid of me to try one of those pretty little devils in that box." Miss Norris let her head sink deeper into the pillows.

"You couldn't have known, ma'am," I said. No, she couldn't have, because what had happened to Lottie Robinson hadn't been made public yet. In light of today, the entire town must be alerted. I had remained standing at the foot of the bed. Now I went around to the side opposite Jesse. "Can you tell us what the petit four tasted like? Was it bitter? Was there anything familiar about the flavor?"

She thought a moment, her eyes closing and her elderly features tensing. Beneath the blankets, her arm slid over her stomach, back and forth. I wondered how much of the pain lingered. "There was nothing but sweetness at first. A lovely flavor I'd never quite experienced before. Almost like candied rose petals. Have you ever tried any?"

"I have," I replied, baffled. How could something so sweet and delicately flavored produce such ghastly results? "You said 'at first.' What happened next?"

Miss Norris's pale lips stretched wide, her nostrils flared, and her eyes squinted nearly shut. "It was horrid. Truly,

truly horrid. Suddenly, there was the most bitter acid burning my tongue, the roof of my mouth, and my throat. I had partly swallowed—the rest I immediately spit out. Manners had no place in that moment."

"No, I can't imagine they did, and a good thing, too." I smoothed a hand over the comforter, found hers beneath it, and gave a little press. "Otherwise, you might be a good deal more ill than you are."

After a brief nod, she turned her head slightly toward Jesse; even that small movement seemed to cost her an effort. "Who would do this to me, Detective?"

"Have you had any disagreements with anyone lately?"

"Why, no, Detective, none that I can think of. Certainly nothing to warrant this."

"And you can think of no one who might hold a grudge against you?" he persisted.

"Not a soul, Detective. I believe myself to be well liked among my peers."

"How well do you know the Van Horn ladies?" I asked.

"The Van Horns?" She blinked in surprise. "You mean Anna Rose and her daughter?"

I nodded.

"Hardly at all." Alarm made her eyes go wide. "Have they also fallen prey to this dreadful prank?"

"No, they're fine," I assured her. She cut me off before I could say more.

"Then surely you're not suggesting they are the ones responsible?"

"We're not saying that." Jesse flicked me a glance and then leaned down closer to her. "I don't know as yet who did this, but I promise you, Miss Norris, I will find out."

Back downstairs, Jesse and I found our way to the breakfast room, where Officers Davies and Osbourn were making notes and checking through the other mail that had been delivered that morning. They came to attention when we entered.

"Nothing else appears tampered with, sir," Officer Davies, the senior of the pair, said.

"That may be, but gather it all and bring it down to the station." Jesse went over to where the petit-four box sat on the table beside Miss Norris's forgotten breakfast. "I want it all tested. Be extra careful with the box."

I came up beside him. "The fact that she didn't eat an entire petit four probably saved her from a much worse illness. From the evidence at Vinland, it appears as though Lottie Robinson ate several at once."

"I can't decide whether this second incident sheds more guilt or less on the Van Horns."

His tone suggested he was thinking out loud, but I commented, nonetheless. "Ada Norris and Lottie Robinson are friends. They sat together at the luncheon. It's possible Miss Norris helped Mrs. Robinson scheme to end Sybil's engagement to Chester Herbert. But while that might make Miss Norris a target of the Van Horns, it doesn't explain the other women who received toxic mail today."

"No." He fell into a ruminating silence for several moments, during which I didn't interrupt him. Finally, he said, "They're all women."

"Yes, they are. So far, at least."

He mused another moment. "Emma, I need you to do something for me. Something not dangerous in the least, I assure you."

I couldn't help but chuckle at that.

He didn't join in my mirth. "Not only are these crimes against women, so far the only *suspects* are women."

I gestured for him to continue.

"I need you to . . . well, to infiltrate and find out more

about these society women. And I don't mean generally. These crimes are personal. What are their loyalties to one another? Who is excluded? Who have had recent run-ins?"

"And you would like me to do this . . . how?"

"Do whatever it is you women do when you're on your own."

"I work at the *Messenger*," I reminded him.

"Ladies clubs, church committees, charity events . . . that sort of thing. Couldn't you suddenly show a keen interest in joining your fellow ladies in civic-mindedness?"

"I am civic-minded." I placed my hands on my hips. "I always have been. Or hadn't you noticed?"

"Of course, I've noticed." With his hand at my elbow, he escorted me out of Miss Norris's house and to his carriage. Once there, he hesitated before handing me up. "Emma, please don't make me beg. This is something we've never seen before. This is beyond ordinary police work."

It was my turn to ruminate. How would I accomplish what he was asking of me? I understood in general terms, but as he had said, this was personal. How would I suddenly show enthusiasm for becoming better acquainted with Newport's society ladies, and would they even allow me into their confidence?

When we arrived at the *Messenger*, I stole a glance through the windowpanes on the right side of the front office. Was Derrick at his desk? I didn't see him, although a glance to the left confirmed that Stanley Sheppard, our editor-in-chief, was hard at work.

"All right, Jesse, I'll see what I can do. But this won't be as easy as you make it out to be. To *infiltrate*, as you put it, I'll need to find reasons to go places I haven't gone thus far and involve myself in matters that until now haven't caught my attention. And I'll need to do it without creating a stir."

His smile would have been infectious if I hadn't had such qualms about this task he had relegated to me. Not only my own qualms, but the anticipation of Derrick's as well. Jesse said there would be nothing dangerous involved. How many times had I believed that in the past? How often had I persuaded Derrick of the same, when all along we both knew otherwise?

Before I'd had a chance to devise a plan, Florence Twombly summoned me back to Vinland.

She invited me to late-afternoon tea, which on the surface sounded lovely. But she had only invited me, not Derrick, and the missive she sent to me at the *Messenger*, via one of her footmen, ordered rather than asked me to be there at five-thirty sharp.

"Does she know we have houseguests?" Derrick asked, taking the sheet of stationery out of my hand and perusing it as he spoke. "Surely she can't expect you to absent yourself when you're entertaining your own guests at home."

I pinned my straw boater into place and tugged on my light kidskin gloves in preparation for our ride home— except in my case, it would be the ride to Vinland. "She can, and she apparently does. Yet this is so unlike her. She and I have always been cordial when thrown together, but we've never been close. Indeed, I believe she has done her best through the years to ignore my existence. And that of my father's, of course."

"Low fruit," he teased, remembering something I myself had said more than once concerning my connection to the loftier Vanderbilts. He handed the invitation back to me. "Any idea what she might want?"

I inclined my head as several possibilities ran through my mind. "Her intentions could be harmless enough. It could be about the Audubon Society, or some other charity she wishes my help with, or . . ." One rather less appealing possibility had me rolling my lips between my teeth.

"Or . . ." His eyebrow raised in expectancy.

"Never mind. I'll find out soon enough."

Having locked his desk drawers, Derrick set his charcoal-gray homburg on his head and adjusted the brim just so. Then he offered me his arm. "Ready to go?"

"No, but let's. The sooner I get this over with, the better."

The ride down Bellevue Avenue, shaded by elm and beech trees, ended all too soon as Derrick steered the carriage over to Ochre Point. The ocean smashed against the cliffs in the near distance, sending up an echo to wend its way along Narragansett Avenue. Gulls cried out, chasing the scudding clouds, or so it seemed from our vantage point. We turned again, passed the massive chateau that was Ochre Court and the Gothic Revival manse called Wakehurst, and turned in at Vinland's gatehouse, decorated in similar Nordic designs as the house. When the carriage came to a stop, Derrick placed his palm against my cheek.

"Remember who you are," he said firmly. With his other hand, he tucked wind-blown strands of hair behind my ear. "Don't let her boss you around. You can always leave and walk over to The Breakers. Telephone me from there, and I'll swing round and get you."

I leaned in, tipped his hat back, and pecked his lips with my own. "That's all right, I'm sure she'll send me home in one of her carriages when she's through with me. Besides, I told Zinnia Lewis not to be afraid of her, that she's flesh and blood like the rest of us. So how can I turn tail and run?"

He showed me his wide, lopsided grin and kissed me in return. "Good luck, then. I'll make your excuses to Miss Carter and Miss Lewis."

After being admitted to the house and relieved of my hat and gloves, I was shown into the drawing room and told

Mrs. Twombly would be with me presently. Rather than sit, I strolled to the windows. The waves beyond the cliffs were brisk, almost jittery things, whipped to sharp peaks by a stiff breeze. The hue of the water had begun to darken as the sun moved across the island and the cliffs cast their shadows. Both the waves and those shadows reflected my current mood.

I heard the clatter of footsteps.

"Emmaline Cross Andrews." Mrs. Twombly, despite her trim figure, seemed to fill the doorway with its carved patterns of Viking knots, twists, and stylized, entwined serpents. "How dare you!"

Chapter 6

She hadn't addressed me as Emmaline since I was a child. That she called me that now instead of Mrs. Andrews made a bold statement about just how upset she was with me.

"I gave you my dear friend's address, believing you were going there in friendship. But what do I discover?" Her mouth snapped closed, while her eyes burned their wrath into me so intensely I expected to hear sizzling. I opened my mouth to reply, but instantly realized her question had been a rhetorical one. "Accusing my friend and her daughter of attempted murder? Have you taken leave of your senses? Or have you simply forgotten everything you ever learned about civility and kindness? You, a Vanderbilt, no less."

She shuddered over my having shamed the family with my unconscionable behavior, then paused for breath. Her normally flawless complexion had turned mottled; a tick pulsed beside her right eye. Had she wielded a battle-ax and stormed toward me I would not have been more astonished. But just as I thought she had finished, she burst out with the worst yet. "What would my brother think of you, if he were alive to see how low you've sunk?"

I winced. She might as well have slapped me. As it was, her reference to Uncle Cornelius, two years in his grave, raised a hot flush to my cheeks and a harsh ringing in my ears. "Mrs. Twombly, please understand . . ."

"You will apologize to them, Emmaline. At the first opportunity. More than that—for words come cheap—you will make this up to them. I don't know how. But somehow. Do you realize what the past year has been like for them? Are you aware of their suffering? Their mortification?" I began to nod, but, once again, she hadn't sought any form of answer from me. She went on, poking the air with an accusing finger. "And you believed it perfectly all right for you to heap further trials onto their shoulders?"

"Mrs. Twombly," I began again, "unfortunately, there are circumstances which do shed suspicion on both Mrs. and Miss Twombly in the case of Mrs. Robinson's illness." I paused only to draw a breath, and then, before she could relaunch her tirade, I asked, "How is Mrs. Robinson today?"

That seemed to drain a portion of the fury from her bearing. "Not well, I'm afraid. Not any better at all. The doctor is trying everything, including purging and administering more charcoal to neutralize the poison. We've also been spoon-feeding her warm milk and honey to help soothe the damage to her esophagus and stomach."

"Has she been conscious, then?" My hopes for Mrs. Robinson rose, even as I used this change in subject to my advantage. At least for the moment, I wasn't being yelled at.

"Barely," she replied. "Just enough for someone to support her head while she swallows. It seems to exhaust her. I don't know that the doctor's treatments are doing any good at all."

"Is the nurse still with her?"

"There are two, one during the day and the other at night, around the clock. If not for that, poor Lottie would have to be moved to the hospital, and I don't want that for her. I want her comfortable and looked after here. Should she . . ." She stopped, her bottom lip trembling in a rare show of vulnerability. "Should she not recover, at least she will end her days here with dignity."

"You mustn't think like that. Of course, she'll recover." Would she, though? My former apprehensions forgotten, I crossed the room to her, took her hands, and led her to one of two long sofas. "Has her daughter been sent for?"

"Yes, I telegrammed yesterday. But it will take her some time to get here all the way from Maryland. I can only hope . . ."

I nodded, understanding. "Perhaps once she arrives and Mrs. Robinson hears her voice, she'll rally."

"That's what I'm hoping as well." She stared down at our hands, still joined. I thought she'd tug free, but she didn't. She simply sat there, regarding me. "I'm sorry I yelled at you, Emmaline."

"It's all right. I understand."

"Do you?" Suddenly, she slid her hand free and sat up straighter, her shoulders forming a perfect T above the severe line of her spine. "What you did was wrong and must be rectified. Why, the very notion that . . . how did you put it? That circumstances have shed suspicion on those refined ladies? What could you mean by that? What circumstances?"

How I longed to be home among friends. But I wasn't, and I had little choice but to try to explain to Mrs. Twombly what happened, without revealing too much about the case.

"It has to do with those very trials you mentioned," I said. I allowed myself a quick glance out the wide windows, searching for strength in the cloud-studded sky. "Those trials ended with a broken engagement and Miss Van Horn's vast disappointment."

"Your point being?"

"Her betrothed married Mrs. Robinson's daughter."

Mrs. Twombly stared blankly back before realization dawned on her slender, aristocratic features. "And you think one of them, Anna Rose or Sybil, is taking their revenge upon Lottie for that? Bah!"

I didn't try to persuade her. I simply let the obvious sink in. Finally, she gave a slight nod. "I suppose one can see why that policeman friend of yours might jump to conclusions. Of course, time will prove him wrong." Her gaze sharpened. "I fail to see why you had to become involved."

I ignored the latter comment and addressed the previous. "I hope time does prove Detective Whyte wrong." And myself, I silently added. "Don't you prefer that I was there to soften the procedure, rather than the Van Horns being interrogated at the police station?"

She repeated the word *interrogated* as if it were an object she wished to dislodge with a flick of her fingertips. She consulted the mantel clock and lightly slapped her thighs, enveloped in rich, russet silk. "Come, tea will be served precisely at six."

She led me into the adjoining dining room, where once again the wraparound saga of Viking passion, warfare, and adventure drew my gaze upward. She saw where my attention had wandered.

"Yes, that frieze." She shook her head. "What on earth was Catherine Wolf thinking when she built this house? Admiring a culture of days past is one thing, but to make one's residence a monument to that culture, ad nauseum, is quite another. Well, it won't be this way much longer. Hamilton and I intend to redecorate soon. We're already drawing up plans."

A footman came and held her chair, then mine. "Surely

you're not going to strip the house of the very elements that give it such character?"

"There will be new elements, ones in keeping with our modern times." She nodded at the head footman, who hurried out without looking hurried at all. Moments later, he returned with two others close at his heels to serve tea. They brought in platters of cold pheasant and sliced ham, deviled eggs, baked squash, a savory bread, and a jellied fruit mold. I marveled that she had gone to so much trouble when there were only the two of us.

"Good heavens," I couldn't help exclaiming. "This is more than a simple tea."

"It's my dinner," she said matter-of-factly. "I eat this way whenever I'm alone. Hamilton is traveling for business right now."

With a nod, I sampled my pheasant; it had been glazed with sweet wine and hints of orange. I wouldn't be hungry for dinner at home, that was certain. "You were saying about the house?"

"Ah, yes. We plan to expand." She pointed to which items on the platters she desired the head footman to spoon onto her plate. "We've found the house is much too small for our needs."

"Will you be adding a ballroom, then?" I wondered if they would build toward the back, closer to the cliffs, or off to the side.

"Yes, between this room and the end of the hallway, between the public rooms and the kitchen area."

I had been about to slice into a deviled egg, but my knife and fork went still. "Between . . . ?"

She nodded. "We're planning to have the house pulled apart and the new room added to the space that opens up."

"Good heavens." My eyes were wide. "Why not simply

sell this house and buy another? I mean, if you aren't keen on the decorations and you wish more rooms . . ."

"Location, my dear. It is everything, and this is one of Newport's best."

How could one argue with such logic? It might shock and confound me, but therein lay one of the differences between myself and other members of the Vanderbilt family. What I considered infeasible, improbable, or downright absurd, they simply made happen.

We spoke of mundane things and enjoyed our tea without further incident, until it was time for me to set out for home. At the front door, while Mrs. Twombly's elegant Victoria carriage trimmed in gold and hung with carved silver lanterns awaited me on the drive, she placed a hand under my chin as if I were a child. "You'll make things right with the Van Horns."

"I will, I assure you."

"How?"

That question took me aback. "I'll think of something. Soon."

On the way to Gull Manor, I prayed an idea would come to me.

Even with Derrick's help, I could think of no way to soothe Mrs. Twombly's ire without opening a chasm of awkwardness between myself and the Van Horns. If I simply went and apologized, would they listen? I doubted they would open the door to me. Besides, what would I apologize for? Helping Jesse do a necessary job?

I spent a restless night, not only pondering my dilemma but wondering why it mattered so much to me. This wasn't Aunt Alice I wished to appease; this was Mrs. Twombly, with whom I had barely exchanged a handful of sentences for most of my life.

This was just the sort of thing I had rarely given a second thought to before Derrick and I married. I wished it didn't matter now. But it did.

With the moonlight diffused by the sheer curtains over our window, I rolled toward him, reached out, and brushed a dark lock off his brow with my fingertips. I smiled. He had made me care about a good many things since entering my life six years ago. With a sigh, I acknowledged I was no longer the same women I had been, but someone new, someone shaped by the sharing of experiences, by coming to see the world from more than one point of view, by the love that had grown slowly but steadily between us.

In the morning, I woke before he did. The filtered moonlight had been replaced by blue-gray shadows creeping across the room. Not wishing to disturb him so early, I slipped out of bed and drew on my dressing gown and house shoes. But before I left, I leaned over him and pressed a kiss to his temple, inhaling the musky scent of his skin deep into my lungs. He stirred, uttered something I couldn't make out, and drifted back to sleep. Still, I knew it wouldn't be long before he sprang out of bed.

Downstairs, I found Katie in the kitchen, kneading dough for the day's loaves of bread. She always rose before dawn, a habit left over from when she was in service—truly in service, for I had made it plain to her that here in my home, she needn't fear dismissal or reprimands. Here, she was part of my household, my makeshift family.

When I pondered what Mrs. Twombly would think about that, I couldn't help grinning.

"Good mornin', Miss Emma." She stood at one of the kitchen counters, up to her elbows in flour. She regarded me over her shoulder. "You're in a good mood in spite o' being up mighty early."

"I didn't see the point of trying to get back to sleep."

"Well, you're not the only one."

"Oh? Who else is up? Surely not Nanny?" I had long ago admonished Nanny not to rise too early, push herself too hard, or try to do the things she had done with ease as a younger woman.

Katie chuckled. "Indeed not." With her chin, she gestured out the kitchen window. "Miss Lewis. She's out there with her paints and such."

"Is she?" I came up beside Katie, reaching into the bowl of shelled walnuts beside the sink. Across the yard, almost to where the property met the ocean, Zinnia Lewis sat on a stool she had borrowed from the vegetable patch, the one Nanny often used while she tended her garden. Her back lay in shadow, but I could see the silhouette of morning sunlight gilding her from the front. Her easel stood before her; she held her paintbrush in one hand, a palette in the other. A wicker hamper occupied the ground beside her feet.

"How long has she been out there?"

Katie shrugged. "Couldn't say. She was there when I came into the kitchen."

"She started painting in the dark?"

Katie replied with another shrug.

Chewing on my walnuts, I headed outside and across the dewy grass, passing the vegetable and laundry yards and the barn where our two horses slept. Though my tread was light, I recognized the moment Miss Lewis heard me by the stilling of her hand over the canvas, though she didn't look behind her.

"Good morning, Miss Lewis," I call out. "I hope I'm not disturbing you."

"Not at all, Mrs. Andrews. Good morning."

As I went closer, some of the details on her canvas took

shape. I recognized the silvers and deep blues, edged with touches of copper and gold, that tinged our ocean at the first kiss of dawn. The ocean spray hitting the boulders along the shoreline just missed us here. Miss Lewis had captured the effect perfectly with her paints. She craned her neck to smile at me, then turned back to her work. With brush to pallet, she mixed dabs of gray, blue, and pink into a single hue of dusky violet.

"I don't mind being watched while I paint. Though I expect it's terribly boring for most people."

"I find it fascinating, especially the way you create such subtle shades. It's something I couldn't do." I studied the painting. The ocean waves in the foreground, framed by boulders, carried depths of charcoal gray and darkest blue, gradually lightening as the perspective approached the sliver of sun on the southeastern horizon. Threads of palest silver gave the impression of choppy waves beneath an indigo sky. "You've captured it exactly. Even the feel of it. How did you do it without a lamp to light your canvas?"

"Thank you." She tipped her head. "I don't know. I suppose I feel as I paint, rather than see. In the full daylight, I can fix whatever I don't like."

I took in her easel, standing on legs that were hinged like human knees, but locked into place. "This looks like a handy contraption. You say it folds up into a carrying case?"

"Yes, all its parts collapse most conveniently, and there's a handle. Invaluable to any landscape artist. It was a gift from Aunt Amity." She dipped her brush into a small can at her feet, swished it around, and rapped it sharply against the rim to shake off excess liquid. Turpentine, I guessed, by the odor that rose momentarily. Then she dabbed her brush into a blob of midnight blue and added a bit of coral pink to it.

I gazed out to the horizon, seeing just that shade spreading into a bank of clouds. "I'm glad you're taking advantage of the view."

"This is an intriguing light. Different from our Florida sunrise." She paused and looked off to one side of the yard. "Aunt Amity's up and about too. Somewhere."

"Here I am!" Amity Carter picked her way along the rocky shoreline from the property next door—her property. My stomach clenched. Was she having second thoughts about the sale?

She carried a pair of binoculars in one hand while the other hand pressed the crown of her wide, floppy straw hat as she bustled across the grass toward us. Patch trotted along at her side. "Good morning, Mrs. Andrews. I hope you don't mind your houseguests prowling about the place before anyone else is up."

"That's why I invited you here, to take advantage of our coastline at any hour you like." After bending down to bid my canine good morning, I gestured to the binoculars. "See anything interesting?"

"Goodness yes! I spotted a long-billed curlew and a whimbrel; they look very much alike to untrained eyes, you know." Before I could comment that I truly didn't know, she counted off a few more species on her fingers, daring to leave her hat undefended against the breezes rolling in with the waves and spray. "A black scoter, a green-backed heron, a great cormorant, and a Caspian tern, among others."

"A fruitful morning," Miss Lewis concluded, without taking her eyes off the churning, undulating view. Even Patch, now playing tag with bursts of ocean spray, failed to distract her.

"And you, Zinnia?" Miss Carter joined me where I stood behind her niece and leaned closer to inspect her progress on the painting. "Oh, splendid. Now, with the addition of a bird or two . . ."

"All in good time, Aunt."

Miss Carter turned to me. "Do you think we might have a chance to venture to other parts of the island for a bit of bird-watching?"

"That's a delightful idea," I replied, and wondered why I hadn't thought of it myself. "I know a couple of perfect spots. We could go later today, if you like. Or are mornings better?"

"Mornings are best for bird-watching." Miss Carter looked apologetic. "But we wouldn't want to impose by getting you up too early."

"Nonsense. Let's plan it. How is tomorrow?"

Miss Lewis dabbed paint to canvas. "We should invite that nice Jennie Pierpont."

"Yes, we should," her aunt agreed, then asked me, "Is Mrs. Hemenway still in town?"

"I don't believe so."

"What about the Van Horns, then?" Miss Lewis suggested, her back still to us as she concentrated on her artwork. The notion startled me, until I remembered she and her aunt had met the Van Horns at the luncheon.

I started to demur. Surely, the Van Horns wouldn't wish to spend their morning with me, especially an early morning. But perhaps an invitation was the very thing to smooth things over with them, especially if I packed a lovely breakfast and made a picnic out of it. Besides—and yes, this might have been the cowardly way out—I wouldn't have to face them alone.

Finally, Miss Lewis leaned away from her painting to gain a slightly different perspective. "I miss dolphins." She turned to catch my eye. "We have dolphins in our ocean, especially in the mornings. Often mothers with their calves. They're such lovely creatures. Although the first time I saw one, I thought it was a shark. The dorsal fin, you realize, can look very much the same."

"And sometimes it *is* a shark." Miss Carter gave a wry laugh. "We never swim this time of day, or at dusk."

"Goodness. But how thrilling. Derrick and I must come for a visit." I tried to imagine the world from all those hundreds of miles away, where the sun rarely cooled and white sand beaches stretched for miles and miles.

Miss Lewis packed up her easel soon afterward. Miss Carter carried her canvas, careful to keep her fingers clear of the drying paint, and I took the hamper. Its clasp hadn't been secured, and as I hefted it, I noticed a sketchbook sitting on top of the other supplies. "Miss Lewis, I don't suppose I could take a peek at some of your sketches when we get inside, could I?"

"Of course you may," she said brightly, and waited for me to lead the way to the house.

In the kitchen, Patch detoured to the bowl of meat scraps Katie had set on the floor for him. Meanwhile, she and Nanny had breakfast waiting for us in the morning room. Derrick was up, already at the table and going through the morning papers. A cup of coffee sat at his elbow.

"Good morning, ladies," he greeted us, setting aside the early edition of the *Newport Daily News* and coming to his feet. He and I always liked to keep abreast of what our competitors were publishing. His eyes caught mine as he held Miss Carter's chair for her, and what I saw in those dark depths brought a smile to my lips and sent a warm shiver across my shoulders. "What have you got there, Emma?"

"Um . . ." What had he asked? Oh, yes. "Miss Lewis's sketchbook." I held it out for him to see. "She's the most wonderful artist. You must see her painting first thing after breakfast. For now, we can have a look at this. Miss Lewis said it would be all right." I chose a place at the table beside his own.

As we flipped through the pages, we were continually taken aback at Miss Lewis's skill, at the detailing she was able to achieve with only a pencil. She had separated the book into sections, each with a different theme. Most were landscapes and close-ups of birds and other wildlife: a chipmunk, a squirrel carrying a nut, an otter sliding through the waters of a stream. Toward the back, we came upon a section for faces, and as we flipped through, one in particular sent a jolt of astonishment through me.

I whisked a hand to Derrick's wrist to prevent him from turning the page. "Why, that's Edith Roosevelt."

"It is," Miss Lewis confirmed with a modest nod. "Do you think it's any good?"

"I most certainly do." I gazed up at her, then back down at the sketch. "Do you know her personally?"

"No, yesterday was the first time I had ever seen her."

"How did you manage such an uncanny likeness?" My finger strayed close to the paper, tracing the line of the Second Lady's chin in the air above the sketch. "You couldn't have achieved this from across that crowded room, surely."

"Oh, but she could." The pride in Miss Carter's tone was unmistakable. "To use your own word, Zinnia has the most uncanny memory. Dates, names, faces, details, sometimes from years ago. I cannot ever win an argument with her when it's about something that occurred a day ago, or five years ago. It can be infuriating!" Her accompanying laughter belied that last claim.

"How extraordinary," I murmured, and Derrick nodded in agreement.

Chapter 7

After breakfast, I hurried back upstairs to the desk in my bedroom to pen a note of invitation for the Van Horns to join us in bird-watching and picnicking the following morning. In it, I apologized for upsetting them during our last meeting. How would my overture be greeted? With contempt, or with forgiveness?

I had little time to ponder as it was time to leave for the *Messenger*. I had plenty of work to accomplish today if I planned to take several hours off the following morning. The answer to my question came that evening, with a reply from the Van Horns waiting for me on the post tray.

Nanny hovered over me as I broke the seal and unfolded the single page. *Dear Mrs. Andrews*, it read, *Thank you for your kind invitation. Sybil and I have quite recovered from the shock of the morning before last, and what is more, we understand the necessity of the detective's questions. We would be pleased, therefore, to join you and the other ladies for a morning of bird-watching. We will watch for your carriage at first light.*

In my letter, I had told them I would send a hired carriage to collect them and Jennie Pierpont, whose accommodations I had tracked down the previous afternoon. Then we would all pile in and be driven out to our bird-watching location.

"Well, I'll be," Nanny commented with a little cluck of her tongue. "They're a gracious pair, I'd venture to say."

Yes, and that graciousness increased the guilt I felt at having been a party to accusing them of attempted murder, or practically accusing them. Nanny apparently saw the remorseful flush that climbed to my cheeks, for she pressed a hand to one of them and smiled.

"Don't worry, lamb. It seems all is forgiven."

"I hope so," I said, but not without an inner acknowledgment that the Van Horns' forbearance might also be an act meant to deflect suspicion away from them. And that thought made me feel even more guilty.

The following morning, Derrick rose with me before dawn, went downstairs, and soon enough returned holding two earthenware mugs of steaming coffee. I thanked him with an enthusiastic kiss. He opened the curtains upon a crisp sunrise that promised a clear, beautiful day. Of course, one could never be certain with New England weather.

"Are our guests up?" I asked.

"Yes, already downstairs enjoying their coffee and the biscuits Katie made last night." He perched on the edge of the bed as I sat up and took the cup from him. He watched me tentatively as I raised it to my lips for my first bracing sip.

I regarded him from over the brim as the strong brew worked its magic. "What?"

The corner of his mouth quirked. "You're going bird-watching in an isolated area with two women, either or both of whom might already have attempted murder. Twice."

"I won't be alone with them. Besides, there are bound to be other nature lovers along the trails."

"Still, I could come along . . ."

I shook my head. "How would that look?"

"As though I enjoy bird-watching as much as the next person." He placed both hands around his coffee cup and stared into its contents. "Have you considered that the Van Horns accepted your invitation a little too readily?"

"I did think about that, actually, last night when I woke up and couldn't get right back to sleep. But they could be hoping that by accepting my overture of friendship, I might be able to intercede for them with Jesse."

"Perhaps." His dark eyes took my measure. "Do me a favor, and stay away from the cliffs."

"Oh . . . well . . . I *had* planned on leading them up to Hanging Rock." I sensed his protest brewing and hurried on. "For bird-watching, it's perfect, with views of both the ocean and inland, and birds of all kinds. Besides, there's no reason for the Van Horns or anyone else to push one of us off the precipice. We'll simply be bird-watching and enjoying the out-of-doors."

"In addition to you asking leading questions," he said wryly. "At least take Patch with you."

"Actually, I rather like that idea. I will, provided there's room in the carriage for him."

It wasn't long before a landau carriage arrived bearing the Stevensons' Livery crest, its canvas top folded down to reveal the Van Horns and Jennie Pierpont, clad in duster coats and hats secured beneath their chins with motoring veils, riding together on the front-facing seat. After I bid farewell to my only slightly mollified husband, the rest of us, having also donned dusters, piled in, taking the rear-facing seat. I'd stowed our large picnic hamper on the box beside the driver, and Patch sprawled out on the floor of the vehicle between everyone's feet. Miss Lewis stood her traveling easel, folded up into its case, on the floor beside her legs, and each of us held binoculars on our laps.

The sun was well up by the time we reached Bath Road and headed down toward the beaches. Which meant, of course, that the best time for bird-watching had already passed, but our high spirits more than made up for that. The conversation along the way centered mostly around Florida, as we discovered that each of my five guests had visited there at one time or another in recent years. If I felt slightly left out, it didn't matter, as this gave me ample opportunity to observe the Van Horns in a casual situation, with their guards down. We passed First Beach, then wound along Purgatory Road, hilly and wooded and dotted here and there with residences and farms, until we descended the sharp hill to Second, or Sachuest, Beach, and Paradise Avenue.

"What an apt name for this thoroughfare, Mrs. Andrews," Amity Carter cried out to make herself heard above the wind and the nearby surf. She held up her binoculars and scanned our surroundings in a slow, circular motion. "With the ocean to our right and such spectacular scenery all around, it is truly paradise."

The others added their agreement. Miss Van Horn said, "Mama, we truly must make a point to explore more of the island. I fear we have limited ourselves to town and thereabouts."

Her mother nodded and thrust out a finger to point. "Goodness, look there!"

"That's where we're going," I announced. Up ahead and to our left, the formation known as Hanging Rock towered above us. Consisting of a tremendous slab supporting another formation that looked as if it had been dropped in place, the two formed a wide, cave-like projection, rather like the gaping mouth of a reptile, under which one could easily imagine wildlife and even native peoples seeking shelter from the elements. A carpet of goldenrod and coastal grasses swept away from its base to meet the road. "That, ladies, is Hanging Rock."

This met with a chorus of oohs and ahs. The carriage jolted us past Second Beach until we took a curve toward the north. The route provided us with splendid views of the formation from two sides. The far side dropped sharply away into a pond surrounded by marsh, while its rocky fourth side stretched beneath the trees and gradually sloped downward into the forest.

"Good heavens, Emma, I believe you're taking us into the back of beyond with the object of leaving us there." Jennie Pierpont laughed as she craned her neck to peer in all directions. Gardiner Pond glistened to our right, its gleaming surface alive with waterbirds seeking their breakfast.

"We're almost there," I replied, "and I think you'll all agree it was worth the ride."

The Hanging Rock area was well used by picnickers, hikers, and bird-watchers, so I didn't doubt my claim to Derrick that there would be others on the trails, especially on a bright morning with such temperate breezes. The entrance to the main trail was well marked, and we started on our way. I carried the picnic basket. Patch trotted along beside me, sometimes bounding ahead and then falling back again. The driver would return for us in three hours' time.

"We did some bird-watching in Florida while we were there," Sybil Van Horn said cheerfully, as she picked her way ahead of the rest of us. She lifted her duster clear of encroaching weeds and stepped lightly over rocks without a break in her stride. I could see already that this outing would do her good, allowing her to forget her troubles and enjoy herself, even if only for a short time. "We stayed right on the beach, in Mr. Flagler's Breakers hotel, as his special guests. He came with us on some of our inland excursions. The birds we saw near the Everglades were spectacular. I remember something called a spoonbill in the loveliest shade of pale pink."

"A roseate spoonbill," Amity Carter supplied. "They aren't nearly as common as, say, herons or egrets, so it's always a treat to spot one."

We had been walking steadily uphill, passing two small parties on their way back down. Now we reached a clearing, and Miss Carter stilled and raised her binoculars.

Her arm shot out. "Quickly ladies! A northern goshawk. A juvenile male, I believe. See it?"

At our sudden halt, Patch dropped to his haunches at my feet. I set down the picnic basket. We all whipped our binoculars to our eyes and followed the line of Miss Carter's outstretched arm.

"I don't see it," Anna Rose Van Horn said, with a sigh of disappointment.

"There, Mother," her daughter said in an urgent whisper. "Ooh, it landed in that tree. That way—look!"

I caught a glimpse of a blue-and-white underbelly before the object of our fascination darted like an arrow from its perch and became lost among the trees.

"A good start," Miss Carter pronounced.

We kept on, following the main trail upward, Patch now running ahead as if to lead us. Perhaps he believed he needed to protect us on this unfamiliar terrain. Breathing heavily from the exertion, I caught up to Miss Lewis and asked her if she had seen the hawk.

"No, but that's all right. My interest is more with the

overall scenery of the area. I'm looking forward to reaching this rock of yours and setting up my easel."

"You'll be delighted with the elevation and views," I promised her. "Although I hope you'll be able to make the climb carrying your equipment. It is rather steep in places, and rocky."

"Well, if I can't, I'll bring my sketchbook and paint the details later."

Miss Van Horn, who had fallen behind us, now caught up. She seemed determined to discuss more of Florida. "I think the most astonishing birds we saw with Mr. Flagler were the flamingos. We northerners don't tend to think of them as real, do we?"

Jennie Pierpont moved up beside Sybil. "Whatever can you mean? Of course, they're real."

"But we so often see stylized drawings of them in story-books and decorative art. To see a living one was such a surprise. And so many of them! Mr. Flagler knew just where to find whole flocks. It was as if the land had turned the most glorious shade of pink."

It must be a particularly fond memory for Miss Van Horn, one of a scant few since her family's troubles began. Apparently, Henry Flagler had long known Mr. Van Horn and invited wife and daughter to his hotel to help them escape the worst of the scandal.

"I'm surprised by that," Jennie said, with a note of derision. She gripped an obliging, low-slung branch to help hoist herself up the incline. "From what I understand, all but a small number of flamingos have disappeared from the state."

"Mr. Flagler has been a most beneficial friend to me." Below us, Miss Carter suddenly halted, held out a hand to stop us in our tracks, and put a finger to her lips. With her binoculars raised, she surveyed the sky between the canopies of the trees. Then her finger darted upward. A bird with a bright yellow body and black and white wings soared across the sky. "A male goldfinch," she whispered with satisfaction. Then she turned to us. "Anyway, as I was saying, Mr. Flagler has been very good to Zinnia and me. He financed my first book on Florida waterbirds and has helped me ever since. From dealing with my publisher to making the public aware of my work, he has proved invaluable. I am most indebted to him."

"And he helped establish our own Audubon Society in Florida," her niece added. "You mustn't forget that, Aunt."

"Quite right, and established a network of wildlife wardens to guard against poaching," Miss Carter continued. "Dangerous work. *Heroic* work!"

"Indeed, yes. I heard a few of them have even been murdered by those poachers." Miss Van Horn's eyes went wide with dread as she relayed this information.

Her mother nodded solemnly, having paused beside Miss Carter. "But Mr. Flagler has seen that their families are taken care of. Isn't that so, Miss Carter?"

"Yes. He's a most generous individual," that woman confirmed with a nod.

While the others expressed their appreciation of Mr. Flagler's philanthropy, Jennie Pierpont scrambled up the steep path ahead of the rest of us. When the trail leveled, she pretended fascination with some object through her binoculars, but I sensed she wasn't looking at anything in particular; she was, rather, avoiding the conversation. I wondered why, but I kept on, waiting until the trees parted and Hanging Rock once more came into view.

"Are we expected to climb that?" she said testily, pointing to the flat summit some dozens of feet above us.

"That is the general idea," I told her lightly, hoping to diffuse her mysterious anger. "The trail winds gradually upward, so it's not as strenuous as it appears, but if you'd rather not, we can find a suitable clearing lower down for our picnic."

"Oh, I say we keep climbing." Miss Carter strode past us.

"I agree." Her niece hurried after her, careful of the easel case she carried at her side. "I cannot wait to see the view from the top."

"I'm for reaching the top as well." Sybil looked eager. She glanced back at her mother, trailing behind the rest of us. "Mother? Can you make it?"

Mrs. Van Horn waved her daughter on. "Go ahead. I'm coming," she said breathlessly. A sheen of perspiration gleamed across her forehead. But I was certain mine was perspiring as well, and moisture had gathered between my shoulder blades and at the small of my back. I had, after all, maneuvered along the trail with only one arm for balance, as I carried the picnic basket in the other hand.

"Fine." Jennie blew out a sigh and followed the others. I waited for Mrs. Van Horn to pass me and took up the rear.

As we reached the summit, I once again heard oohs and ahs.

"This is spectacular, Mrs. Andrews." Atop the flat expanse of stone, Amity Carter slowly turned in a circle. "Don't you think so, Zinnia?"

"Outstanding. Thank you, Mrs. Andrews." Miss Lewis had made it all the way up by strapping her easel case to her back. Now her aunt helped her wriggle free. She set down the case, opened the latches, and began unfolding her easel. She adjusted the legs at varying heights to compensate for the uneven surface, and so she could stand while she worked. Next, she took out tubes of paint, her palette, brushes, rags, and a small canvas, only about twelve inches square, that looked as though she had prepared it earlier. Lastly, she took out a jar of what I assumed to be turpentine and a container to pour a small amount into.

Miss Carter wasted no time in searching the skies, walking from one edge of the flat slab to another, gazing down into the treetops. The Van Horns followed her like schoolgirls on a field trip, taking her cues on where to aim their binoculars. Patch alternated between following the four ladies, trotting back to me, and following his nose in pursuit of his own interests. When Miss Lewis began her painting, Mrs. Van Horn made herself comfortable on a nearby rock to watch. Sybil and Amity Carter announced their intention of going back down to follow the trails for a while longer. They set off in high spirits.

Only Jennie Pierpont appeared discontent. After finding a relatively smooth place to set the basket and spreading out a thick blanket—the padding of our petticoats would also come in handy—I made my way over to her.

"Jennie, is something wrong?"

She didn't look at me, pretending interest in something out over Sachuest Bay. "I'm sorry. I suppose I'm still smarting from the luncheon at Vinland and taking things overly to heart."

"What things? I thought the luncheon went well."

"Appearances can be deceiving. I'm sure, as a reporter, you're aware of that."

"You're right, I am. But what happened to bring you so low?" I thought I knew. While the attendees had enthusiastically welcomed Edith Roosevelt and even Harriett Hemenway, many of them had verged on rudeness during Jennie's speech. But I'd have thought a woman of Jennie Pierpont's spirit would have a thicker skin. And why fret about it now?

"It was the donations. I suppose I shouldn't have set my hopes so high."

"You mean the donations were less than adequate?" I found it hard to believe that anyone invited to Florence Twombly's home—which many considered quite a coup, socially speaking—would have been less than generous in supporting whatever cause was touted that day.

"It would appear the ladies of the Four Hundred are not as enamored of birds as we might wish. Perhaps it was because most of them hail from New York and are only in Rhode Island a few weeks in the summer. Or"—she clamped her lips shut and scowled—"perhaps they simply don't want to give up their plumage."

"Their plumage? You mean the feathers used in decorating their hats."

"I do. It's shameful, their lack of regard for life in the name of frippery and vanity."

"You're right, Jennie. They need to be educated. An Audubon Society, if I'm correct, will help to do just that. We'll find your funds for you. I'll do everything in my power to help. That includes using the *Messenger* to further your cause." Her anger continued to puzzle me, and I couldn't help trying to satisfy my curiosity. "What was said this morning that upset you? You seemed happy enough during the ride over."

With her gaze, she followed the path of a bird soaring too high to be identified, adding the flat of her hand to her hat brim to shield her eyes from the sun. "Henry Flagler."

"What about him?"

She dropped her hand and faced me. "He's no naturalist, nor any friend of Florida wildlife, flamingos included."

"But Miss Lewis just said he helped establish the Florida Audubon Society."

"Yes, a hollow effort, meant to distract from the truth. The man's hotels and railroads disrupt breeding grounds and destroy habitats. I've seen firsthand the results of his *philan-*

thropy." That last word dripped with sarcasm. "He creates a problem, then covers his complicity by sponsoring so-called solutions. He and his wildlife wardens. Bah!" Waves of ire turned her face crimson. Her words darted like a barrage of bullets, nearly prompting me to duck out of their way. "He's no better than my own distant cousin, J. P. Morgan, or your Vanderbilt relatives. They're only interested in the natural world so far as they might exploit it for their own financial gain."

To deny her charges would have been a lie, and a condescending one at that. She was right. My relatives *did* exploit everything from the natural environment to poor workers to any perceived weaknesses in their industry rivals, all in the name of profit. However much affection I felt for my cousins as people, even as philanthropists, as businessmen they left much to be desired.

"I understand now why you took issue with Miss Carter's praise of Mr. Flagler. But perhaps, as a naturalist, she feels it's better to befriend him. That way she might sway him to her point of view more often than not."

"Perhaps." Her acknowledgment was both reluctant and begrudging. "But when I think of all those women at the luncheon, so set in their ways, selfish and uncaring, shortsighted and ignorant, and believing they need answer to no one"—her fists curled around the binoculars hanging from her neck and the fire climbed into her cheeks again while her eyes became icy—"I'd like to strangle them all with their own finery."

She whirled away and stomped off, her booted feet scattering pebbles and fallen leaves. She found a path downward and disappeared among the trees. I stared after her, gaping. Her anger startled and alarmed me, and I wondered how fervently she meant those last words. Would she resort to violence to further her cause? Had she already?

Once again, I thought back to the luncheon. Yes, many of the women had been impatient for Jennie's speech to end, preferring to move on to the delicacies offered by Mrs. Twombly's French chef. But in one thing they hadn't erred: they hadn't worn feathers. Not even Lottie Robinson or Ada Norris. So if Jennie had wished to teach these women a lesson, why choose them in particular? Then again, there had also been those letters sent to other ladies of the Four Hundred. Perhaps Mrs. Robinson and Miss Norris were meant to set a frightening example, while the others were less severely punished for their sins of vanity.

As I set out our picnic, I considered that, while I had hoped to observe two suspects today, I now found myself with three.

Returning home in reverse, our hired carriage dropped off my houseguests and me at Gull Manor first before swerving north on Carroll Avenue to take the Van Horns to their boardinghouse and, finally, Jennie Pierpont into town. We waved goodbye, each of us in seemingly high spirits. I believed Mrs. Twombly would be glad to hear of our excursion and its outcome, at least when it came to the Van Horns and my transgression against them.

Yet, the moment I glimpsed Nanny's grim expression, I knew something was wrong. She beckoned me alone into the dining room and handed me an envelope. "It's from Vinland."

"Perhaps it's another invitation." I slipped my finger beneath a corner of the flap and tore it open.

"I don't think so."

I spared Nanny a glance before reading the note. My stomach sank; Nanny had proved correct. "Mrs. Robinson has succumbed to her illness. Oh, Nanny, this is horrible."

"I thought as much. I heard from Agnes Singleton again, a

little while after you left. Word has gotten around that the poor woman was showing no sign of recovery."

I heard a gasp behind me, and Zinnia half-stumbled into the room. Her face had gone white. "She died?"

"I'm sorry, yes." Nanny compressed her lips and assumed a sorrowful expression.

Though I didn't say it aloud, my thoughts seemed to echo through the room and were reflected in our faces. This was now a murder investigation.

Chapter 8

❦

Nanny and I spent the next hour soothing our guests, who were shocked by this development and believed themselves to have narrowly escaped a similar fate. We adjourned to the parlor with a pot of Nanny's strong Irish tea.

"It could easily have been one of us," Amity Carter said, her gaze pinned on her niece. "We were at the luncheon, and it seems luncheon guests were targeted. That we emerged unscathed . . ." She reached out and stoked Zinnia's cheek. "That you are unscathed, my dear, I most heartily give thanks."

Miss Lewis placed her own hand over her aunt's where it continued to cradle her cheek. Both women closed their eyes a moment as if in silent prayer. Then they both collected themselves.

"You as well, Mrs. Andrews" Miss Lewis said. "And Mrs. Twombly. Oh, and so many others. How strange that some were singled out and not others. What do you think it means?"

I shook my head. "I wish I could say. We can only hope

the police will find the answers to such questions." My mention of the police brought me to my feet. Surely, they had been notified. "If you're both feeling a trifle better..." It was a question, and both ladies nodded.

"We are, Mrs. Andrews." Miss Carter held her cup and saucer on her lap. "You've already spent a good portion of your day with us. We understand you lead a busy life. If there are matters you must attend to, please do not let us keep you."

"Nanny and Katie are here to see to any needs you might have." I glanced over at Nanny, ensconced in one of the easy chairs. She nodded. I said to her, "I'll need Katie to help me hitch Maestro to the carriage." Then I nearly slapped a palm to my forehead. "What am I thinking? Derrick took the carriage into town, didn't he?"

"As a matter of fact," she replied, "he did not. He left it here for you in case you wished to meet him at the *Messenger* this afternoon. He called over to The Breakers carriage house to borrow one of theirs."

It was yet another advantage of being on such cordial terms with my Vanderbilt relatives—at least, the Cornelius Vanderbilts. Whatever I needed, they were more than happy to provide. Over the years, I had kept my requests to a minimum. I hadn't wished to take advantage of their generosity, true, but I had also learned that sometimes generosity came with strings—such as Aunt Alice trying to find me a husband or convince me I shouldn't pursue such an unladylike occupation as journalism.

Or drive my own carriage.

But in this case, I could have kissed Aunt Alice for her unfailing kindness. In fact, I would, next time I saw her. "Wonderful, then I'll just find Katie . . ."

"It's already done," Nanny said with a smile. "As soon as

this note came from Mrs. Twombly, I asked Katie to ready the carriage for you."

Another considerate family member for whom I was grateful. I hugged and kissed her, bade my guests good day, and soon set out for Vinland. When I arrived, I saw several police vehicles, Jesse's carriage included, as well as the hospital rescue wagon, there to take Mrs. Robinson's body to the morgue at Newport Hospital. A morbid thought struck me that, with the help of an autopsy, they might learn more about this deadly toxin.

A footman admitted me to the house. I walked into a scene of controlled chaos, with servants and police streaming up and down the staircase and drifting in and out of the service area. I saw no sign of Mrs. Twombly, but a hunch sent me across the hall into the drawing room. She stood at the French doors, staring out, her back to me.

She must have heard me come in. Without turning, she asked, "Have they taken her out yet?"

"Not yet." She must have believed me to be one of her servants, for, at my reply, she quickly turned. "Oh, Emmaline. You're back."

I went closer, until the two of us stood framed against the view outside, the endless sky and clouds and the distant, watery horizon. "I received your note. I'm so sorry."

"She didn't deserve this, Emmaline."

"No one does."

"Yes, but why her, a widow who lived a quiet life, who wanted nothing so much as to see her grandchildren grow?" She reached out, her fingertips tracing the curving line of the curtain framing the doorway. "Why has someone done this?"

The little noise she made in her throat indicated she didn't expect me to answer, that she had only been voicing her thoughts aloud. In fact, I knew more than I wished to reveal just then; at least, I'd stumbled upon a possibility or two.

One of those possibilities is what had brought me there. "I saw Detective Whyte's carriage out front. He is upstairs?"

She nodded.

"I'm going to go up to speak with him. Then I'll come back down. Are you . . . are you all right on your own?"

"I won't be alone for long," she said. "Alice and Gladys are coming. You go on up. See what you can learn."

Jesse stood in the upstairs hallway, issuing orders to a pair of his men. Inside the room that had been Lottie Robinson's, a hushed voice issued directions that involved the removal of the body.

"Easy now. Lift her gently onto the stretcher. That's right, no need to jostle her . . ."

The pit of my stomach clenched in pity and desolation. No matter how many times one experienced death, the reality of it—the sheer, brutal reality—remained crushing.

I waited on the landing until Jesse finished with his men. They nodded as they went by me to the staircase. Jesse beckoned me over to him.

"It's now a murder," he said.

"I know."

He whispered an oath, then looked sheepish. "Sorry. This one doesn't make any sense, Emma. None at all. She wasn't involved in anything nefarious—I'm all but certain of it. We've been looking into her life these past months. There's nothing. The sale of her house, her plans to move nearer to her daughter. That's it. Her finances are in proper order, and her name certainly isn't attached to any kind of scandal."

"Except that of her daughter marrying the man who had promised himself to Sybil Van Horn."

"Yes, that. If this was Sybil's doing . . ." He didn't finish the thought. I knew well enough what awaited Sybil if she was found guilty of murder.

"I have something to tell you. Not about Sybil, but another of the luncheon attendees." I leaned forward and craned my neck to see into the guest room. The coroner and his assistants had positioned Mrs. Robinson's body on the stretcher and covered it with a sheet, the edges tucked in beneath it to prevent a hand or foot inadvertently slipping out on the way to the ambulance. I straightened. "Not here. Can we go back downstairs?"

He nodded and let me lead the way. Voices came from the drawing room; Aunt Alice and Cousin Gladys had arrived. We hurried past the doorway and turned into a smaller room at the end of the hall that also adjoined the library. I stuck my head into the latter room, saw no one, and closed the door. Jesse did the same with the door into the hall.

This room faced the front of the house. From the driveway came the sounds of voices and the ambulance doors opening. I steeled myself not to look out and turned instead to Jesse.

"I took a group of ladies bird-watching this morning." Before I could say more, he gave me an incredulous look.

"This is the important thing you wished to tell me?"

"Please, listen. The group consisted of my houseguests, the Van Horn ladies, and Jennie Pierpont. It's her I wish to tell you about. Jesse, the things she said, the bitterness I heard in her voice. Her dedication to protecting birds might even border on disturbed. She is furious about the industry that encourages the poaching of birds for the sake of women's fashion, and that anger extends to the women themselves. Especially those who attended the luncheon but didn't seem to take the subject seriously. She actually said . . ." I felt myself becoming overly impassioned; I paused to collect myself and lower my voice. "She said she'd like to strangle those ladies with their own finery."

"That's a motive if ever I heard one." He touched his fingertips to a spot on his chin where he had nicked himself shaving that morning. "The only question is, why would she physically harm the very women she wishes to win over to her cause?"

"That's a good question, but if you'd heard her earlier, you'd be inclined to believe she wasn't thinking altogether rationally."

"That was a good plan, by the way, gathering all those women together like that. How did the Van Horns seem to you?"

"Relaxed. They seemed to enjoy themselves. And they seemed to have forgiven me for barging in on them the way we did. You, however,..." I shrugged. "I can't say how they feel about coming under Detective Whyte's scrutiny."

"They needn't forgive me. I've grown a thick skin," he said dismissively. "Were they within your sights the entire time?"

"No, Sybil Van Horn and Miss Carter set out for a time together on the trails, and after Jennie's tirade she went ... somewhere. I don't know if she joined the other two or not. I didn't ask when they all returned, other than to inquire if they'd spotted any interesting birds."

"And did they?"

"Do you truly care?" I knew he didn't, but nonetheless, I replied, "Anytime one is with Amity Carter, one will see feathered creatures one didn't even know existed. Her enthusiasm brings magic to the simple act of bird-watching."

"Agreeable enthusiasm, as opposed to Jennie Pierpont's anger."

"Precisely."

"Don't be alone with her, Emma. Or with the Van Horns, for that matter. Not until we know more."

I told him I wouldn't, but wondered whether I would be able to make good on that promise.

* * *

That Sunday morning, Miss Carter and Miss Lewis joined me and the rest of the household at St. Paul's Church for services. Once again, we had leased a larger carriage, with plenty of room for all of us.

At the church, I sat beside Derrick, our hands joined on the seat between us. I allowed my eyes to fall closed as the pastor's words washed over me, bringing me a sense of peace. For a few precious moments, the questions running through my mind were stilled, the suspicions silenced. I drifted with the rise and fall of the hymns and savored the respite.

It was after the service, when many of the congregants mingled in the large church basement, that a new idea came to me. Several of the ladies were forming a committee to raise money to help feed Newport's poor during the coming winter. I pledged my support and raised the notion of approaching other congregations in town with the hope of forming an organized, citywide effort. I volunteered to speak with the appropriate ladies at Trinity Church.

On our way out, as the others walked ahead of us to the carriage, I heard Derrick's chuckle in my ear. "More schemes, Emma?"

I glanced up at him in mock surprise, not at all startled that he had gleaned my ruse. Still, I pretended to have taken offense. "Do you have an objection to my helping raise money for those in need?"

"I don't object at all, not even that you're using the fund as an excuse to do exactly what Jesse asked you to do, which is to find out as much as you can about our society ladies' private lives. Why else would you have volunteered to speak to the women at Trinity Church?"

I laughed at his astuteness in having caught me out. "Yes, you're right. It's a good pretext to get me through the doors of Trinity Church without arousing suspicions. But it is also a good cause, and one I'd support even if I didn't have an ulterior motive."

"My darling, of that I have no doubt, but I do sometimes enjoy teasing you."

At the carriage, Derrick helped all the ladies climb aboard. I waited, taking my turn last, and as he took my hand, he leaned in and whispered, "Just be careful, I implore you."

Aunt Alice proved helpful in my quest to visit Trinity Church. She told me most committees met on Tuesday at the vestry house close by. After checking in at the *Messenger* with Derrick and attending to a few articles and other matters, I walked down Spring Street to the church, armed with a list from the meeting at St. Paul's that included dates when food and clothing would be distributed. The windows of the vestry, once a private home set between a dry-goods store and a shoe-repair shop, had been thrown wide, and the main door stood ajar to the temperate weather. I let myself in.

I found several groups of ladies occupying different corners of what had once been the parlor. There were many faces I recognized among both the Four Hundred and our wealthy year-round residents. The signs of affluence met me everywhere I looked, from the sumptuous fabrics and embroidered embellishments of the ladies' afternoon dresses to their elaborate hats trimmed in silk and feathers—yes, feathers had made a reappearance. The scene here was a far cry from St. Paul's modest congregation. I pricked my ears for any snippets of gossip as I walked through.

"Emmaline!"

I turned to behold a slender redhead, her hair and bright green eyes set off by a walking suit of amber silk embroidered with green and gold leaves. A picture of stylish elegance. I gasped in delight at the sight of my friend and cousin by marriage.

"Grace! I didn't know you and Neily were back in town." Grace Wilson Vanderbilt and I embraced and kissed each other's cheeks. I noted that her hat boasted no feathers, but rather supported an intricate bow made from a generous length of wired velvet ribbon. "When did you arrive?"

"Over the weekend. We returned from Paris last week, gathered up the children, and here we are. I was planning to call on you very soon."

I had no doubt Grace told the truth about planning to call on me. She and my closest Vanderbilt cousin, Cornelius III—or Neily, as we called him—had married several years ago, much to the dismay of his parents. It had caused a rift that even now appeared unbreachable, as Aunt Alice blamed the pair for Uncle Cornelius's declining health and eventual death. Their objection to Grace Wilson, that she hailed from an upstart family of gold diggers, had always struck me as the greatest of ironies, as those were the very reasons Caroline Astor had attempted to permanently exclude the Vanderbilts from polite society over a decade ago.

"How are little Corneal and Grace?" I asked her, always delighted to hear about their two young children. "Are you at Beaulieu again?"

She laughed at my eager questions. "The children are quite well, thank you, but you'll see them for yourself soon enough. Yes, we've leased Beaulieu again for the remaining weeks of the summer." Taking a breath, she slipped an arm around my waist and drew me toward a group of ladies occupying a table beneath the mullioned windows on the room's north side. "Now, what brings you here? I know you don't worship at Trinity."

After the other ladies at the table greeted me, I explained to them all about St. Paul's project to feed Newport's less-privileged residents in the coming winter months. "There is always great need," I added, "and while I understand many of you aren't in Newport for the winter, you're still very much a part of the community, and I've no doubt you'll want to ensure the well-being of the very people who work for you and keep Newport beautiful while you're here in the summer." I included this last, hoping a touch of guilt might inspire their generosity.

Tessie Oelrichs snapped to attention. "As anyone can tell you, Mrs. Andrews, Trinity Church already has funds set aside for Newport's poor. I simply don't see the point of casting our largesse any farther." She caught the glances of the other ladies. "I'd say that would be spreading it rather too thin. Wouldn't you all agree?"

She, along with her husband, Hermann, had purchased the estate called Rosecliff on Bellevue Avenue a few years earlier, had torn down the house, and were currently having a mansion resembling the Grand Trianon at Versailles built in its place. The house was already three years under construction, and they still had at least another year to go, but Tessie was in no rush to unveil what she called the most graceful and genteel house in Newport.

Surely, Mrs. Oelrichs needn't fear spreading her or her friends' finances too thin.

"What St. Paul's is proposing," I calmly explained, "is an interchurch program, coordinating efforts to be certain that needs are met throughout the city at all times, with no gaps in the services we can provide."

"Why, you make us sound like some sort of charity organization," Mamie Fish said loudly. "As though Newport were the Lower East Side and all of us Sisters of Mercy or some such."

While the ladies chuckled over this, Grace stood up from her seat. "Aren't we exactly that? A charity, I mean. Is that not what churches are supposed to do? Besides provide a place for worship, of course." She looked down at me, her green eyes filled with fondness. "What our Emma suggests makes good sense. It will not only coordinate efforts to help the city's poor, but eliminate wasted dollars in duplicating those efforts."

She sat down, and I mouthed a thank-you in her direction. She had silenced the chuckles and prompted the ladies to take my suggestion seriously. From behind me, I heard another voice call my name. I turned to see yet another Vanderbilt relative, "Aunt" Alva, former wife of Uncle Cornelius's brother, William, now married to Oliver Belmont. I hadn't known until that moment that she had returned to town; last I'd heard, she and Mr. Belmont were traveling through New England. I stood to greet her.

"Nice to see you as well, Emmaline. I heard something of your idea as I came in, and it sounds like an ideal one." She sent a sharp gaze around the table at the others, the pure white feather in her hat swaying as she tilted her head. "I don't appreciate anyone disparaging my dear niece's ideas. Now then, let's get down to business."

Little by little, the other groups in the hall joined us, including Mrs. Wetmore and her two daughters, Maude and Edith. I was glad to have them there; as year-round residents as well as dedicated philanthropists, their assistance could be counted upon. Aunt Alva took up the task of compiling Trinity Church's own list for distributing necessities, in accordance with the list I'd brought from St. Paul's. Soon, we had a solid plan, but we needed to do more. We needed to recruit the rest of Newport's congregations in order to do the most good for the city.

"Well, that looks like everything." In addition to making a schedule, Aunt Alva had also penned a list of pledges from various ladies and the tasks and donations they would oversee. It never failed to amaze me how efficient and effective these women could be once they'd taken on a challenge. Suddenly, all frivolity vanished, and they were as astute as any of their husbands in their boardrooms.

With business concluded, the ladies vacated their seats to mingle. I linked my arm through Grace's and strolled away from our table. "Have you heard about the recent packages and letters delivered around town that contained a toxin?"

"What? No." Grace looked sincerely taken aback. "We've been so much on the move since arriving back in the country, I haven't had a chance to catch up on anything."

I explained what had been happening, and about Lottie Robinson's passing. I'd barely finished when I heard Aunt Alva's voice at my shoulder. "And you're trying to track down the source, aren't you, Emmaline?"

Rather than answer Aunt Alva's question, I asked one of my own. "You haven't received any of this mail, have you?"

"If I had, I wouldn't have been harmed." Aunt Alva smiled shrewdly. "Mamie told me what's been happening. I'm having my secretary open everything for me, and she's doing it while wearing gloves."

"Good. But do make sure your secretary is using the utmost care. Whatever this toxin is, it's highly dangerous. And yes"—I lowered my voice—"I'm helping to find out who's responsible."

"How can we help?" Grace drew us farther into an open area where a good number of the ladies were mingling and our voices would blend in with the rest.

"Yes, Emmaline, I'm willing to help in any way I can."

Aunt Alva drew herself up taller. "Oliver, too. I can speak for him as surely as I can speak for myself."

I had no doubt Aunt Alva could persuade her adoring second husband to do anything she asked of him. "It's information I need. That's partly why I'm here today, although the Interchurch Fund, as we're calling it, is real and vitally important. But I'd also hoped to"—I shrugged—"hear the latest gossip, I suppose."

"Wait one moment." Aunt Alva's expression turned wary. "Are you saying you believe it's one of us?"

"No, not exactly." I gave a firm shake of my head. I saw no need at this point to pit woman against woman by arousing their suspicions of one another. "It's just that every victim has been a woman of the Four Hundred. Someone obviously has some kind of grudge against our wealthy summer set. Which is why you must be very careful."

"What kind of information are you seeking?" Grace asked. I could see her warming to the notion of helping. She had helped me once before and had found it a great adventure—until the dangers became real.

"Have there been any unusual disagreements among your circles lately?" I turned to Grace. "Since you've only just arrived, you probably won't have heard of anything yet, but if you do . . ."

"I'll let you know immediately."

"As will I, but"—Aunt Alva eyed me speculatively—"it sounds to me like you suspect one of these ladies"

"Do you, Emma?" Grace wrapped a hand around my wrist. "Who? You can tell us."

Aunt Alva was scanning the faces around us, her fingers moving as if she were taking a count of the attendees. "Everyone here appears to be getting along just fine." She guffawed, drawing the attention of several of the ladies nearby. "Well, on the surface, that is. There is always some amount of subterfuge afoot." She crossed her arms and regarded me. "You might as well tell us whom you suspect."

As I gathered myself to reply, Grace and Alva tightened our little huddle. I sighed and whispered, "Anna Rose and Sybil Van Horn had a grudge against Mrs. Robinson"—here I lowered my voice still more—"but Ada Norris has also been targeted. Did either of the Van Horns have anything against her?"

"Other than being given the cut direct from a lot of our peers in general, no." Aunt Alva wrinkled her snub nose as she considered. She fingered the fox fur draped over one shoulder. "They come to Sunday services, but that's all these days. I can't say I blame them, poor things." She nodded at Grace and me. "The three of us know what it's like to be excluded, don't we? To be outsiders even among those who are supposed to be our family."

"We most certainly do," Grace agreed. Her mouth fell open, then quickly closed, and her eyebrows surged. "So the Van Horns are suspects?"

I shushed her.

"They are," she whispered, reaching her own conclusion.

"Please don't make me regret confiding in you," I whispered back. "No one can know any of what we've just discussed, or more women could be hurt." I wagered that last would induce my gregarious aunt Alva to hold her tongue. Of Grace, I had no doubts.

Aunt Alva gave a decisive nod. "You needn't worry. I am the soul of discretion." At that moment, the dessert table was unveiled, and the women began gravitating toward it. Aunt Alva whispered in my ear, "I've got an idea." She took my arm and briskly walked me over to the Wetmore ladies, who were poring over a wide platter filled with colorful, artistic cakes that were almost too pretty to eat. Yet all I could think about was whether they might be toxic.

"Mrs. Wetmore, Miss Edith, Miss Maude," Alva said in a singsong voice, "would you be so kind as to look after my dear Emmaline for a few minutes? I've got a thing or two that needs doing."

"Of course, it's our pleasure," Mrs. Wetmore graciously said. "We hardly had a chance to chat at Florence Twombly's luncheon, and Edith wasn't there at all. Come, Mrs. Andrews, let's catch up."

As we seated ourselves at one of the tables with several other ladies, I watched Aunt Alva, who had recruited Grace, circulate through the room, for all appearances chatting casually. Then a latecomer stepped through the doorway, prompting an abrupt silence to fall over the room. Aunt Alva sent a pointed glance across the room at her, then shifted her gaze to me. She winked, and I knew I'd be leaving there today with an answer or two.

Chapter 9

"A school for girls, you say." Mrs. Wetmore caught her daughters' gazes. They nodded to each other and turned back to me. "A capital idea. Please count us in. We'd love to be of help."

Though their offer of assistance in establishing my new school pleased me no end, I couldn't take my eye off the woman who had lately joined the proceedings. She had a rather barrel shape but carried herself with grace, her chin elevated a fraction. She appeared middle-aged, of similar years to my aunts Alva and Alice. Dressed modestly yet tastefully, her outfit spoke of wealth without any of the ostentation displayed by some of the other women here. She moved from table to table, from group to group, but as far as I could see, she spoke little and no one spoke to her. In fact, as the women physically snubbed her by turning away, my face heated in sympathetic mortification.

"A finishing school?" Mamie Fish said brightly, taking up where Mrs. Wetmore had left off. "I like the idea of our girls staying in this country rather than being shipped off to

Switzerland or some such place. Too many families are all too ready to hand their daughters over to the Europeans."

It was no secret that Mamie Fish didn't subscribe to the notion that wealthy Americans should emulate European aristocracy. That was why her cottage, Crossways, was modeled on colonial American architecture rather than French or Italian renaissance or English Gothic Revival.

"While I thank you for your support, Mrs. Fish, it won't be a finishing school. Rather, a high school with a full course of subjects." I took a bite of an apricot tartlet and waited for her response. It wasn't long in coming, nor anything other than I expected.

"Then surely this school won't be for our daughters." She put emphasis on the word *our*, implying that the daughters of the Four Hundred were to be considered separately from "ordinary" girls.

"No, it's for anyone who wishes to attend." While my tone exuded confidence, I was beginning to realize that most wealthy families thought as Mamie Fish and Aunt Alice did, that while girls needed to be educated in the arts—dance, music, literature, etc.—they needed only the most basic knowledge of other subjects. Just enough to hold interesting dinner conversations.

"I don't see how you'll keep such a school open," Mrs. Fish went on. "Seems to me you won't have enough paying students to make up for the ones who can't pay, nor enough wealthy investors." She eyed me sharply. "I'm assuming you wouldn't turn away a girl because her family can't afford the tuition."

"No, I wouldn't wish to do that," I agreed.

"Then, without our daughters"—once again, she emphasized *our*—"and without the support of society families, you won't have the funds to maintain your teachers' salaries. Will you?"

"My husband and I are prepared to—" Before I could state Derrick's and my willingness to contribute funds of our own, Mrs. Wetmore cut me off, though not unkindly.

"I don't believe that what you're saying is true, Mamie." She assumed a tolerant expression, one that suggested her patience had its limits. "Had such a school existed when my Maude and Edith were young, I would certainly have sent them."

"And I would happily have attended," Edith Wetmore added eagerly.

"I, too," her sister Maude put in with equal enthusiasm. "If women are to eventually have the vote, they'll need a proper understanding of politics and economics."

"I believe Aunt Alva might even have sent Consuelo," I said, but I wondered. Would she have, or was I merely making a hopeful claim? Consuelo Vanderbilt had been educated exceedingly well, more than most of her peers, but she had been taught at home by tutors, not at a school.

But Mamie Fish had alerted me to an essential fact: I must painstakingly think through the school's finances and develop a sound plan to keep it running in the event we lacked enough tuition-paying students and the financial support of the community. As I had begun to say, Derrick and I were prepared to fill in funds where needed, but for the long-term success of the school, we would need ongoing resources.

"We'll find donors willing to contribute to scholarship funds." I heard the stubbornness in my voice. One way or another, I would make this school a success.

Mrs. Fish apparently heard and understood my tone of voice. "My dear Emma, I'm not saying I would not support you. I will, of course. I am only playing devil's advocate and pointing out that, with such a school, you might not find the backing you'll need."

"Why do you all look so serious?" Aunt Alva had returned with Grace at her side. Before waiting for an answer, she continued. "I must be off. Emmaline, walk out with me? Grace, you, too."

On our way to the door, I scanned the room for the mysteriously excluded woman who had attempted to find a place for herself here, but who apparently had not been successful. She was nowhere to be found.

Finally, we stepped outside and walked up toward the church. We paused beside the graveyard, where birdsong replaced the female chatter at the vestry. The trees cast their shade over the headstones, and the church's white clapboard tower scraped a partially clouded sky. On Spring Street, carriages half-clogged the road as they waited for their mistresses to finish their meeting. An automobile slowly inched past them, its engine puttering and its driver scowling and mouthing words it was best we didn't overhear.

Before either Aunt Alva or Grace could say anything, I asked a question. "Who was that woman who came late and seemed unwelcome among the others?

Aunt Alva grinned triumphantly. "Mina Wallingford. It is she I wish to speak to you about now."

Despite not having recognized her, I knew the name and something of her history. Mrs. Wallingford was one of our wealthier local Newporters. A widow, she had inherited the millions her husband made from his shipyards along the New England coastline from Connecticut to Maine. "Why was she given such a cold shoulder?"

Grace let out an excited little breath, but she waited for Aunt Alva to explain.

"She's been cast out," she said with a snap of her fingers. "Two weeks ago, some of the ladies here at Trinity banded together and told Mina Wallingford she was no longer welcome to serve on any church committees."

"No longer welcome—to volunteer her time and money?"

That sounded preposterous to me. "Why on earth did they do that?"

"Because they say she is impossible to work with. Isn't that so, Grace?"

"I wouldn't know exactly. I haven't been spending as much time in Newport these days . . ."

Aunt Alva cast a glance at Grace that quieted her immediately. "From my own experience," she said, "Mina can be difficult. She likes to be in charge, and she insists things go her way. She also enjoys taking credit for other people's accomplishments. Apparently, two weeks ago, the ladies finally decided they'd had enough."

"Yet she came today anyway." I gazed over my shoulder toward the vestry, where ladies had begun trickling out the front door.

"I'm surprised she had the gall to show her face," Aunt Alva said. "Yet part of me says good for her."

"I agree." Grace's gloved hand made a little fist. "Good for her. As you said earlier, Mrs. Belmont, you and I certainly know about being shunned."

"Indeed we do, my dear." Alva's blunt features, which had always reminded me somewhat of a French bulldog, hardened with determination and defiance. It was Alva who had forced Caroline Astor's hand in accepting the Vanderbilt family into society. After she divorced Uncle William, not only did the entire Vanderbilt family turn against her, but society rejected her as well. For a time, Alva's marriage to Oliver Belmont helped restore her position, at least partially; Alva's tenacity and sheer audacity had done the rest.

No wonder she felt sympathy for yet another society outcast. "What happened when Mrs. Wallingford was asked to leave?" I asked. "How did she react?"

"According to what I was just told, she was livid." Aunt

Alva slapped her handbag against her skirts. "Utterly morti-fied and bent on getting even. According to Eliza Stevens and Margaret Chandler, who heard her with their own ears, she said she would see their committees burn in . . . you know where."

My eyes widened in disbelief. "Good heavens, she didn't."

"Tell her the rest," Grace urged.

I spared her a glance, then returned my full attention to Aunt Alva. "Please, don't keep me in suspense."

"The two loudest voices against her . . . were Lottie Rob-inson and Ada Norris."

My mouth dropped open.

"So you see, Emma," Grace murmured in my ear, "the Van Horns may yet be vindicated."

I frowned. "But would Mrs. Wallingford . . . ?"

Aunt Alva gave a careless shrug. "Would Anna Rose and Sybil Van Horn?"

"One moment, though," I said as a thought occurred to me. "This doesn't rule out the Van Horns at all. They've been abandoned by many of their longtime friends, many of whom were at this meeting today. Their chief argument might have been with Lottie Robinson, but that doesn't mean they have no cause to resent the rest—or want revenge against the very women they hoped would rally around them in their time of need."

"You do make a valid point, Emma." Grace tugged at one of her lace gloves. "We haven't ruled out anyone, then. We've merely added a suspect."

"Very true." Aunt Alva sighed loudly. "At least Anna Rose and Sybil are no longer the only suspects."

But how much longer would the list grow? Suddenly, a weariness overcame me, and I wanted nothing more than to be at home with my feet up, sipping some of Nanny's strong tea and letting her reassure me, as she had done all my life, that all would be well. Instead, I hurried back to the *Messenger* to continue the day's work.

That evening, Derrick and I sat side by side in the parlor, sipping sherry, while Nanny and Katie put the finishing touches on dinner. Like the newlyweds we were, we leaned shoulder to shoulder and entwined our hands while we discussed the day.

"Jesse says they still haven't identified the toxin." I had telephoned over to the police station before leaving the *Messenger* and endured the impatient huffing of Jesse's partner, who obviously resented having to play telephone operator, as he had put it. When Jesse came on the line, I told him what I had learned at Trinity Church concerning Mina Wallingford.

"A bit of revenge that got out of hand," Jesse had mused. "Yes, she may have had a motive. I don't suppose . . . ."

"That I'd help you question her?" I'd chuckled into the buzzing coming over the line. "Yes, of course. Tell me when."

Then he had told me his frustrating news concerning the toxin. "The police lab in Providence has only determined that it's not one of the usual substances tainting the petit fours. Not a poison such as arsenic or strychnine, nor a household cleaner such as carbolic acid, bleach, or lye. Now they're testing for poisonous plants. They've consulted with Dr. Agassiz, but he said it could be one of a thousand different plants laced into those cakes. That makes the toxin nearly impossible to pinpoint."

Dr. Alexander Agassiz, who owned the Castle Hill estate in the far southwest corner of the island, held degrees in various sciences, including chemistry, zoology, and botany. He had traveled the world many times over, identifying species and collecting specimens. If he couldn't identify the toxin, it was doubtful anyone else could.

"Whatever it was, it had to have been added to the petit fours after they were prepared." Derrick's thumb traced the palm of my hand as he considered. "An invisible substance that was possibly poured over the icing. Which implies a liquid of some sort."

I nodded. "Yes, that's what the police believe, too. Although, it could also be something granular, like a glazing of sugar."

"Have they considered peppers?" Derrick and I both looked up at the doorway as Nanny came into the room. "I don't know why I didn't think of it sooner. Well, I do know why—it's because I don't cook with such peppers, nor does anyone else I know of. But in some countries, they use peppers that are so hot they burn the skin if held too long. And when someone isn't used to eating them, they can cause severe dyspepsia."

"Really?" I traded a surprised glance with Derrick. "What kind of cooking would call for such harsh ingredients?"

"I've only read about it, mind you," she said and she took a seat, "but in South American countries, and in the islands, I've heard tell they flavor dishes with a good amount of spice and heat."

"Eat at one's own risk," I joked, then turned serious. "But how could a pepper be used without being obvious?"

"By grinding it to a powder, like many spices," Nanny said, "or squeezing the juice from it."

"I see. And where would someone here obtain such a pepper?"

"In this country? I'd say most likely in a large city with a diverse population," Derrick offered with a shrug. "Like New York, Boston, perhaps even Providence."

"Places members of the Four Hundred frequent," I concluded. "Thank you, Nanny. It's quite possible the police aren't thinking along these lines, that something common in exotic cooking could have been used to poison the victims."

From down the hall came Katie's voice, bidding us all to come and eat. Nanny shifted forward in her chair; before she got any further, Derrick was on his feet and helping her up. Our houseguests hurried down from their room upstairs, chattering as they came. They had apparently spent the afternoon sightseeing along the Cliff Walk and had gone up to rest before dinner.

Derrick had taken to shedding his coat upon arriving home each evening. Now, because of our company, he retrieved it from the back of his chair, but before he shrugged back into it, I gave in to the temptation to rest my cheek against his shoulder. At the sensation of his starched shirt-sleeve, framed by the edge of his vest against my skin, a deep sense of contentment spread through me. Nanny walked ahead of us out of the room, but I noticed her peeking at us over her shoulder and grinning.

I concealed a start as I realized that only a few short weeks ago I'd felt self-conscious at displaying our affection in front of Nanny and Katie. Gull Manor, long my home, hadn't felt like *our* home. It had been strangely disorienting to have him here—a man, where only women had dwelled for so long. When did that change? I could not say; I had not noticed any gradual easing of my reservations concerning my newly married state. I only knew that, as Derrick and I strolled to the table together and were greeted by fanciful smiles from Nanny, Katie, Miss Carter, and even Miss Lewis, I no longer felt any need to slip my arm free of his or open space between us.

Following dinner, I returned to the parlor with the ledger book I'd kept since inheriting Gull Manor, along with a modest annuity, from my great aunt Sadie. My parents had imparted to me an appreciation for art and culture; my father was an artist, and he and my mother had often hosted small parties of other artists, poets, and writers at our house on the Point while I was growing up. Though a child, I had nonetheless absorbed their enthusiasm for creativity and something more: a freedom of thought and expression, which I credit for my journalistic ambitions. But it was Aunt Sadie, and surely not my parents, who had taught me how to manage my personal finances, and how to balance my salary with expenditures so that I never went into debt.

Despite a second and more substantial inheritance from Cornelius Vanderbilt, I had not lost sight of Aunt Sadie's lessons. I continued to record each expense, large or small, in my household ledger, and what's more, I took into account only my own resources. I had pledged to myself upon my marriage that I would not depend on my husband's money to cover costs I could not. He had chuckled over it at first, until he had seen my determination. Respect had taken the place of amusement in his dark eyes.

Tonight, I was going over my charitable endeavors. St. Nicholas Orphanage in Providence had topped the list for several years. Now I decided to increase my donations. There were organizations here in Newport that I supported as well, such as the Women's Work Project, which helped poor women, married and unmarried alike, find work as seamstresses, laundresses, shopworkers, and the like, and provided care for any children too young to attend school. Again, I decided to increase my support. Only when I was satisfied that I was making fair contributions to my community did I turn my attention to Gull Manor's future school, for I didn't wish to sacrifice one for the other.

Miss Lewis and Miss Carter soon joined me, though when they saw me concentrating over my open book, they offered to go elsewhere.

"No, please stay." I closed the ledger, using its ribbon to mark my place. "I was just finishing up. Were you outside?"

"We were," Miss Carter replied, with an appreciative expression. "Watching the first stars come out. The air is so fresh here, so crisp at night."

"We're not used to that, not at this time of year," Miss Lewis supplied with a laugh.

That made me curious. "How do you withstand such hot weather in the summer months? Why, I think half the women in Newport would faint dead away in the first minute."

"One grows used to it." Miss Carter draped her skirts just so over her knees. "And we live quite close to the coast, where we benefit from the ocean breezes. Farther inland, there's nary a breath of air to be found. Our indigenous population, however, seems to have mastered the heat, for they live in the flat wilderness at the very center of the state and, for all appearances, thrive there."

Miss Lewis arched a dubious eyebrow. "They were given little choice, Aunt. One learns to make do with what one has, doesn't one?"

Miss Carter shrugged to concede her niece's point. I had detected the faintest note of bitterness in Miss Lewis's statement and couldn't help wondering if she had been thinking of something in addition to the fate that had befallen Florida's Indian population. Perhaps something in her own life?

I discreetly regarded the pair. They posed a rather commonplace picture, a young woman serving as a companion to an elder aunt. Amity Carter appeared happy with her choices. As a single woman, she had achieved what most married women could never dream of. She immersed herself in a topic that fascinated her—that of Florida's natural environment—and had published several books on the subject, with plans for more.

But what about Zinnia Lewis? Yes, she painted and seemed to derive satisfaction from her hobby. But could it ever be anything more? Would her paintings find an audience? Would she ever have the chance to exhibit them? And what about her future—would she find a husband? Did she want one? It would be wrong to assume that what made her aunt happy would necessarily make Miss Lewis happy.

Then again, none of it was any of my business.

A telephone call first thing the following morning sent Derrick and me on a detour to Beaulieu, the Bellevue Avenue home of Neily and Grace Vanderbilt. Her secretary had made the call and asked me to come as quickly as possible; her employer desperately wished to see me, she said. When, with my heart pounding in my throat, I inquired after the matter, the woman would only repeat that it was imperative I arrive there soon.

I did my best to resist snatching the carriage reins out of Derrick's hands and urging Maestro to a gallop. My lower lip nearly bled, I bit it so hard along the way, while my fingernails left half-moons in my palm, even through my lace gloves.

Derrick brought the carriage to a halt in front of the steps leading up to the entrance of the French chateau–style mansion built in the middle of the previous century. A footman awaited us outside and opened the door without our needing to tell him who we were. Inside, across the black and white marble-tiled hall, I saw Neily leading the children in from the terrace. They spotted us and came running.

"Auntie Emma!" Neily's three-year-old son, wearing knee britches and suspenders half falling from the shoulders of his lawn shirt, shrieked in greeting and barreled toward us, making me certain he'd slip and fall on the tiles. Behind him toddled two-year-old Gracie, resembling a floating tuft of lace in her smock dress with its wide, puffed sleeves.

I knelt down to gather them to me. "Hello, you two! Goodness, how big you're both getting."

"I am," young Corneil declared proudly, "but Gracie is still just a baby."

I met his adorably defiant gaze. "That's right. And that's why she needs her big brother to take care of her."

With a solemn expression, he nodded in agreement and turned his attention to Derrick, who picked him up and tossed him in the air. Corneil shrieked with laughter and begged for more. Meanwhile, with Gracie balanced on my hip, I took the hand Neily offered me and came to my feet. His features were grim.

"What's happened?" I asked my cousin, barely aware of Gracie's tiny fist tugging at the brim of my straw boater.

Before he answered, he said to Derrick, "You'll watch them for a few moments? Their nurse will be down directly."

"Of course," Derrick replied heartily. "Tell her not to hurry. What shall we do, children?" With Corneil balanced on one hip, he reached out with an arm to gather Gracie to his other side. I couldn't help grinning at the picture he made, flanked by two chubby, dimpled faces.

To me, Neily said, "Come. She's upstairs."

He said nothing more until we reached Grace's room. Although Derrick and I shared a room, Grace and Neily had deferred to the common practice among the wealthy of establishing separate bedrooms, connected by a dressing room and a kind of inner passageway off the main hall. It allowed maids and valets to move discreetly from one room to another; it allowed husbands to do the same.

Neily tapped at Grace's door, then opened it without waiting for a reply. My stomach clenched in dread as I followed him inside. I didn't immediately see Grace, and all I could think of was Lottie Robinson and Ada Norris. Would I find a similar fate had befallen my friend?

My gaze darted to the bed, an elaborate, gilt-framed affair draped in satin and ruffles. It reminded me of Aunt Alva's queenly bed at Marble House, although presently she resided at Belcourt. A breath of relief escaped me when I saw that Grace's bed lay empty.

"Emma, thank goodness you're here."

Her voice had me whirling in the opposite direction. I crossed the room to where she reclined on a chaise-longue that was nearly as fussy as the bed. She sat half-upright against a pile of pillows, with her feet propped on yet more. She held the edge of a light blanket against her bosom. Her hands were wrapped in strips of linen.

Neily came up on her other side and leaned low to kiss her cheek. "How are you feeling, my dear?"

"It still burns, but the ointment is helping."

I reached out. "May I see?"

She allowed me to unwrap her hands. Red splotches enwrapped her fingers, especially those of her right hand, although both hands had been affected. Then I noticed a patch of raw skin to the right side of her mouth. "Grace, what happened? Were you sent tainted baked goods?"

"No, not baked goods. A letter. It must have been in the ink." She shut her eyes a moment and shook her head. "So stupid of me. You warned me of what was happening. I knew better, yet I still had Miss Havens, my secretary, bring me my mail this morning. She hadn't yet had a chance to go through it, but I said it would be all right. I often go through it myself. But if she had, it would be her experiencing this horror, and I'd have been riddled with guilt!"

While I wouldn't have termed her injuries a horror, I recognized the burns as the same that had inflicted the other women. I took her right hand gently and turned it palm up to better view the burns on the pads of her fingers. "It looks like you smoothed the page open and kept your hands on the paper as you read."

"Yes, I did exactly that. And then I suppose I touched my face, and that's how I got this." She pointed to the burn below her cheek. "I don't remember doing it, but you know how that is. We touch our faces all the time without realizing it. My hands started to burn first, and then this spot on my face became fiery." She gripped my forearm and pulled me closer. "Emma, do you think it will leave a scar?"

"I'm sure it won't, Grace." I wasn't sure at all, but I didn't wish to alarm her. "Have you telephoned for a doctor?"

Behind me, Neily spoke. "Yes. I can't say what's taking him so long to get here." He drew his fob watch from his vest pocket and consulted the time. "I'll go down and wait for him. And save Derrick from the children."

That last got a chuckle from Grace, a good sign. She leaned her head back against the tufted chaise. "I feel so foolish about this. But why was I singled out? I only recently arrived in Newport. I certainly didn't attend Mrs. Twombly's luncheon like the others."

That was a very good question. Grace hadn't attended the luncheon . . .

But she had been present for the meeting at Trinity Church. And so had Mina Wallingford. Had she seen Grace with me, and perhaps overheard some of our conversation about the toxin? Or about Mrs. Wallingford herself?

A sudden fear for Aunt Alva filled me, until I remembered Alva Belmont was not a woman to forget a vital detail such as tainted mail arriving along Bellevue Avenue.

"Do you have any clues as to who is doing this?" Then, as if having read my mind, she asked, "Do you think it was Mrs. Wallingford? It is highly likely, isn't it?"

"It's possible, but not a foregone conclusion," I cautioned. "It so happens I intend to call on the woman—soon."

"Will you bring up my name?"

I gave this some thought. "I'd like to mention you to see if she exhibits any reaction. But I wouldn't give her the satisfaction of letting her know you fell prey to this cruel act, if indeed Mrs. Wallingford is responsible."

"You'll be careful, won't you, Emma? It wouldn't do for something like this to happen to you. I'd never forgive myself."

I gave her forearm a reassuring squeeze. A knock at her door announced the doctor's arrival, and I bade her good morning.

Chapter 10

"Emma, I don't like it. I wish you wouldn't go."

Later that day, Derrick blocked the path from my desk to my office door. He planted his feet wide and crossed his arm.

"There's nothing to worry about. I'm simply calling on the woman. Seeing her at the committee meeting at Trinity Church gives me the perfect opportunity. She won't know I'm there to question her."

"Jesse should go with you." His voice held finality, as if there could be no further argument. It was a tone I had heard from him before, but rarely directed at me.

My hands went to my hips. I could be as stubborn as he. "Then she would know she's being questioned."

"She is being questioned!" His voice rose. He stopped, took a breath, compressed his lips, and began again more calmly. "Why must it always be you?"

"If not me, who?"

"The police, for heaven's sake."

"You know how that always goes in such situations. She'll

simply refuse to answer his questions. Besides, I owe this to Grace."

"Do you?" His arms fell to his sides. He circled the desk, coming to a stop only inches away from me. He gathered me to him in that way of his—a way that always melted my anger and softened my resolve. "I don't want you in harm's way. I want you safe. If Mina Wallingford is responsible, who is to say she won't serve you up the same deadly toxin?"

I angled my chin to smile up at him. "I won't have anything to eat or drink."

His lips pinched tightly together while his eyes blazed with admonishments. I relented.

"I'm sorry, I didn't mean to make light. But truly, I don't have to accept tea and cookies from her. I'll tell her I've lately eaten. Besides, I won't be entirely alone. Jesse will be outside and a few houses down in his carriage. If I'm not out in twenty minutes, he'll come to my rescue."

The hard line of his jaw relaxed, and I knew our argument had ended. I stood on tiptoe to plant a kiss on his cheek. Ruefully, he said, "I didn't really think I could change your mind."

I kissed him again, fully on the lips. Then I gathered up my things and left.

Mina Wallingford lived on Catherine Street in a tree-shaded house behind low stone walls, its weathered-brick façade clad in lush ivy. At the front door, I showed my calling card and was immediately ushered into a conservatory at the rear of the house, first passing through a sumptuously furnished drawing room. I was not kept waiting long.

"Mrs. Andrews, I am told." As on the previous day, Mina Wallingford wore a subdued, yet tasteful and obviously expensive ensemble, this time in cobalt-blue silk. Although a widow, she was apparently long out of mourning. Her hair had been drawn back to her nape in a bun, with curls fashioned at the sides. She looked the epitome of a respectable, wealthy, and dignified woman.

I had been standing at one of the floor-to-ceiling windows framed by potted palms. I walked toward her and extended my hand. "Mrs. Wallingford, I hope you'll forgive the intrusion."

"May I ask what brings you to my home?" Her gray eyes regarded me with curiosity, and with wariness. She shook my hand briefly, her palm cool and dry against mine.

"I was at the Trinity Church meeting yesterday."

"I see." Her lips pursed. One eyebrow twitched as she assessed me. "Won't you sit down?" She motioned me to a wrought-iron chair, its seat and back heavily cushioned in a burgundy and cream striped fabric. She sat facing me. "And what might I do for you, Mrs. Andrews?"

"Nothing, Mrs. Wallingford. It's simply that . . . well . . . I saw how the others behaved. That is what prompted me to call on you." Not entirely a lie, I told myself.

"How kind." She sounded dubious. "Or are you merely curious about Newport's latest pariah?"

"I would hardly call you that, ma'am." I set my handbag in my lap and removed my gloves, in essence making myself comfortable. Or, at least, giving the impression that I was comfortable there in that house, speaking with a woman who continued to hold me in her shrewd gaze. "But you see, I understand something about not being accepted by society. I'm a Vanderbilt relative—a poor one, if the truth be told—"

"I thought I recognized you. You're Emmaline Cross, aren't you? Or you were before you married."

"That's right. I—"

"You're a reporter."

I breathed out slowly. "Mrs. Wallingford, I am not here as a reporter." Again, not entirely a lie. I was there at Jesse's behest. "I am here as someone who, as I said, understands a bit about what you are going through."

Her gaze swept me up and down. She appeared amused in a haughty sort of way as she waited for me to continue.

"My Vanderbilt cousins always made a point of including me whenever they were in Newport. But that didn't mean their acquaintances saw me in the same light. To many of them, I was that poor relation who didn't belong. And now, my own in-laws are less than pleased about their son choosing me as his wife. His mother, at least, has yet to come around and possibly never will. So you see, I know what rejection is."

"And you are here to commiserate? I assure you, Mrs. Andrews, I certainly don't need your pity."

Goodness, I thought, was she entirely impervious to overtures of kindness or friendship? Suppressing a sigh, I continued trying. "I simply didn't like what I saw yesterday. I found the behavior of most of the other ladies reprehensible."

"Did you discover the reason for it?"

I raised my chin and spoke the truth. "In my view, there is no good reason for rudeness."

"Then you've heard what they say about me." She scoffed. "Trying to organize most of those hens is like trying to organize . . . well . . . a flock of hens. They don't take well to being led, however much they could benefit from my guidance."

My mouth nearly dropped open. Only a quick catch on my part prevented my astonishment from being revealed. And yet, she had provided me with just the inroad I needed.

"But you keep trying, don't you, Mrs. Wallingford? You aren't ready to abandon your fellow philanthropists. Otherwise, you wouldn't have gone to the meeting yesterday, would you?"

"Indeed, Mrs. Andrews." She pulled herself up taller. "One must do what one can, despite obstacles."

"It's quite noble of you. Especially when people can be so cruel. Surely, ma'am, it does anger you?"

"Of course it does. Especially when one is being criticized by"—she broke off and sniffed—"one doesn't like to use the word *inferiors,* but sometimes one must."

My back stiffened as I envisioned Aunt Alva's likely response had she heard that last comment. I leaned forward, assuming a confidential air. "Were there ringleaders? Ones who egged the others on?"

Blowing out a breath, she raised her eyebrows in a long-suffering gesture. "There are always ringleaders, but I wouldn't deign to speak of them. Besides, one of them can no longer make trouble."

She pronounced this with such audacity that another shock went through me. She spoke, of course, of Lottie Robinson, no longer of this world. Did Mina Wallingford send her the petit fours to punish her? Did she punish Grace today?

"Perhaps there is a way to mend broken bridges," I suggested, attempting to sound naïve and well-meaning.

"Bah. Didn't I try yesterday simply by going to the meeting? By showing them all that I'm above taking their insults to heart and am willing to put the good of the community above my own personal feelings?"

"Yes, I'd say your attendance yesterday implied as much. My relative, Grace Vanderbilt, holds nothing against you. Perhaps she can help you reestablish your position."

Her brow wrinkled. "Mrs. Vanderbilt? Well, I suppose she also knows what it's like to be held at arm's length, what with the way the family treated her when she married young Mr. Vanderbilt."

"Yes, that's true. Do you know her well?"

"Not well at all, Mrs. Andrews, and I would never impose my problems on a young woman barely of my acquaintance. I would consider that the height of ill manners."

I had watched her closely during this exchange. She exhibited none of the usual signs of discomfiture or uncertainty that usually accompany lies. No heightened color, no dilation of her pupils, no fidgeting. My bringing up Grace had puzzled her, but hadn't unsettled her. "Mrs. Wallingford, this alienation can't go on forever. The other committee members must accept you back into the fold eventually."

"Must they?" Her tone suddenly turned bitter, where previously it had been indifferent. I had managed to strike a chord after all, just not the one I'd hoped. "They are a backstabbing, spiteful lot, and most of them deserve whatever misfortunes fate turns their way."

Good heavens. "Perhaps that's a bit harsh. Some of them are—"

"Most are calculating social climbers, Mrs. Andrews, and it would serve you well to remember that."

I let that go unobserved and eased into a new tack. "Perhaps turning your attention to other matters entirely might help smooth things over."

"What are you getting at?"

"I'm thinking of a hobby, perhaps, rather than a philanthropic project. Something that doesn't require such structure. Something enjoyable."

"Ah." She tilted her head at me. "You mean something that doesn't require leadership—something where the other women won't resent my expertise."

I held back a sigh of frustration and smiled. "Yes, that's it exactly."

"Such as what, Mrs. Andrews?" She sounded less than convinced.

"Well ... for instance, my houseguests are avid bird-watchers. Perhaps you'd care to join them in that endeavor."

"What for? If I want to see birds, I'll walk out onto my own terrace."

"Or gardening, perhaps. Have you any interest in botany, ma'am?"

A deep furrow formed above her nose. "I appreciate trees and flowers as much as the next person, but I leave the particulars up to my gardeners. That is what I pay them for."

"Then you wouldn't know about some of our native flora here on the island, or farther afield? Never been out for hikes in our natural areas?"

She let out a huff. "Mrs. Andrews, this is the most ridiculous conversation. How odd you are. Do you really think a woman such as myself would don a pair of rugged boots and set out into the wilderness—to do what?" She came to her feet. "Thank you for your visit, but I have a stack of correspondence on my desk that needs my attention."

Once she had closed the door at my back, I breathed a sigh of relief. She had to be the most irascible individual I'd ever had the misfortune of attempting conversation with. I now had a full understanding of why her peers had ousted her from their church committees, deeming her impossible to work with. Could she be responsible for the poisonings? I hadn't come to a dependable conclusion either way, but at this point I wouldn't have put it past her.

But did she possess the knowledge to find and use a toxic plant to poison others? Her bafflement when I brought up botany and hiking rang true, but one could never be certain. Did she have motive? Yes, potentially. Did she have opportunity? Very possibly. Therefore, she could not be ruled out.

* * *

The next days passed quietly. I checked in regularly with Grace, who reported that her hands were healing nicely. They were now taking strict precautions with all correspondence and unsolicited deliveries that arrived at Beaulieu. In the meantime, while the police continued their investigation, Derrick and I engaged lawyers to draw up the sale agreement for Miss Carter's property. Although she was advised to ask more than she had originally stated, Derrick and I had no difficulty meeting her price. A hitch did arise, however, when it was discovered that the will naming her as the inheritor of the property had not yet been fully executed.

The job of executor, apparently, had fallen on Miss Carter's brother-in-law. Miss Carter's sister had died five years prior, and the uncle had left the property free and clear to Miss Carter herself, yet it seemed this brother-in-law continued to drag his feet among his own lawyers in hopes he might find a way to share ownership of the property, if not take possession outright.

"I never did much like Ezra," Miss Carter announced at dinner that evening, after explaining the problem to us. "For that matter, I never much liked my sister, Katrina, either. She sided with my parents when it came to the prospect of my marrying and helped them make my life miserable."

"Aunt," Miss Lewis murmured, leaning closer to her in a confidential way, "I'm sure our hosts don't wish to hear about all that."

"Oh, and why not?" Miss Carter flourished her fork in the air over her plate. "I have a feeling Mrs. Andrews understands what it's like for her family to oppose her chosen lifestyle." Her eyebrows went up as she pierced me with a quizzical look.

I laughed. "Indeed I do. But it was never my parents who disapproved. My dear Aunt Alice—Mrs. Vanderbilt, that is—was forever trying to persuade me to give up reporting and settle down with a nice, wealthy man."

"Which is what you did," Miss Carter pointed out. Her lips momentarily pursed, as if in disapproval.

"Yes, in the end I did. Happily so." Derrick and I traded fond looks. "But it was my decision and not Aunt Alice's, and I'm still actively reporting."

"I wouldn't have had it any other way," Derrick said matter-of-factly.

"Well, then, bravo." Miss Carter paused for a piece of braised lamb shank. "Not many women would have prevailed in that manner. I needn't point out that you and Mr. Andrews are not at all the norm. I keep telling Zinnia—"

"Yes, yes," her niece singsonged, "'treasure your independence and protect it.' Truly, Aunt Amity, I've learned that lesson well. You have driven it deeply home."

Miss Carter's gaze sharpened, but fleetingly, like the disapproval she'd exhibited a moment ago. She reached over the table between them and patted her niece's hand. "Just remember that everything I have will be yours someday. And then you'll need rely on no one."

Miss Lewis nodded. But I continued to wonder what the younger woman aspired to do with her life. Did she find contentment as her aunt's companion? Or did she feel trapped? Miss Carter implored her to protect her independence, but did she truly possess such freedom—freedom to live as she saw fit? Did she wish to meet a man, marry, and have children? And if so, would her aunt interfere? Miss Carter, I realized, was the very antithesis of Aunt Alice, wishing quite the opposite for her niece of what Aunt Alice had wished for me.

I decided to change the subject while continuing to focus the conversation on our guests. "What sent you all the way to Florida, if I may ask?"

"My family. My parents were still living then. Over the years, I'd had more than enough of their scheming to send me down the aisle with the appropriate candidate and finally moved out of their home." She sipped her wine, then stared into the crystal goblet thoughtfully. "I sold off some of my jewelry and gowns to raise money, and a dear friend and I moved into a tiny flat in New York's East Village. Oh, how we loved it there. We were on the top floor of a brownstone and could see the treetops lining the street outside our windows. I'm sure the other tenants, indeed the neighbors up and down the street, thought we were hopelessly fast. We weren't. We attended musicales and poetry readings, and I met several writers who helped me develop my own literary style. It was a wonderful time of self-education."

She sat back against her chair. "Soon, though, my money began to dwindle, and I hadn't anything more to sell. My parents, who always seemed to find out everything about me, swooped in to persuade me to return home. I refused. Then the uncle who eventually left me the property next door made me an offer. He had gone to Florida to work with Henry Flagler on developing his hotels. Uncle Cecil offered me a position as his secretary. I seized the opportunity. My parents never forgave him—or me. But I have never regretted my decision."

"Nor have I, Aunt, in joining you." Miss Lewis smiled wistfully at me. "I hail from a branch of the family without much in the way of resources. From an early age, I prepared for life as a governess or schoolteacher. I wouldn't have minded terribly. There are worse ways for a single woman to earn her keep. But there would have been little time and no money for my art."

We took our tea in the parlor, an interesting brew we hadn't had before. It had a rich, almost earthy flavor I didn't remember ever tasting before. I resolved to ask Nanny about it later and continued the discussion by inquiring of Miss Lewis, "What about marriage? Is that in your eventual plans?"

Her face became shuttered. "As my aunt has said, independence is far more important. Marriage tends to strip a woman of her own identity. Her own dreams."

"But as you can see, it isn't always that way," I persisted, believing at my very core that Zinnia Lewis had traded her own dreams for those of her aunt. Could Amity Carter be so jealous of her niece's attentions that she guarded against anyone else encroaching on Zinnia's time? I purposely avoided Miss Carter's gaze as I waited for Miss Lewis to comment. But the conversation was cut short.

Derrick cleared his throat. "Have you made plans for tomorrow?" he asked our guests.

"We haven't decided yet. Any suggestions?" Miss Carter undoubtedly welcomed the change in subject. At the same time, I wondered at my impertinence in attempting to force the issue with her niece. Why had it become so important to me?

"Since you toured a portion of the Cliff Walk today," Derrick said, "perhaps you'd like to see Sachuest Point. It's not far from Hanging Rock, but more directly overlooks the ocean. Much like the Cliff Walk, but farther out and without the houses and civilization."

"That sounds perfect," Miss Carter exclaimed. "What do you think, Zinnia?"

She had taken a book of plant sketches off the shelf and sat with it open on her lap. Without looking up, she replied, "As long as there is a good spot to set up my easel."

"Plenty of excellent spots," Derrick assured her.

"But we've imposed enough on you and Mrs. Andrews," Miss Carter said with a tsk. "We couldn't possibly ask either of you to put off your work another day to escort us around the island."

"Not to worry," I told her. "I'll call over to my relatives' stables and ask that a carriage and driver be sent over for you in the morning. Goodness knows, they have plenty on hand."

"There, then it's settled." Derrick paused, and I suddenly felt his scrutiny upon me. His next words surprised me. "Are you quite all right, Emma?"

"Me? Yes, of course. Why would you ask?"

He reached out and grazed my cheek with his knuckles. "You're looking tired, a little pale."

Nanny chose that moment to saunter into the room, Patch trotting along behind her. "Emma, tired? I was thinking the same thing during dinner."

I let out a laugh. "I do believe I'm being insulted."

"Not at all." Derrick hadn't taken his eyes off me. "We're just a little concerned. Especially in light of what's been going on."

"I feel fine," I insisted. "Yes, a bit tired, perhaps, but—"

"Of course you're tired." Nanny came over and pressed a palm to my forehead, the way she used to do when I was a child and had a fever. "You've taken on far too much lately, what with the newspaper, these plans for the school, the church project, and this case for Jesse . . ."

"And houseguests," Miss Carter said with a note of regret. "Dear Mrs. Andrews, I fear Zinnia and I are only adding to your burdens. Perhaps it would be better if we—"

"I wouldn't hear of it." I pressed to my feet. "There's no need for anyone to worry about me. Perhaps Nanny's right, and I'm simply doing too much lately. I think I'll go up now and get a good night's sleep. You'll all see. I'll be my usual chipper self in the morning."

After bidding everyone good night, I did indeed climb the stairs, with Patch leading the way. He stopped once or twice when I lagged behind. Truth be told, I was feeling fatigued, but as Nanny had said, I was simply stretched thin these days.

I had no idea when Derrick came up to bed, for I didn't stir until first light, when I opened my eyes to find him asleep beside me. Sitting up and stretching my arms over my head, I felt renewed energy surge through me. It seemed a good night's rest had set me to rights, and I was ready for another busy day at the *Messenger*.

Fate, however, had other ideas.

Chapter 11

The message from Vinland arrived as we and our guests were finishing up breakfast. It wasn't from Mrs. Twombly this time, but from her daughter, Flora. She asked me to come there as soon as possible.

"We'll stop on our way into town." Derrick gathered up some papers and his hat, while I retrieved my handbag from the hall table. Before he and I could slip out the front door, Nanny came running down the stairs carrying my embroidered silk shawl, a gift from Derrick when we were in Italy on our honeymoon.

"Here, wear this." When she reached the bottom of the stairs, she crossed the hall to me and tossed it around my shoulders. "To keep the draft off your shoulders and neck."

"It's August," I patiently informed her. "It must be at least eighty degrees already. I assure you I'll be quite safe from drafts."

"Just humor an old woman, thank you."

"All right, Nanny." I kissed her cheek. "I'll wear it if you promise not to worry about me. I'm fine."

She nodded and changed the subject. "You'll let me know later what your cousin wants."

She was referring to Flora, and her unusual request that I come to Vinland. Though she and I had always gotten on well enough, we were not close, not truly friends as I was with my other Vanderbilt cousins. That could only mean her summons had something to do with Lottie Robinson's death.

Flora awaited us just inside the front door, and as soon as the butler admitted us and walked away, she pressed a finger to her lips. "Thank you for coming. Mother isn't awake yet. She doesn't know I sent for you."

As she had spoken in a whisper, I did likewise. "What is this all about?"

Her gaze darted back and forth between Derrick and me. "Come this way."

We followed her into the library, which, like the drawing room and dining room, faced the rear of the property. It was another beautiful summer day, and the brightness of a perfectly manicured lawn, flawless sky, and glittering ocean outside the large windows nearly had me shading my eyes, especially in contrast to the dark interior of the book-lined room.

"Please, have a seat." As soon as we had done so, Flora held out an envelope that I hadn't noticed she had been holding. "Quickly, read this. I'll need to put it back where it was before Mother awakens."

"Flora, you're beginning to frighten me a little." I opened the flap and withdrew a single, folded sheet of paper. As I read the words written in a slanting script, my eyes widened.

Derrick leaned to read over my shoulder. "What is it?" His eyebrows climbed high on his forehead. "I see. Where did you find this?"

We had read an angry retort aimed at Lottie Robinson,

citing her cruel, meddling ways and concluding with a wish that she would learn a harsh lesson in what it meant to suffer.

The missive was signed by Sybil Van Horn.

"Our housekeeper found it tucked in among some of Mrs. Robinson's personal effects when she cleaned out the dresser and armoire in her bedroom."

"The police obviously missed it," I mused, reading the words once more. "This is important evidence." I looked up at Flora. "Why the secrecy? Does your mother know about this?"

"She does." Flora drew in a breath and then pinched her lips in disapproval. "But she didn't intend to give it to the police. She wants to protect Sybil and her mother, and I understand why, but I thought this was simply too important to ignore."

Derrick said gently, but firmly, "It most certainly is."

"Flora, I thought I heard voices. Why, Mr. and Mrs. Andrews . . ." Florence Twombly, looking regal in a satin morning gown and elaborate coif despite the early hour, swept into the room. At first, she looked puzzled; then, upon seeing the letter I held, her civility dissolved into a mask of anger. "Flora, what is the meaning of this? Mrs. Andrews, I'll have that letter, please. This instant."

Derrick and I came to our feet. Flora followed our example. "Mother . . ."

"Mrs. Twombly, something like this can't be kept from the police. It's too important—"

"So, Mrs. Andrews, I see you still wish to accuse my friends of that heinous act. Neither Anna Rose nor Sybil is capable of harming another human being. I know this with certainty. As I told you before."

"Mrs. Twombly," Derrick calmly said, "no one is accusing anyone of anything."

Her chin jutted in defiance. "Aren't you?"

"No." He walked several strides toward her. "We merely believe that nothing should be withheld from the police. To do so would be to interfere with the case and obstruct justice. This note does not mean anything conclusive. It does not mean Sybil Van Horn murdered Mrs. Robinson and hurt all those other women."

"No?" That steely chin quivered as my relative groped her way to a chair. "Then what does it mean?"

I went to her and crouched by her chair. "It means Sybil has suffered terrible disappointments and is both hurt and angry. And that she held Mrs. Robinson at least partly to blame."

Her gaze met mine. "And you believe that's a motive."

I said nothing. I didn't have to. Mrs. Twombly surely understood the obvious.

She rose and drifted through the room, running her fingertips over the top of each piece of furniture she passed. "Lottie wasn't responsible for Chester Herbert's change of heart when it came to Sybil. I know Sybil and her mother believe she was, but Lottie assured me she never interfered. But I suppose it was natural for them to believe she was to blame."

"Who holds my mother to blame, and for what?" Another individual stood in the doorway, a young woman I knew by sight, if not by acquaintance: Mrs. Robinson's daughter, Charla Herbert. Unlike Mrs. Twombly, she was dressed to go out in a black crepe mourning outfit, though she had not yet donned hat and gloves. The slight roundness beneath the skirt of her dress revealed her pregnancy. She held the doorjamb on either side of her as if to hold herself up. "Have you discovered who killed my mother?"

As Mrs. Herbert regarded us, her eyes demanding answers, Flora looked about to cry. "I'm sorry," she murmured to me. "I should have told you that Mrs. Herbert arrived yesterday to arrange for her mother's body to be taken to Maryland for burial."

Yes, she should have, but I said nothing. Instead, I quickly folded Sybil Van Horn's letter and inserted it back into the envelope, and then held it half-hidden in the folds of my skirt. This very woman before us now, Lottie Robinson's daughter, stood at the root of Sybil Van Horn's unhappiness, whether Lottie Robinson had interfered or not.

The moment, strained and filled with an agonizing silence, seemed to stretch forever. Finally, Mrs. Twombly found her voice. "No, Charla, they have not found the person responsible for your mother's death. Not yet. But the police are working hard to find the answers. And these people . . ." She gestured to us. "These are my relatives, Emma Andrews and her husband, Derrick. They're helping the police."

"Are you?" Charla Herbert looked us up and down. "Why?"

"We own a local newspaper," I explained. "Investigating is part of our job, and there are times my husband and I are welcome in places the police are not, and may speak with people who otherwise would not deign to converse with detectives."

"I see." That seemed to mollify her, for she released the doorframe and allowed her arms to fall to her sides. "Thank you for that. Please promise me you won't rest until you know who did this."

"We will do our best, I promise." I felt Mrs. Twombly's stare burning into me. Did she think I would reveal Sybil Van Horn's letter to Mrs. Herbert? When I didn't, she, too, seemed to relax, at least a fraction.

"Charla, dear, please come with me," she said. "We'll have some breakfast. I'm sure you could do with a cup of coffee. Cook makes it good and strong but without a hint of bitterness."

"Yes, and I could use something to eat. Funny, how we think we'll never want to eat again when something terrible happens, yet we always feel better when we do."

They started out together, but Mrs. Twombly stopped, excused herself a moment, and quickly crossed the room to me. "All right, take the letter to the police. I suppose it's the right thing to do. But you must give Sybil and Anna Rose a chance to explain and not simply condemn them for this burst of temper. Who could blame Sybil, with all her hopes crushed so?"

"You have my word." I told her, and Derrick took her hand and made the same pledge.

After she left us, Flora began apologizing. "That didn't go at all as I expected. I never thought Mother would be up so early. Mrs. Herbert either. And I'm sorry I didn't warn you that she was here."

"It's all right, really." I took her hands in mine and gave them a reassuring squeeze.

"At least you have the letter. You'll give it to the police?"

"Yes, we'll take care of it. It was brave of you to go against your mother's wishes."

"I think even she would agree with that." Flora gave a small chuckle. She walked us to the front door, and we said our goodbyes.

Outside, as we climbed into the carriage, Derrick asked, "The police station?"

I didn't answer immediately. Mrs. Twombly had asked us to give Sybil a chance to explain. She needn't know we had the letter, only that we had seen it. "I think another detour first. To where the Van Horns are staying."

Derrick turned the carriage in that direction, which brought us closer to home than to town. On the way, a new thought occurred to me. "I wonder . . ."

"What?"

"What if Sybil Van Horn didn't write that letter? We have

two forged cards, one from Edith Roosevelt and the other from Harriet Hemenway. This could be an attempt by the killer to frame Sybil."

"It should be easy enough for the police to determine whether it's Sybil's handwriting. In the meantime, we can gauge her reaction to it. She might even admit to having written it. As you said, darling, it doesn't mean she killed anyone."

We arrived at the house on Carroll Avenue, secured the brake on the carriage, and went to the front door.

No one answered our knock.

"That's odd." I tapped the knocker again. "Where would the Van Horns go so early? And why wouldn't the landlady be home?"

Derrick stepped away from the front door and peered in through a front window. "Looks dark and still inside."

I knocked yet again. Then I tried the knob, which turned. The door opened.

"Even more odd. No one home, but the door left unlocked?" I crossed the threshold. "Hello? Is anyone here?"

"We can't simply go in." Derrick nonetheless followed me into the little front hall. "This is trespassing."

"Perhaps the landlady went out, and the Van Horns didn't hear our knock."

"Or they're still abed, or don't wish to receive company."

I glanced at him over my shoulder, gave a shrug, and continued toward the back of the house, where I knew the Van Horns' room to be. The house felt unusually still. The shadows bore down heavily; the silence was stifling. As I reached their door, a certainty filled me that something was wrong. Terribly wrong.

Once again, I knocked. "Mrs. Van Horn? Miss Van Horn? Are you here? It's Emma Andrews."

"It seems obvious they're not home."

"Then why was the front door unlocked?" I shook my head and gripped the knob, which also turned at my prompting. I pushed the door open. At first, all I saw was the darkened room; there were no lights on, and the window curtains were closed. Just enough light filtered through the edges of the curtains for me to make out the basics. The accommodation was small—merely a bedroom with two brass bedsteads, each covered in an appliquéd quilt, and two chairs with tufted seat cushions set before a small, round table. The beds were made, and there were no signs of breakfast or anything else that signified the Van Horns had been here recently.

"Emma . . ." Derrick's hand brushed my arm. I was about to turn to leave when something caught my notice.

One of the quilts lay askew on its mattress, as if half dragged off the bed after it had been made. Then I noticed a hat lying upside down on the rug near the foot of that same bed. I went all the way in and crouched to pick it up. It was a straw sun hat with a wide brim, a yellow silk lining, and a wide hatband to match. Two feathers, downy, and snowy white, curled about the crown. But where they had been secured to the hatband, a small tear suggested there had been yet a third feather.

Derrick crossed the threshold with softly thudding footsteps, as if he feared disturbing the inhabitants. "What have you got there?"

I turned to show him. He shrugged and lifted his hands, his expression saying he was impatient to be gone. I turned back toward the nearest bed, and I saw it.

A hand, gripping the missing feather. Quickly I rounded the bed, and there, sprawled between it and the wall, lay Sybil Van Horn.

*   *   *

I stayed at the house while Derrick took the carriage and doubled back to Gull Manor to use the telephone. That seemed faster than driving into town, or knocking on doors in hopes a neighbor might be connected to the phone lines. Staying behind with Sybil's corpse was not something I relished, but we couldn't simply leave her there alone, and if her mother or the landlady came home in the interim, someone needed to be there to explain what happened and lessen the shock.

Derrick returned before Jesse got there. When Jesse finally arrived, about a quarter hour later, he brought his partner, Gifford Myers, with him. The coroner, he said, would also come shortly. I gave Jesse the letter Sybil had sent to Mrs. Robinson. With Sybil's death, her angry words toward the older woman only confused matters, for this all but proved Sybil had not been guilty.

She might very possibly have known who was.

Derrick and I waited in the parlor while the police inspected the Van Horns' room, looking for any clues left behind: a shoe print on the area rug, a fiber from a piece of clothing, even a stray hair. But I had already discovered what I believed would prove the most telling clue of all: Sybil's hand clutching the feather missing from her sun hat.

Had the killer placed it there? Would he or she have left such a piece of evidence behind? I didn't think so and told Jesse as much. I believed Sybil had reached for the hat herself and torn the feather loose as a clue.

Because she had known she would die. Alone.

Where was her mother? The landlady returned not long after the police's arrival. She was now in the kitchen brewing tea for everyone. She had been upset at the news, of course, but not distraught, not grief-stricken, more dismayed that this had happened in her home. She hadn't known the Van

Horns well at all, she said, as they'd mostly kept to their room during their stay.

"We still don't know what killed her," I commented to Derrick. I remembered a vase on the floor not far from where Sybil lay, flowers and water strewn beside the hearth. Had it fallen during a struggle, or had someone used it to bludgeon Sybil? It looked to be deeply cut crystal, with a gilt base. Heavy.

Derrick nodded, his hand tightening around mine. "Jesse will tell us soon."

"Why was she alone? Where is her mother?"

"Poor Mrs. Van Horn," he said. He released my hand only to slip his arm around me. "This, after everything else she's had to endure."

"Are you talking about the mother?" Gifford Myers turned the corner into the room. "She's the main suspect."

"What?" Derrick and I said at the same time. Then I continued. "Why on earth would you suspect her mother of this?"

The detective ambled through the room, studying the porcelain curios, the photographs in their silver or gilt frames, the collection of thimbles on their tiered rack hung beside the mantle. "It certainly looks like the mother is our killer, doesn't it? Started with that Robinson woman, then the others, and now her daughter. Miss Van Horn probably realized what her mother had been doing and confronted her. That's always a mistake."

"Don't you think you're jumping to conclusions, Myers?" Derrick reclaimed his arm from around me and came to his feet to face the other man levelly.

Detective Myers looked him over, then shifted his gaze to me. "What does the famous Miss Cross have to say about it?" His tone mocked, as it usually did when he addressed me.

"Mrs. Andrews," Derrick corrected him in a tone that warned caution.

"It would seem the missus has you well trained, Andrews. Do you ever disagree with her?"

I sucked in a breath and braced for Derrick to take a swing at the other man. As it was, he spine went rigid, and the muscles in his upper arms bulged beneath his coat sleeves. "I'm going to pretend you didn't say that, Myers. Jesse's got enough to do investigating these murders. He doesn't need another one to distract him."

Detective Myers started to snigger. I couldn't directly see Derrick's face, but I did see the line of his jaw turn to steel. His expression must have been such that the detective immediately stifled his impulse to laugh and backed a step away. "All right, Andrews. No need to be so touchy."

"If you're done with your business in this room, Myers, I suggest you vacate it. Immediately."

Gifford Myers shoved his hands in his trouser pockets, swept the room with another insolent glance, and turned on his heel. He didn't run from the room, but he didn't drag his feet either. As soon as his footsteps receded down the hall, the landlady came bustling in with the tea.

"I'm sure you could use this." She set the tray down on the sofa table. "I'm so sorry about your friend. She was your friend, wasn't she?"

"We . . . were acquainted," I replied. "She and her mother are friends of one of my relatives. Do you have any notion of where Mrs. Van Horn might be?"

"I've already told the detectives, dear. I haven't seen her this morning. Nor yesterday dinnertime, either."

"When did you last see her?" Derrick asked.

"Yesterday morning, at breakfast. But it's nothing unusual, really. She sometimes is absent from the house. Poor dear. She can have no idea what has happened to her daughter. What a dreadful thing to come home to."

"Yes," I agreed with a sad shake of my head. "When did you last see Miss Van Horn alive?"

"Yesterday evening, when she had her supper."

"And after that," I asked, "did anyone visit her?"

"I couldn't really say, as I retired early. I don't think so."

"The front door was unlocked when we arrived here earlier," I said. "Do you ever leave the door unlocked when you go out?"

"Was it? Good heavens, it shouldn't have been. I lock up every night before I go to bed, and if Miss Van Horn had a guest, she certainly knew to lock the door after they left. This morning, I went out through the kitchen, something I often do. And I most certainly locked the door behind me."

"Have they had any guests while they've been here?" I kept on, knowing Jesse probably asked or would ask most of these same questions. Still, I felt an urgent need to understand what had happened.

"Well, there was you, of course, the other day." She clasped her hands together. "And that other young lady. Although I use the word *lady* loosely. I'm quite sure I don't care for that one."

I darted a questioning look at Derrick, who returned it, and asked, "Whom do you mean?"

"Miss Point . . . Pont . . ." She scrunched up her nose.

"Pierpont?" My heart started thumping. Had Jennie visited the Van Horns?

"Yes, that's it. Miss Pierpont. She's a brash one. I don't like the way she talks. Too loud, too forceful. Thinks too much of herself, that girl does. I suspect she's fast." She uncovered a platter of what looked like shortbread cookies and gingersnaps. "Help yourselves, and if you need anything, just give a holler."

We poured ourselves some tea, but left the cookies untouched. Jesse came in a few minutes later. "I'm nearly certain whoever did this used the vase. It's a heavy piece, as I'm sure you could see. It's that metal base more than the crystal, although that's heavy, too. Combined, it's an effective club."

"Effective," I repeated.

Jesse must have heard the derision in my voice. "Sorry. I forget sometimes that not everyone is accustomed to seeing such matters objectively." I nodded and waved for him to continue. "Other than the vase, we did find other signs of a struggle. The shoe marks on the rug look as though a scuffle took place, and there's a small table near where Sybil fell that has been shoved against the wall. Again, the marks on the rug show where it should have been." He eased into a chair.

"How horrible," was all I could say.

Jesse reached for a cookie. "Any word about the mother?"

"The landlady hasn't seen her since yesterday morning," I told him.

"Then, at this point, without her mother to identify the handwriting, we don't know if Sybil actually wrote that note to Mrs. Robinson." He took a bite of his cookie and ruminated for several moments. "Could the first victim's daughter have done it?"

The notion startled me. "Mrs. Robinson's daughter, Charla?"

"Wrote the note and put it among her mother's things to be found by the housekeeper," Derrick said, in attempt to clarify what Jesse meant.

He nodded.

"Good heavens, I never would have thought of that," I exclaimed. "My cousin told us she arrived in Newport yesterday and is staying at Vinland. So . . . yes, it's possible, I suppose, but probable? I don't think so. And surely you're not accusing her of coming here and murdering Sybil this morning."

"She would have a strong motive if she believed Sybil sent her mother those petit fours."

"What about the other victims?" Derrick set his cup and saucer on the table before him. "And Mrs. Robinson herself? We know Charla Herbert can't be responsible for any of that. Doesn't it make more sense that the same murderer killed Miss Van Horn?"

"She had to have discovered something important." I also set my teacup aside. I rose to my feet and began to pace. "Something that made her dangerous to the killer."

"It was someone she knew," Jesse said. "That much is obvious by how little the room was disturbed beyond the scuff marks and the table out of position. She trusted her visitor enough to admit them to the house and to her room."

"Do you believe, as I do, that the feather in Sybil's hand is a clue she herself left for us?"

"I'm not so sure, Emma. She might have simply gripped the first thing her hand touched—the hat, sitting on the bed beside her—to try to anchor herself and keep from falling, and the feather simply came loose in her hand."

His counter theory was a sound one, I couldn't but admit. But if Sybil tore the feather from the hatband as a message to the police, it could very likely be pointing to one particular person. "We just learned from the housekeeper that Jennie Pierpont has visited Sybil."

Jesse had started to rise but let himself fall back against the chair. "And you're only just telling me this?"

"We only found out right before you came in," I protested in Derrick's and my defense.

"Emma, between this and what Miss Pierpont said to you during your outing to Hanging Rock, she's certainly a suspect—a stronger suspect than previously."

"Yes, I know. That's why I'm mentioning it." I stared down at the carpet's flowered pattern.

Jesse pushed to his feet. "I'd better go have another talk with the landlady and see if she remembers specifically when

Miss Pierpont visited." He hesitated. "There is also Mrs. Van Horn, disappearing to no one knows where while her daughter lay dead."

"A mother, murdering her own daughter?" Derrick made it sound ludicrous. "It doesn't surprise me that your partner would believe that, but you?"

"If Mrs. Van Horn sent the toxin to the victims, and her daughter discovered the truth and threatened to tell us, then yes, perhaps the mother saw no choice but to silence the daughter." Jesse's shoulders hunched beneath the strain of the investigation. "I'll be posting an officer here in the hope she comes back. And I'll be contacting police stations on the island and the mainland. Until we know more, both Jennie Pierpont and Anna Rose Van Horn are wanted women."

Chapter 12

"Yes, I did see Sybil last night." Jennie Pierpont spoke defiantly, as someone does when they feel they have nothing to hide. Or when they're doing their best to appear so.

I had come to the police station after learning from Jesse that Jennie had been found at the inn where she'd been staying and brought in for questioning. He had already interrogated her, but when I arrived, he gave me permission to speak with her alone. We sat in a small room used for such purposes to the rear of the main room, near to where a hallway led to the holding cells. It pained me to think of young, lively Jennie Pierpont behind bars.

"We had planned to meet," she continued. "She wished to help me with the plans for the new Audubon Society. In fact, she was very excited about it. She said it provided her with renewed purpose, as this past year had left her foundering. I told all of this to the detective." The defiance, which had momentarily lapsed, returned in full force.

"You planned to meet at her boardinghouse last night?" I asked, knowing she had already made this detail clear, but knowing, also, that details often changed when a person wasn't being truthful. "Why not earlier, in town?"

"Several reasons, Mrs. Andrews." Her use of my surname sent an immediate message; we were no longer on friendly terms. I hoped to remedy that before I left, but for now I let her talk. "For one, I had meetings yesterday with potential doners. Here in Newport and elsewhere on the island." She paused, and then added, with an edge of vitriol, "I can supply the names of the individuals who can corroborate that, as I also told the detective."

I ignored her anger. "You said there were other reasons you met when and where you did."

"Mrs. Andrews, does it not occur to you that meeting in town would have meant going to a restaurant or other public place, where Sybil would have been obligated to order a meal, or something to drink at the very least. She could ill afford such outings, and I endeavored to spare her both the expense and the humiliation of coming up short. My coming to her at her place of residence did just that, and I'd brought us a little repast to share. She was delighted by the arrangement and said as much."

If Jennie had meant to arouse guilty feelings in me, she had succeeded. But I needed to remain objective "So you arrived there after dinnertime? What time exactly?"

"I already told the police."

"Please, humor me. What time was it?"

She made a noise of frustration. "I don't know . . . perhaps eight-thirty?"

"And how long did you stay?"

"An hour? No, closer to two."

"Did the landlady let you in when you arrived at the house?"

She shook her head. "No, Sybil did."

"Did you see the landlady?"

"No, Mrs. Andrews, I did not. I don't know where she was. Up in her bedroom, one supposes. I had the distinct impression from a previous visit that she doesn't care for me."

The landlady had said as much to me. "And Mrs. Van Horn?"

"What about her?"

Was Jennie purposely being obtuse? "Was she at home when you called?"

"No." She showed a frown of perplexity. "I did think it strange for her not to be home at that time of night. Sybil said something about her visiting friends, but . . ."

"Yes, but what?"

"It was a bit strange. Awkward. Sybil didn't say where her mother went, or with whom, and she didn't seem particularly pleased that her mother had gone out. In fact, she changed the subject immediately."

"What was Sybil wearing last night?"

The question appeared to startle Jennie. "Why do you ask? The police didn't."

Jesse should have, I thought. "Please, just answer the question."

"I don't know . . ." Her brow furrowed as she thought back. "I believe it was a tea gown. Yes, a pale-rose tea gown. Informal. Comfortable."

Perhaps Jesse hadn't asked the question yet because he was waiting for the coroner to estimate the time of death. According to Jennie's description of Sybil's attire and what I'd seen that morning, Sybil hadn't changed her clothes between last night and this morning. Meaning she hadn't gone to bed; meaning she had more than likely died last night, sometime after the landlady had gone to bed.

Yet, another possibility nudged its way into my logic: With her wardrobe now limited, perhaps Sybil simply donned the same gown upon rising that morning.

"After she dismissed your curiosity concerning her mother," I said, moving on, "what did you talk about?"

She continued to view me with a puzzled expression, but she said, "The Audubon Society. One of my goals is to enlist as many interested people as possible as bird-watchers who will catalog the various birds in their areas. The more volunteers we have, the more accurate the numbers and varieties of birds that are currently calling Rhode Island home. We'll especially need the help during the migratory seasons."

"I see. And Sybil thought she could help you with that?"

"She might have lost her footing among her peers, but she most certainly was not helpless or cowed. She intended to start her life over and . . ." She broke off suddenly. Up until this moment, she had remained either angry or stoic. Now her eyes filled with tears. "She's really gone, isn't she?"

I reached across the table between us and clasped her hand. "I'm so sorry, Jennie."

"I barely knew her, really, and in all honesty, if she hadn't been in such reduced circumstances, she and I probably would never have interacted socially. Despite my illustrious distant cousins, I don't hail from great wealth. But she and I did interact, and I quickly grew fond of her. Poor Sybil . . ." She slid her hand free of mine, and with her elbows on the table, she dropped her face into her hands and wept.

I allowed her several moments before returning to the matter at hand. But I didn't give her quite enough time to compose herself. My next question required an unguarded answer. "Jennie, at Hanging Rock, you said you would like to strangle society ladies who wear feathers with their finery."

Her sobs abruptly ceased, and she raised her reddened eyes to meet mine. "You've come to throw my words back in my face."

"You threatened violence against women of the Four Hundred, of which Sybil was most certainly a member. An ostracized one, but still a member."

"I didn't think of her that way, not the Sybil I met."

Didn't she? I wondered. The sun hat with the missing feather flashed in my mind. Had Jennie only pretended to befriend Sybil, only to murder her for her fashion preferences?

"Yet prior to her downfall, she dressed as fashionably as any wealthy young lady. And that includes wearing items from nature that you would disapprove of." Besides feathers, wealthy women wore fur of all kinds, tortoiseshell, and ivory, not to mention fueling the discord involved in the gemstone industry with their love of precious stones. "What did you mean when you said that to me?"

"Only that it angered me," she said impatiently. "I never meant I would hurt anyone. Surely you've said such things in anger."

"Yes, I have. And for now, we'll let that go. Think, Jennie. Had Sybil ever spoken about which friends her mother visits? She has so few, her options are limited."

Her eyes narrowed. "Why all these questions about Mrs. Van Horn?"

"She hasn't been home since yesterday."

"Do you mean . . . she doesn't know about Sybil?"

"Not yet, I'm afraid. Do you have any idea where she could be?"

"No. As I said, Sybil didn't want to discuss it. She became almost morose when I inquired after Mrs. Van Horn. As soon as I let the matter drop, her mood improved."

I thought back to that first interview with Jesse and the Van Horns. They'd claimed to have been window-shopping in town on the morning Lottie Robinson took ill, but I'd sensed a secret between them, something they didn't want to reveal. How I wish we'd pressed them.

"I didn't kill her, Emma." It was Jennie's turn to reach across the table. She gripped my hands. "I swear I never harmed Sybil. I wouldn't have. I couldn't."

I returned the pressure of her hands. "I promise you I'll find out what happened."

It wasn't a promise that I'd see her exonerated, and the knowledge of that registered in her eyes. Still, it was the most honest promise I could make, and that knowledge, too, crossed her features. She drew a steadying breath.

"Then I'll have to stay here until you do, won't I? I'm to be put under arrest."

"I don't yet know what Detective Whyte plans to do, but I do know what I'm planning. And that's to get to the bottom of who has been targeting our Newport ladies. I won't stop until I have the answer."

I left her and joined Jesse at his desk in the main room. On it sat the basket of necessities and small luxuries I'd brought for Jennie. I had left it with the officer at the front desk, who must have gone through it before delivering it to Jesse.

"Did you learn anything?" he asked as I sat across from him.

"Nothing she hadn't already told you, except for what Sybil was wearing last night when Jennie visited her." I paused, but before Jesse could ask, I continued, "The same as what she lay in this morning. But she might simply have donned the same dress in the morning."

He absorbed with this a nod. "How did Miss Pierpont seem to you? Do you think she was telling the truth?"

"She sounds and looks sincere. And I want to believe her. According to her, she lost a friend in Sybil. She appears to be grieving. And frightened about being accused, of course."

"We don't have conclusive evidence against her yet. And I'm not ruling out Mrs. Wallingford yet, either."

I felt a little burst of hope for Jennie's sake. "Then you'll release Jennie in the meantime?"

"I'm afraid not. We're going to hold her a day or two without formally charging her. I want her where I can keep an eye on her while we search for Mrs. Van Horn. With any luck, she'll turn up soon, and we can sort this out. Did Miss Pierpont have any idea where that lady might have gone?"

"None. She said when she commented on Mrs. Van Horn's absence last night, Sybil didn't want to talk about it."

"Interesting."

"Remember when we visited them together, and I got a sense they were hiding something?"

"I do. And it appears we should have delved deeper at the time."

"Don't worry." I came to my feet. "I've got another idea how to find out where Mrs. Van Horn might be." I raised my eyebrows and grinned. "Florence Twombly." But I immediately sobered as my stomach sank. "I just realized she doesn't yet know about Sybil. I'll have to tell her. She's going to be dreadfully upset."

When I returned to the *Messenger* from the police station, I telephoned over to Vinland and left a message with Mrs. Twombly's housekeeper that I would be stopping by later that afternoon. I didn't say why, I but emphasized that it was important.

I arrived there with Derrick in the late afternoon, when the sun's slanting rays set flame to the red sandstone exterior. We were escorted to Mrs. Twombly in the drawing room, where she was arranging flowers in a vase.

She turned at our approach. "Back so soon? I hope you're not here to tell me Sybil has been arrested."

I caught Derrick's gaze with a mournful expression. Neither of us relished this task. "No, that's not why we're here. May we sit?"

"Would you care for tea?" she asked, more by rote, it seemed, than genuine cordiality.

"No, thank you."

"Flora's gone out," she informed us.

"That's probably best, for now," I murmured.

Obviously puzzled by my comment, she motioned us toward the seating arrangement near the French doors. "What did Sybil have to say about that letter?"

"Mrs. Twombly." I paused and swallowed. "About Sybil. When we arrived at her lodging house we discovered . . ."

When I hesitated, she made an impatient gesture. "Yes? Out with it. I've never known reporters to vacillate."

"Sybil is dead," I blurted.

Her face drained of color. "What?"

"She was murdered," I told her more gently. "We found her in her bedroom. It appears she was attacked—bludgeoned to death."

Her hands went to her mouth to muffle the small cry she uttered.

Derrick placed his hand over mine and took over explaining. "It happened sometime last night or early this morning, we believe. When we got to the house, we found the front door unlocked. The landlady was out, but she had gone out the back and never knew the front had been unlocked. The police believe Sybil knew her assailant, as there were no signs of breaking and entering."

"How dreadful. Oh, my poor, dear Sybil. And Anna Rose! How is she? She must be beside herself."

"That's just it," I said. "We don't know where Mrs. Van Horn is. She's been missing since yesterday. Do you have any idea where she might have gone?"

"I can't begin to imagine . . ." Her fingers drummed on the carved arm of her chair. Then she froze in alarm. "Surely the police don't think Anna Rose had anything to do with . . . with what happened to Sybil?"

Derrick spoke gently. "Right now they only want to find her."

"How much worse can this possibly be?" Mrs. Twombly passed the back of her hand across her brow. "Such a nightmare. I wish I'd never come to Newport this year. I should have gone to Florham and had Anna Rose and Sybil join me there. They would have been safe at Florham. I could have prevented all of this."

"You couldn't have prevented all of it," I reminded her. "There are the other ladies as well. There is Mrs. Robinson."

"But Sybil would be alive."

I shook my head. "They might not have wished to go to Florham. I believe they came to Newport hoping to see and be seen, because by not hiding they were showing everyone they had done nothing wrong. It wasn't right that they suffered for Mr. Van Horn's actions."

"Emma's right," Derrick said. "They could have stayed away from Newport if they had wished to. It was their choice to come here. They had their reasons."

"It was a disastrous choice," she said in a harsh tone.

"Yes," Derrick agreed, "but neither they nor you could have foreseen any of this."

After a pause, Mrs. Twombly stood. "Thank you for coming and telling me. For saving me from finding out from the newspapers or some other source. I do appreciate that."

Despite her undoubted sincerity, we were being dismissed. Derrick helped me up. She walked us across the hall, and at the front door, she surprised me by kissing my cheek. Then she patted it, turned, and before I could say anything, she walked away.

Before dinner that evening, Derrick and I sat with Nanny and Katie in the kitchen. He and I watched as they prepared dinner, and whenever Nanny asked for this or that ingredient, he or I would rise and go find it. As was their custom, our guests were upstairs resting before the meal. Their trek to Sachuest Point had been a success, with Miss Carter spotting a wide variety of seabirds and Miss Lewis accomplishing a colorful new seascape. They had arrived home flushed and happy, until I told them about Sybil Van Horn and her missing mother.

Now I was glad for some time alone with my small family. Once again, we went over the facts of the two deaths and the attacks on the other women.

"It's gotten so the ladies and their secretaries are afraid to open their mail," Katie said as she stirred a pot on the stove. "When Julie and Mary and I went to market this morning, we heard lots of whispers that some of the grand ladies have told the lesser servants to open everything." Having referred to two of her fellow servants at neighboring estates, she glanced at me over her shoulder. "So now everyone's afraid, Miss Emma. I didn't want to say that you haven't assigned that task to me. They'd be resentful."

"I'd never ask you to do something I was afraid to do," I assured her. "But as a precaution, before we open anything that arrives at the house, it's prudent to don gloves first."

"Of all things. Land sakes," Nanny muttered. She hefted a sack of dried beans and scooped some out with a tin measuring cup. She then poured them into a pot of water to soak overnight. "What is this world coming to when folks are afraid of the daily mail?"

Katie tapped her wooden spoon against the side of the pot she'd been stirring and set it down on a trivet. "Do you think this Jennie Pierpont is responsible, Miss Emma?"

"There are several particulars that do point in her direction," I replied with a sigh. "That feather . . . I wish I knew what it meant. And whether Sybil tore it from the hat or if her attacker did, as a message."

"Isn't it obvious?" Nanny came over to the table. Before she could pull out a chair, Derrick was on his feet and pulling it out for her. He scooted it back in as she settled.

"That Jennie Pierpont is a champion of wild birds. She's angry about women and their fashion choices. She told you so herself." She said to Katie, "Bring me the peas when you have a moment, love."

"That's true," I agreed, "but it doesn't prove she did anything about it. There's no direct link between her and the victims. Jesse said so."

"Yet," Derrick pointed out, "a lot rests on the police identifying the toxin."

"Which they haven't been able to do yet," I reminded him, "and might never do. There are simply too many possibilities. It could be anything growing anywhere on the island or have come from somewhere else."

Katie came to the table with a basket of peas still in their pods, along with two empty bowls. Nanny began shelling. Derrick reached over and grabbed a handful, and I did likewise. Soon we were all tossing peas and pods into their respective bowls.

"Think back to the luncheon," Nanny said, without pausing in her task. "You said that's when this began, or the very next day, anyway. Something must have happened there."

My fingers paused. "All I can remember is that a good number of the ladies were less than polite when it came time for Jennie to speak. As if Mrs. Roosevelt and Mrs. Hemenway had stretched their patience to the limit and they had none left for Jennie. Or they didn't deem her important enough to listen to. I don't know." I finished splitting open a green pod, rolled the peas into the proper bowl, and slapped the rest with the discards as if it were somehow responsible for my frustrations.

"I remember you saying that Mrs. Robinson and Miss Norris were among the most visibly rude." A pod in hand, Derrick sat back and regarded me. "And they were the first and most affected victims."

"Hello, all. I'm not intruding, am I?" Zinnia Lewis entered the kitchen, looking refreshed after a nap. She had donned an informal dinner gown of pale blue muslin with darker blue trim and a high lace collar. She appeared pretty and youthful and might have been mistaken for a daughter of the Four Hundred. I had little doubt the sparkle in her eye had something to do with the dress, something she never could have owned if not for her aunt's patronage.

Derrick stood and drew out a chair for her. "Not at all. Care to shell peas?"

She let go a little laugh. "I would love to. Aunt Amity will be down shortly, by the by." We shelled in silence for a few moments, until she said, "Forgive me for eavesdropping, but I couldn't help overhearing as I came down the hall. You were discussing the luncheon and the reactions of the ladies to Jennie's speech."

"We were." My hands stilled. "You were more in the middle of everyone than I was. Do you remember anything specific among the guests that day?"

"Such as what?"

"What it was they were muttering under their breath," Katie leaned in and clarified, making us all chuckle.

"Yes, that," I agreed, and waited for Miss Lewis to consider. My eyebrows drew together as I remembered something her aunt had revealed about her. "If anyone can remember something important, it would be you, Miss Lewis."

"First, would it be all right, do you think . . . that is to say, I'd be pleased if you'd call me Zinnia. And I know Aunt Amity would not mind being on a first-name basis either."

"Splendid," I replied eagerly. "And by now you know all of our names."

With that happily settled, I allowed her to think back on the luncheon. According to her aunt, Zinnia never forgot a detail, no matter how small. What an extraordinary gift, I thought.

"As you already mentioned," Zinnia said, "attention had begun to lapse by the time Jennie came to the podium. Now, I did notice that Sybil and her mother paid close attention to all the speakers, Jennie included. Sybil appeared quite excited about Jennie's ideas for establishing her Audubon Society in Rhode Island."

"That concurs with what Jennie told me today," I said. "She and Sybil had formed a friendship in recent days, and Sybil wished to be involved in the society."

"Yes, but Mrs. Van Horn more than once tried to quell her daughter's enthusiasm. I'm not sure why, exactly." Zinnia tilted her head as she considered, then shrugged.

"I can guess." I noticed the pods in Nanny's bowl were diminishing; we had almost finished shelling. I grabbed a few more. "If they were in Newport to try to salvage their reputation among society, Mrs. Van Horn might not have wanted her daughter involved in anything even slightly controversial."

"But all ladies of the Four Hundred are involved in charities and causes. We're only talking about birds, Emma." Nanny regarded me from over the rims of her spectacles. "Why would she object?"

"It's one thing to support a cause through one's church or social club, but an Audubon Society has political ramifications beyond simply counting bird populations. Their ultimate goal is to change the laws to protect birds from hunters and industries that seek to profit from their deaths."

"Such as ladies' fashion," Derrick concluded. "It's an important cause, but I can understand how someone in Mrs. Van Horn's position wouldn't want her daughter bringing that kind of attention to herself. They'd had quite enough attention due to Mr. Van Horn's activities."

"Exactly." I pulled a pod apart rather too vigorously, and the peas went flying. They landed in the center of the table with a rapid tap-tapping. "Especially with a woman like Jennie Pierpont." When the others cast me puzzled expressions, I explained. "She's very outspoken. Even if she is innocent of these current crimes, there are plenty of people who will find her far too assertive for a young woman. Mrs. Van Horn certainly wouldn't have wanted Sybil associated with such an individual."

"I see. That would explain what I overheard between them," Zinnia said as she reached to scoop my fallen peas into her palm.

My heart thumped against my breastbone. Could mother and daughter have argued the point? Perhaps Sybil refused to heed her mother's demand that she not involve herself with Jennie or the Audubon Society. In the face of her daughter's defiance, did Anna Rose strike a death blow?

Chapter 13

Later that evening, while the others went outside to watch the first stars pepper the sky, a chill sent me upstairs for a shawl. My guests' door was ajar, and as I passed it, I caught a glimpse of Zinnia's canvases leaning against the wall. I hesitated, while curiosity urged me to enter the room. Would it be wrong to peek? Zinnia had already said she didn't mind people watching her paint. One would assume that also meant she didn't mind people viewing her finished paintings.

I stole inside. Although the sun had set, enough light came in through the open windows that I could make out most of the details. There were three completed canvases. I recognized the area around Hanging Rock, and a section of the Cliff Walk near Rough Point. Another showed the rocks and views from my own property. Then I noticed a fourth, smaller canvas stacked behind the rest. This one had been rendered in dark colors, mostly grays, blues, black, and touches of silvery gold where the moonlight hit the waves. A nighttime seascape. It obviously hadn't been finished, unless

Zinnia meant for the images to fade raggedly around the edges and the waves to appear to melt into the sky.

When had she painted this? And where? It felt familiar. Perhaps from her aunt's property next door? The angles of the headland in that direction were just enough to create a very different perspective from my property.

I put the canvases back the way I'd found them and tip-toed out of the room, although why I chose stealth I couldn't say, as everyone else was outside. Although I only looked at the paintings, I felt as though I had been spying. I could easily ask Zinnia about her night scene, but that would have been to admit I'd gone into the room uninvited, and that seemed wrong. I vowed not to do it again, to respect my guests' privacy in the future.

At work the following day, I had an unexpected visitor. One of our newsboys led another youth into my office. Ethan was there, typing out his latest article on the summer's parties and balls, when the two youths appeared in our doorway, holding their caps in their hands.

"Miss Cross?" the younger of the pair said in an uncertain voice. He was one of our own delivery boys; the other boy I didn't recognize. I gestured for them both to come in. Ethan's hands stilled on the typewriter. A sudden silence fell over the room. "Yes, Jake, what can I do for you?"

"I hope we're not bothering you. This here is Harry. He's got something he wants to talk to you about. I tried asking him what it is, but he won't tell me. Only you." Jake's gaze angled toward Ethan.

The second boy, taller, ungainly, and obviously in his middle teen years, stood fidgeting with the pocket of his trousers and shifting from one foot to the other. He was red-haired, freckled, with summer sky–blue eyes. Those eyes didn't meet mine.

"Hello, Harry," I said. "What is it you'd like to talk to me about?"

"Um . . ." He, too, eyed Ethan, then shot Jake a suspicious look. "Not in front of anyone else, ma'am. In secret, like."

"Secret," Ethan repeated. When I turned to look at him, he waggled his eyebrows and compressed his lips to hide a grin. Then he quickly rose from his chair. "I'll just be in the back, checking on . . . um . . . things."

When Jake showed no sign of leaving, I came to my feet and went to the door. "If you'll excuse us." I grasped Harry's forearm to draw him farther into the room, while at the same time blocking Jake's path so he had no choice but to back into the hallway as I closed the door.

I turned to regard my young visitor. "Do you have a last name, Harry?"

"Yes . . . um . . . it's Walsh, ma'am, but I'd rather not be . . ."

"Let's not worry about that right now, Harry." I took in his dark blue jacket and the flat cap in his hands. "You're dressed like a newsie. Which paper do you work for?"

Once again, he looked distinctly uncomfortable answering another question. After a brief hesitation, he said, "The *Newport Chronicler*, ma'am."

I didn't think he'd come to the *Messenger* for a job; if he had, he would have been talking to Mr. Sheppard in the front office. "Why are you here? What do you have to tell me?"

"It's about that lady who died, and the others who got hurt, ma'am. You see, I . . ." His hands fisted around his cap until it bunched into a tight ball between them, the brim crushed. "There was this lady, ma'am. She asked me . . . that is . . . she hired me to do an errand. A few errands. That's all I thought it was, ma'am. Otherwise, I wouldn't 'a done it."

"Done what, Harry?" Before he could answer, I said, "Wait. Let's sit." I went around to the typing table and rolled the chair closer to mine, positioning it so we would be face-to-face. I sat and bade Harry to do the same. "Now then, what did she hire you to do?"

"I saw it in the newspaper just this morning, ma'am, your article about how ladies have been getting mail that hurt them, and those other two ladies who got cakes. I never would have if I'd known . . . I didn't mean to . . ." Yet again, his voice faded. A flush of color climbed in his face.

"Slow down, Harry. It's all right. Just tell me what happened." I could feel my own face growing hot as my heart pumped furiously in anticipation of what he'd say next.

"This lady, she hired me to buy the cakes at two different bakeries. Then she told me to meet her again the next day. When I did, she gave me the same two packages and told me where to deliver them. But she said they were to be a surprise, so she wanted me to slip them in with something else being delivered to the houses."

My mouth had fallen open; I had to force my lips to close. This was exactly the scenario I had envisioned regarding how the petit fours had arrived unseen at Vinland and Miss Norris's house. "Do you mean to say you waited in the service driveway at each residence until you were able to add your packages in among others being delivered?"

"That's it exactly, ma'am. That's what she told me to do."

I sat leaning forward with my hands on my knees. "Let's back up a little. How did you meet this woman?"

"I was in town, carrying my newspapers to my street corner, when she came up to me. Said she needed help with something and she would pay me."

"That must not have seemed out of the ordinary," I said, and he nodded vigorously.

"Could always use some extra coin, ma'am."

"What did she look like?"

"Hard to say. She wore widow's weeds, with a hat and a veil. I couldn't hardly see her face at all."

"Can you describe the dress? Or the hat?"

His brow puckered, and then he shrugged. "They were both black."

"Plain or elaborate?" When furrows again began to appear above his eyes, I clarified, "Was the dress fancy? Did it have flounces or braided trim or jet buttons?"

"I guess."

I sat back and sighed. He didn't remember, that much was clear. Or he never took note in the first place. Typical of boys. "Could you at least make out if she was old or young?"

"Not really, ma'am."

"What about her voice? Was it high or low, strong or whispery?"

As I said *whispery*, his finger came up. "That one. She talked in almost a whisper. Weak, like. Scratchy. So maybe she was old. That makes sense, right, ma'am?"

It did, unless this woman had been attempting to disguise her voice.

"Harry, I'm going to ask you to be brave and come with me to the police station."

His eyes opened wide, and he pushed back in his chair so hard it rolled backward. "Please, ma'am, don't make me do that. I only came here 'cause it seemed like the right thing to do. But I don't want to get in trouble. My family needs me. They depend on my wages."

"Coming here *was* the right thing to do, Harry. And you won't get into trouble because you didn't do anything wrong. The woman who hired you did the wrongdoing, and we have to find her before she hurts anyone else. You want to do that, don't you? Help find her and make sure she pays for what she did?"

"I . . . um . . . yes, ma'am."

"Good." I stood, prompting him to do the same. He came awkwardly to his feet and rolled the chair back to the typing table. Meanwhile, I retrieved my handbag from the desk drawer I had stowed it in and took my hat from the coatrack in the corner. Before we left, I fished a coin from my change purse and held it out. "This is for you, a reward for being so brave."

He started to protest, but I pressed the coin into his palm and would hear no more about it. In the front office, I quickly explained my errand to Derrick. He looked as though he wished to accompany us on the walk down Spring Street and across Washington Square, but he remained at his desk. As Harry and I walked out the street door, I heard Derrick lift the receiver of his telephone and ask to be connected with the police station. Good. They would be expecting us.

Faltering over the words, Harry repeated his story for Jesse, Gifford Myers, and Police Chief Rogers. Scotty Binsford took notes. The poor boy seemed overwhelmed with such an audience, and who could blame him? He seemed all too happy to say his goodbyes and exit the building.

I followed him out to the sidewalk. "Thank you, Harry. You've been a tremendous help."

"I hope they find her, ma'am. I don't like being used like that." He squinted in the sunlight as the breeze ruffled his hair. "Next time someone wants to hire me for something, I'll ask more questions."

"Don't worry. I doubt anything like this will ever happen to you again." I hated to think of anyone so young, perhaps only fifteen or sixteen, becoming so jaded. "But if the same woman should approach you again—"

"I'll come directly here, like I promised Detective Whyte," he finished for me. He slapped his cap on his head. "But I won't let on to her."

"Good. Thank you, Harry."

After he left me, I went back inside and rejoined Jesse at his desk. "Has Jennie said anything more?" I asked him.

"Not much. She's still adamantly denying everything. Her story hasn't changed."

"A sign she could be innocent."

"Or a good liar." Jesse sifted through some papers on his desk, found whatever he was looking for, then shuffled the rest into a neater pile. "We've already searched through her room at her lodging." He scanned a typewritten list on the page before him. "There was a black dress, but nothing resembling widow's weeds. But that doesn't mean she hasn't gotten rid of them."

"Most women do own at least one black dress," I pointed out. "What about the other suspects? Will you go through their things as well?"

"Once I have a warrant." He raised an eyebrow as he regarded me. "I need a warrant, but you don't. The Van Horns' landlady would almost certainly let you in."

"Under what pretense? And what if Mrs. Van Horn should return while I'm there?"

"You'd think of something. You always do."

He had a point. Once I'd sneaked into the bedrooms of a suspect's home disguised as a maid. I'd been seen by someone who knew me but didn't recognize me at the time. Somehow, I'd managed to hide within a shadow and then excuse myself before she became any the wiser.

But I could hardly arrive at the Van Horns' boarding-house dressed as a maid.

"Any luck with the toxin yet?"

Jesse shook his head. "It's a bit like searching for a needle in a haystack. With something like arsenic or other known poison, there are tests that can be done to detect it. Doesn't seem to be the case this time. The laboratory is trying anything and everything they can think of. But we might never know what it is."

Jesse's dismal assertion followed me back to the *Messenger* and then across the island as Derrick and I made our way home. We took an inland route along Carroll Avenue, which brought us back to the house where Sybil Van Horn died.

I had decided on a simple, if rather unimaginative, reason for our return. As Jesse had proposed, a uniformed officer had taken up position across the road in a plain carriage. We waved to him, and he waved back, knowing full well who we were.

When the landlady answered our knock, I said, "We're sorry to bother you again. I fear I dropped something in the Van Horns' room. Would it be all right if we came in to look?"

"Oh. Yes . . . I should think that would be all right." She stepped back to allow us both to enter.

"Thank you. I don't suppose Mrs. Van Horn has returned?"

"No, I'm afraid I have neither seen nor heard from that poor lady." She motioned toward the officer keeping guard as she closed the door. "I've brought that good fellow lunch and tea, and I suppose I'll make him a plate for supper, if he's still here. I have to say, despite what happened earlier, I've never felt safter."

"You needn't have any fears, ma'am." Derrick had doffed his hat and held it at his side. "It's highly doubtful whoever did this would have any reason to come back."

"But why Miss Van Horn?" the landlady fretted. "Such a refined, lovely girl. I'll never understand it."

"Nor will we," I said, then gestured down the hallway. "May we?"

"Yes, of course. I'll just unlock the door for you."

The good woman didn't follow us into the room, but

asked us to let her know when we were leaving. Our time would be limited, for how long should it take to ascertain whether my lost object lay in the room? I pointed Derrick toward the armoire.

"Check in there. I'll take the bureau."

It didn't take Derrick long to confirm what we suspected. "Two black dresses, neither of which I would term widow's weeds. They look to be silk, one with velvet piping and braiding, the other with ivory lace." He quietly closed the armoire doors.

Likewise, I closed the last drawer I'd searched through in the bureau. "And nothing resembling a widow's veil."

I stood in the center of the room, casting my gaze all around me. The furnishings that had been knocked out of place had been straightened and the strewn flowers cleaned up, but the vase was missing. The police had taken it.

The table and chairs in the corner held little. Nothing tossed over the backs of the chairs, no organized mess on the tabletop. Only a portable writing desk in a pretty cherry-wood trimmed in brass. I went to it. A small brass plate pronounced this the property of Anna Rose Van Horn. I attempted to lift the lid, but the clasp held fast.

"Let me try." Derrick took the money clip from his inner coat pocket and slid the bills free. Then he fiddled with the piece, bending it until the back of the clip, the unornamented side, formed a wide V with the front. He sat at the table and inserted the edge into the narrow gap between the box and its lid. After several minutes, during which I grew convinced he wouldn't succeed, I heard a click. Derrick grinned up at me.

My hands went to my hips. "I didn't know you could do that."

"I didn't either. Come. Sit." As I took the other seat, he opened the box. It proved to be quite an elaborate one. Inside were what one might expect: pens, pencils, a small jar of ink, tightly sealed, all neatly stowed in their own compartments. A hinged, leather-covered writing surface opened to reveal stored correspondence. Derrick met my gaze. "Should we?"

"I know it's wrong, but I believe we must. If we have time." Standing, I moved to the door and listened for sounds the landlady might be returning. The ticking of a clock echoed along the hallway. I hurried back over to the table. Derrick was already shuffling through the letters. "Most appear to be from friends . . ." He showed me one, with a French postmark. "Or bills of lading."

"The Van Horns must owe a great deal of money." Reaching, I took the last few envelopes from the stack to hurry our task along. Something from the very bottom of the pile fluttered to the table, a loose piece of paper, folded in half. I smoothed it open and beheld a sketch of a tree bearing round, apple-like fruit. A close-up representation of a branch, its leaves and fruit rendered in minute detail, occupied one corner. "What could this be?"

Derrick glanced over my shoulder, then took the sketch to study it closer. "Perhaps it's a tree on the property they lost recently. Perhaps Mrs. Van Horn had seen it planted and hated to leave it behind, so she sketched it, or had a sketch made of it. Perhaps it meant something special to her and her husband."

"Hmm . . ." I retrieved the paper from his hand. "What kind of tree would that be? It's unfamiliar."

"It looks like some breed of apple, doesn't it? Maybe crabapple."

"Crabapple trees don't usually carry much sentiment. And it's not something I've seen here in Rhode Island. It looks almost stunted, and rather too dense."

"There are countless breeds of apples, and the Van Horns

were wealthy enough to import a tree of any variety they chose."

"I suppose you're right." I hesitated. "Should I put it back?"

"Yes. No." Once again, our gazes connected. Derrick shook his head. "I don't know why we shouldn't put it back, but don't."

"You don't think . . ." I studied the sketch again.

"A poisonous apple? I've never heard of any. Except in fairy tales."

"Those poisonous apples had an antidote, and the stories had their happily-ever-afters."

He leaned over and kissed my lips, a gentle peck. "Like our story?"

I smiled briefly and set the paper down. "Not for Lottie Robinson, nor for Sybil."

We tidied the signs of our snooping. I slipped the sketch into my handbag. Then I removed a glove and slid off the opal ring Derrick had given me in Italy. On our way out, I showed it to the landlady. "I found it," I lied. "It had slipped from my finger and fallen to the rug."

"Oh, you must be relieved."

"I am." Any guilt I experienced at lying was tempered by my desire to keep the reason for our visit from Anna Rose Van Horn, should she return to the house. I didn't wish to alert her that I or the police considered her a suspect in her own daughter's death.

Did I truly think she did it? No, but the timing of her disappearance, along with having a possible motive for the other attacks, made it impossible to rule her out.

When we reached Ocean Avenue, I asked Derrick to turn west, rather than east toward Gull Manor.

"Where are we going?"

"I'm hoping Dr. Agassiz is at home at Castle Hill."

"Dr. Agassiz? But the police have already consulted with him."

"I want to show him the sketch we found."

"It's a long shot that it means anything."

I pressed my hand to his forearm, my fingers curling around the muscle beneath his sleeve. "Humor me. What was so important about this sketch that it was hidden beneath all that correspondence at the bottom of Mrs. Van Horn's traveling desk?"

"My darling, perhaps it wasn't hidden at all, but simply tossed in and forgotten."

"Again, humor me."

He released the reins with one hand and raised my hand to his lips. "Of course. Always."

The housekeeper at Castle Hill told us that Dr. Agassiz and his son, Rodolphe, were both at home. She led us through the cool, paneled interior of the house, into a conservatory flooded with sunlight and out onto the lawn overlooking Narragansett Bay. The house, a shingled Victorian at the crest of a broad hill, boasted a gracefully peaked roofline and a lofty turret, the views from which I could only imagine. Perhaps Derrick and I would include just such a turret in the house we would build.

Down the slope of the lawn, toward the rocky shoreline, we saw a semicircular grouping of wooden reclining chairs, a half dozen in all, two of them currently occupied. Two men lounged in the low chairs, with their legs stretched out in front of them; each held a glass of something that flashed amber in the lowering sun. The housekeeper bade us follow her and set out across the grass.

The two men, obviously father and son, heard us coming, carefully placed their glasses on the wide arms of their chairs, and stood to greet us.

"Mr. and Mrs. Derrick Andrews to see you, sir," the housekeeper said.

"Very good. Thank you, Mrs. Nelson. Please send Travers down." The doctor circled the chairs and came toward us with his hand extended. I knew Alexander Agassiz to be in his sixties, a fact attested to by the grizzled hair wreathing his bald pate, yet he moved across the grass with the spry nimbleness of a younger man. His travels and exploring apparently kept him fit. "Good to see you both again. Have you met my son, Roddy?"

"It's lovely to see you, Dr. Agassiz," I said, "and yes, Mr. Agassiz and I met a couple of years ago on the polo grounds."

That gentleman, only a year or so my elder, was not only an avid polo player but a highly skilled one. He might have walked off the polo grounds only minutes ago, as he was attired in breeches, boots, and a tweed coat and vest. He, too, extended his hand. "It was Miss Cross last time. My congratulations."

We exchanged niceties, and a quick reshuffling of the chairs placed four of them in closer proximity, facing one another.

Mr. Agassiz retrieved his glass and held it up for our perusal. "A predinner aperitif. What would you both like?"

It was then I heard the discreet footsteps in the grass behind us, and a glance over my shoulder confirmed the arrival of an obliging footman. "Thank you, but nothing for me," I said.

"Nor me," Derrick said, holding up a forestalling hand. "We're due home for dinner, but we stopped by to see if you might be able to help us with something."

"If there is anything I can do, I'd be most pleased to help. What is it?"

"We hope you might be able to identify a certain tree for

us." I opened my handbag, and before I could fish out the sketch, Roddy Agassiz chuckled.

"You've certainly come to the right place. If anyone can be of assistance in such matters, my father can." He slung one leg over the other knee. "Are you planning new landscaping at Gull Manor?"

"No, nothing like that," Derrick replied, but with a slight wink in my direction, as we would indeed be landscaping the property next door once it became ours.

"You're sure you won't join us in a drink?" Roddy asked, and when we both again cordially declined, he waved a hand, sending the footman away as stealthily as he had come.

"Now, then," his father said heartily. "I love a challenge. What is this tree you'd have me identify? Is it anything to do with the matter the police have been investigating?"

"It might be." I unfolded the paper and passed it to him. As he studied it, Roddy leaned to view it as well, his eyebrows gathering.

"Is it a species of apple?" Derrick asked.

Dr. Agassiz didn't immediately reply, but continued scrutinizing the artwork with his lips compressed and his eyes narrowed. He studied the close-up sketch in the corner of the page. Finally, he said, "No, not an apple, although I can see why you might think so. You see the branches?" He held the sketch toward us. "They are thinner and more flexible than those of any variety of apple tree, and do you see the overall rounded shape of this tree, how uniform it is? The shape of an apple tree is more haphazard." He turned his gaze on his son. "Is it familiar to you?"

Roddy took the paper. "I'm not sure, Father . . ."

"If it is what I think it might be, you and I encountered them along the South American Atlantic coast." He raised his eyebrows in expectation and watched his son.

"Do you mean . . . manchineel?"

His father slowly nodded, then turned back to Derrick and me. "This is merely a sketch, so it is impossible to be certain. But had the police showed me this when they consulted with me about possible toxins, I likely would have had an answer for them. As it was, I only considered more local plants."

"What is a manchin . . ." I trailed off as the rest of the word eluded me.

"Manchineel," Dr. Agassiz repeated for me. "Very dangerous. Highly poisonous. Many an unwary sailor, new to the Southern Hemisphere, has perished making the same mistake you did." He spoke to Derrick. "Believing it to be a species of apple, and eating a piece of its fruit, would most certainly result in death."

Chapter 14

"Where on earth did you get this?" Dr. Agassiz tapped the paper.

"I . . ." I paused to consider my reply, and then continued. "An acquaintance had it, and I was curious."

He flashed a cunning smile. "Can't divulge your sources in crime solving, Mrs. Andrews?"

"In helping to solve crimes," I corrected him. "I simply have a hunch this could prove significant to the case."

"Yes . . ." He drew out the word and glanced down at the sketch again. "But I don't know where someone in Newport would have come by this. It doesn't grow anywhere near this state. And transporting it . . . that, too, would be dangerous. Would they have brought whole fruit? Leaves? Sap? Your culprit, if indeed they used any portion of the manchineel tree, would have to have known what safety precautions to take."

Derrick leaned forward. "Then you're saying any part of the tree is toxic to humans."

"Any and all parts," Dr. Agassiz clarified, "to humans and all creatures."

"In the old days, the Indians used it to poison their arrow tips," his son informed us. "And what Father said about sailors believing it to be eatable? It's said the fruit bears a deceptively sweet taste that fools the unsuspecting until it's too late. Then it acts like acid in the body. A horrible death, from what I understand."

"The Spanish call it *manzanilla de la muerte*." Dr. Agassiz raised his drink for a sip, and during the pause, his son translated.

"Little apple of death. Simply standing under one of these trees during a rain will result in serious burns on the skin. Blindness, should any get in the eyes."

A breath whooshed out of me. I recalled Miss Norris's description of tasting a petit four: first sweetness, almost like candied rose petals, followed by acrid bitterness and intense burning. "This has to be what was used. But then . . ."

I didn't wish to voice the thought that echoed through my mind. Anna Rose Van Horn had most likely drawn this sketch. She had hidden it. And with her daughter now dead, the woman had gone missing. I shook my head and let my eyes fall closed.

"Where in South America is this tree found?" Derrick asked as my disbelief battled with what we had just learned.

"In the northern and central regions," Dr. Agassiz said, "as well as on the Caribbean islands and in Florida. It grows among the mangroves."

"Florida," I repeated in a whisper. Anna Rose and Sybil Van Horn had been to Florida only months ago, guests at Henry Flagler's hotel. And then I remembered that the Van Horns were not the only suspects who had recently been in Florida.

* * *

Once back at home, I telephoned the police station. Jesse wasn't in, but I left a message that I wished to see him the following morning. I wouldn't have told him what we had learned over the phone. The lines were less than private, true, but I had another reason. Although we had previously discussed this case in front of our houseguests, I no longer wished to do so.

All signs pointed to Anna Rose Van Horn as the culprit, but with great sadness I acknowledged that I no longer fully trusted Amity Carter or Zinnia Lewis. What about Mina Wallingford, dismissed by her peers from the committees at Trinity Church? Had she, too, been to Florida? The police wouldn't have asked her such a question. Until now there had been no reason to.

The evening passed like any other, with one of Nanny's sumptuous yet simple meals, conversation, and a lively game of charades in the parlor afterward. As the clock struck ten, Nanny yawned and excused herself. I stood up to do likewise and expected our guests to follow.

"Aunt Amity, let's go outside and look at the sea and stars a while." Zinnia Lewis gave her aunt's hand a little tug when the elder woman hesitated. The younger turned to me. "You don't mind, do you?"

"Of course not. Shall I join you?"

"Only if you wish, but you look rather tired." She appealed once again to her aunt. "Come, we don't have very many days left to enjoy the northern skies."

"Yes, my dear, you're right." Miss Carter came to her feet. Linking arms, the pair wished the rest of us good night and headed outside.

My heart began to thud with excitement. Once they were outside and beyond hearing, I found Katie in the kitchen. "Let me know when they come back inside," I said hurriedly. "Call me from the bottom of the stairs—ask me something about tomorrow's breakfast or some such."

She eyed me quizzically, but asked no questions. She merely raised an eyebrow and nodded. I made my way upstairs.

Derrick met me on the landing, having just gone up himself. He regarded me with narrowed eyes. "You suddenly don't look particularly tired."

"An opportunity has fallen into my lap," I said in explanation and led the way to our guests' bedroom.

"What are you—" Derrick followed close on my heels, but went no farther than the threshold after I opened the door and stepped in. "What the blazes are you doing?"

I'd stopped short, wondering where and how to begin. I knew I wouldn't have long, and I couldn't turn on a light. The gas sconces in the hallway would have to do. I went to the bureau and opened the top drawer.

From the doorway, Derrick hissed a breath. "You can't do that."

I ignored his reprimand, finished flipping through items of clothing, and moved on to the next drawer down.

"Emma, please." He sounded exasperated. "This is wrong."

Having slid open the third drawer, I stopped and faced him. "They're from Florida."

"So are a lot of people."

"Not very many of them are here in Newport at the moment." I returned to my task, sliding my hands beneath camisoles, stockings, and other personal effects. If Derrick believed I felt no guilt, he was wrong. My cheeks flamed with culpability, my heart raced with blame. "Listen for Katie. She's to let me know when they're coming back in the house."

"You've got Katie in on this..." He shook his head,

something I only glimpsed out of the corner of my eye as I moved to the nightstand.

Once I'd exhausted the furnishings in my search, I turned to the cases they had brought with them. There was a travel desk, like the one we had found in the Van Horns' room. It, too, was locked, and I decided there mightn't be time to pry it open. Zinnia's paintings still lined the wall where I'd found them previously. Her easel stood near them, folded and packed into its case. After a brief hesitation, I crouched and opened it. The typical painter's accoutrements met my scrutiny. I opened two of the tubes of paint and sniffed the contents. Nothing but the oily odor of pigment met my inquiry. Likewise, the contents of two glass containers and one larger, metal one revealed turpentine inside.

After replacing each item exactly as I had found it, I stood up and scanned the room. Another wooden case sat on the dressing table. It was about the size of the travel desk, though its shape was more of a jewelry box. It immediately caught my interest, as I hadn't seen either woman wear any jewelry other than what they had worn upon their arrival at Gull Manor. This suggested the only such ornamentation they had brought had been what they were wearing. So what resided in that box?

I moved to the dressing table. The lid opened easily enough, revealing slotted compartments, a dozen in all. Within each compartment, I discovered paper packets, folded like envelopes. I chose one and opened it.

When a sweet aroma drifted beneath my nose I almost dropped the little package. I gasped, bringing Derrick into the room.

"What is it?"

"It's sweet . . ." My heart pounded in my temples. Choosing at random, I drew out another packet. I sniffed, then frowned. The sharp-sweet scent of aniseed permeated the air. Another yielded a spicy blend of cinnamon, clove, and allspice. My breathing steadied. "Tea."

"What?"

"I believe it's only tea. They must blend their own and travel with it," I explained.

"Nothing lethal, then," he replied, with a touch of mockery.

"No. Nothing lethal." I replaced all three packets, closed the case, and repositioned it carefully on the dressing table.

"Good, then let's go." He started toward the door.

"Wait." I had caught sight of Zinnia's sketchbook on the windowsill. I went to it, careful not to stir the curtains lest either of our guests happened to gaze this way. I lifted the sketchbook and began flipping through it.

"Now what?"

"I'm just seeing if there's anything new."

"Such as a sketch of a manchineel tree?"

I shrugged. I didn't believe there would be one, but I simply couldn't leave until I'd given the room a thorough search. And that included a peek into what and where Zinnia had been sketching. Yet page after page yielded nothing new or remarkable. I started to put the book down where I'd found it, but the back cover fell open to reveal a likeness I hadn't seen before.

It was of a man. The details were lovingly rendered, matching or even surpassing the image Zinnia had sketched of Edith Roosevelt. I carried the book closer to the light in the hallway. Derrick followed, his breath heating my neck as he gazed over my shoulder.

"I wonder who he is," I mused. A brother? No, the lines she had drawn around his eyes and mouth suggested an older man, perhaps a good twenty years older than Zinnia. Her father? An uncle?

"No one I recognize," Derrick murmured.

"No, me neither."

"Then put it back where you found it." His voice held impatience and more than a little perplexity. He was used to my inquisitiveness, but not this manner of shameless prying.

I had started to close the book when I noticed, in the hall light, a smudge a couple of inches in length in the bottom right corner. On closer inspection I realized something had been erased. I held the page up to the light, hoping a trace remained of the words that had been written there. Judging by the grooves in the paper, it appeared as though the words had been crossed out before they had been erased.

Who was this man? I might never know, for unless Zinnia allowed me to look through her sketchbook again, I could never ask her. The look on Derrick's face said it was none of my business. Perhaps not, but that didn't stop me from contemplating the closed wardrobe doors. Would I find evidence of Harry Walsh's widow's weeds? I took one step, but froze as Katie's voice drifted up the staircase.

"All finished outside, ladies? Can I get you anything?"

My time was up.

I didn't need to go the police station the following morning, as Jesse turned up at the *Messenger* shortly after Derrick and I arrived. I hadn't even had time to pass through the front office into the rear of the building before the street door opened behind us and Jesse stepped in, removing his derby.

Bypassing the usual greeting, he said, "A woman matching Anna Rose Van Horn's description was seen at the train station in North Kingstown the night before her daughter was found dead. Late."

"You mean before Emma and I found her dead," Derrick corrected him in a harsh tone. He came to his feet, having settled in at his desk only the moment before. He seethed at Jesse. His attitude didn't surprise me, yet it puzzled me. He never showed this kind of resistance to my involvement in police business when it was the two of us alone. Only when Jesse was present. The old rivalry, I supposed.

"Yes, yes," Jesse replied impatiently, quite used to Derrick's bluster when it came to me being involved in police-work. "But at least now we have a direction and a time frame. The woman apparently boarded a northbound train sometime after ten o'clock. There's more, nothing positive, but . . ." He paused, as if for dramatic effect. It worked, as my pulse sped in anticipation.

"Don't keep us in suspense," I said rather testily.

"We can't be certain," he went on, "but a woman was seen on the Fall River Line Ferry that left Newport earlier that same evening, heading to the mainland, wearing a mourning veil."

Both Derrick's and my mouths fell open on gasps. He asked, "Seen by whom?"

"A ticket collector. We inquired with the line after you found Miss Van Horn, but the man was working on another ferry at the time."

We pondered this in silence for several moments. Then I asked, "If this was Anna Rose Van Horn, why would she have obscured her face for the ferry ride but not once she reached the train station?"

"It's obvious," Derrick replied. "She didn't wish to be seen leaving Newport. Once she reached the mainland, especially at that time of night, she must have judged it safe to remove the veil."

"That's what I'm thinking, too," Jesse said. "But as for where she went after reaching North Kingstown—" With a shake of his head, he slapped his hat against his thigh.

"You said the northbound train, but she could have doubled back toward New York." I fell silent as a trolley went past our windows, its bell clanging and its wheels clacking on the tracks.

Jesse waited until it had passed. "We don't think so, but

we've sent telegrams to the central New York City police stations nonetheless, as well as several points along the way. My hunch, though, is that she hasn't gone far."

Derrick folded his arms and leaned against the edge of the desk. "What makes you think so?"

"For one, she traveled lightly, only one small valise."

"If she was looking to make her escape, she wouldn't have packed a trunk," I pointed out.

"Would she have packed at all, though?" Derrick spoke as if thinking out loud, his face drawn tight. "Daughter confronts mother, mother strikes back. Does she then pack her things, or does she simply run?"

I sighed. "Depends on the mother. Is she as cold as ice? Ruthless? Is she sorry for what she did?"

"If she did it," Derrick reminded me.

I gazed down at my feet, then back up. "This suggests Mrs. Van Horn was still in Newport after Jennie Pierpont visited Sybil—"

"After Miss Pierpont claims she visited Miss Van Horn," Jesse corrected me. "She could have been lying about when she arrived at the house."

I nodded my concurrence, then fished the sketch of the manchineel tree out of my handbag. As I did, our editor-in-chief arrived. I greeted him, then glanced at Jesse in question.

He regarded the older man briefly. "It's all right. I think we can trust Mr. Sheppard to be discreet." Stanley Sheppard nodded and went to his desk. He moved a stack of papers from his inbox to a spot in front of him, but his attention remained on us.

I handed the sketch to Jesse and launched into the description from Dr. Agassiz and his son.

"Simply by standing beneath the branches in the rain?" Jesse asked, incredulous that any substance could be so toxic. Stanley Sheppard expressed his astonishment with a low whistle.

"That's what he said," I confirmed. "Natives in the area used it on the tips of their arrows long ago when they fought the Spanish. But the question is, how would someone transport such a poison from so far away?"

"Surely, if someone did, it was because they intended to use it. This rules out a crime of passion." Jesse continued staring down at the sketch. He angled it to peer more intently at the close-up details in the corner. "Except, perhaps, in the case of Sybil Van Horn, who was possibly murdered because of what she knew. But I'm sure the mother never planned on having to kill her own daughter."

"It does appear methodically planned out." Derrick unfolded his arms, then picked up his pen and tapped it against the desktop. "But getting back to Anna Rose, if she didn't catch the train south, she could still be in Rhode Island."

Jesse nodded. "That's what we're hoping."

"If she's innocent," I murmured, "think of what she'll come back to . . . her own daughter . . ." I shook my head in dismay, then wondered why I believed Mrs. Van Horn to be innocent with so much evidence against her. "Each of our suspects has been to Florida."

"Each?" Jesse frowned in puzzlement. "Jennie Pierpont has been our main suspect. This"—he held up the sketch— "only muddies the waters. Without Mrs. Van Horn's disappearance and the fact that this was found among her possessions, Miss Pierpont would be indicted."

I didn't wish for either woman to be guilty. I caught Derrick's eye, questioning him silently. Should I reveal my further suspicions to Jesse? Did I have any basis for those suspicions other than my houseguests hailing from Florida? They had also attended the luncheon. And they habitually left the house on excursions of their own, morning and evening, supposedly to view the wildlife and scenery. Were they always together? The answer, I realized, remained in question.

Derrick's dark eyes communicated his qualms to me just as silently; he hadn't approved of my searching their bedroom, and when I turned up nothing, it seemed his disapproval had been justified.

"What are you two conspiring about?"

Derrick closed his eyes and nodded to me. I said, "If we're to consider recent travelers to and from Florida, shouldn't we include Amity Carter and Zinnia Lewis?"

Jesse's eyebrows shot up. "Your guests? Do you have any reason to suspect them?"

"None," Derrick said. "And yet Emma has a point. They recently arrived from Florida."

Jesse turned his attention back to me. "What do you know about them?"

"Admittedly, not much. Miss Carter, by her own words, is happily single and independent. She enjoys what she does—that is, studying nature, particularly birds, and writing books on the subject. I feel she has no regrets about the choices she's made."

Jesse studied me, then said, "And Miss Lewis? Do you believe she has regrets?"

How well he had come to know me in recent years that he could make such a conjecture. "I'm not sure, but sometimes she seems . . . pensive. Wistful, perhaps. She might not relish the prospect of remaining single all her life, and being with her aunt doesn't afford her much opportunity to meet eligible men. But that doesn't give her a motive for murder."

"Does she share her aunt's enthusiasm for the natural world?" he asked next.

"In a way, yes, but as an artist, not a naturalist. She's been painting since she's been here, and sketching."

"Sketching, you say?" Jesse rubbed a hand under his chin and once more regarded the paper in his hand.

"Yes. She keeps a sketchbook with her. I've had the opportunity to glance through it. Most of the pictures depict scenery, the types of things she likes to paint."

"I see." Jesse's frown returned. "Do aunt and niece get along?"

"Splendidly, from everything we've seen," I said.

"No arguments, no complaints?"

"Not a one." This time, it was Derrick who answered. "They've been delightful guests, not a bit of trouble."

"And have they interacted with any of our local people?" Jesse set the sketch on the desk, took out his notebook and pencil, and jotted a few lines. "Other than at the luncheon."

Derrick looked at me, and I said, "We went bird-watching at Hanging Rock with the Van Horns and Jennie Pierpont. Miss Carter strolled the area with her binoculars and instructed the others on what to look for. Miss Lewis set up her travel easel and began a landscape."

Jesse's pencil paused. "And nothing of note was discussed then? No grievances against anyone?"

I inhaled slowly. "The only member of our group to have any complaints against anyone was Jennie. As I've already mentioned, she was angry at many of the luncheon attendees for their lack of concern for the topic at hand. She also resents men like Henry Flagler. The topic of Florida had come up—naturally, since my guests are from there—and she insisted industrialists, for all their philanthropy and outward concern for the natural environment, are the most culpable when it comes to destroying habitats and endangering species. But you know all that."

"And neither Miss Carter nor Miss Lewis joined in the conversation?" Jesse asked. "They didn't air any opinions on the matter?"

"No, the conversation with Jennie was for my ears alone. The others were already engaged in their own activities. Miss Carter had praised Mr. Flagler for his friendship and generosity, and I had noticed that this upset Jennie. I asked her why."

"Speaking of whom," Derrick put in, "are you releasing her now that there are other suspects in the mix?"

Jesse didn't surprise me when he shook his head. "I can't, not yet. And we also have to remember that Miss Van Horn died by means other than the toxin. We haven't yet ruled out a second killer."

"What?" I exchanged an incredulous glance with Derrick. "You must be joking. How could Sybil's death not be connected to the other incidents?"

"I understand your sentiments, Emma. Had Miss Van Horn died of the same toxic substance as Mrs. Robinson, then yes, we would know for certain that there had been one killer. And yes, the two deaths probably are connected and committed by the same person. But probably isn't good enough in a case like this. We'll need more evidence before we can reach any definite conclusions."

My stomach sank on Jennie's behalf. "I see your point. May I visit her later today?"

He nodded. "I see no reason why not. Maybe you can get her to reveal something."

At that, Derrick shot him a lethal look. Jesse and I both shrugged it off, and I said, "Even if Jennie is innocent, she can't very well harm me at the police station."

Derrick slanted his lips in a dubious gesture. "What about the other suspects? What do you intend to do about Miss Carter and Miss Lewis? Will you be invading Gull Manor?"

"That's something else Emma can do," Jesse said. "Have you searched through their belongings? Looked for the items Harry Walsh described the mystery woman wearing?"

Derrick and I exchanged another glance, a rueful one on my part.

"What now? You two are always passing secrets between

you." Jesse shook his head and raised his eyes toward the ceiling.

"Yes and no," I replied. "After hearing Dr. Agassiz's description of the manchineel tree and learning it grew in Florida, I did take a look through their bedroom. But I was more concerned about finding evidence of manchineel."

"Did you search the closet?"

"I ran out of time, I'm afraid. But I will."

Derrick blew out an impatient breath. "I wish you wouldn't."

I turned to him, reaching for his hand. "I understand. But with so much at stake, we can't afford to be chivalrous, can we?"

"I suppose not," he conceded with a shrug. His fingers tightened around mine.

"All right, perhaps tonight, then." I gave his hand a shake, as if we had struck a bargain. In the meantime, I had work to do, and so did Derrick.

Chapter 15

That afternoon saw me back on Marlborough Street, at the police station, asking to see Jennie. Although Jesse was out, he had cleared it with the officer at the front desk and with Chief Rogers. They took her to me in the interrogation room. She entered warily, until her gaze fell on me.

"Emma!" She rushed to the table and sat opposite me. "Do you have any news? Have you found anything that will get me out of here?"

We linked hands across the table. "Not yet, I'm afraid. But suspicion has fallen on a few others. The focus isn't only on you now."

"Oh, but that is good news. They'll let me go, then, won't they?"

I studied her face. Sleeplessness had produced deep shadows beneath her eyes. Her youthful features had aged, her worries and fears tracing lines that hadn't been there previously. Pity welled inside me. "They can't, Jennie, not just yet. You're still a viable suspect."

My heart squeezed as hope drained from her expression.

"But you just said the focus isn't only on me. Surely that means there is doubt, that they don't have solid evidence against me."

"Jennie, please be patient a while longer. You must have faith."

The worry lines above her nose deepened. She avoided my eyes.

I leaned closer to her. "You've had some time to think. Can you remember anything that might be helpful?"

"Such as what?"

"Such as . . . you were at Hanging Rock with the rest of us. Did anyone say or do anything that struck you as odd?"

"Hanging Rock . . ." She appeared mystified. Then her features smoothed. "Do you mean to say the others that day are also suspects? Anna Rose Van Horn, your friends from Florida . . ." She scrunched her nose. "Why would your two friends hurt anyone here? They barely know a soul."

I ignored her questions and, hoping to catch her off guard, bluntly asked, "What do you know about poisonous trees that grow in Florida?"

She eyed me askance. "What do you mean?"

"Please, Jennie, answer the question."

"The toxin—the police believe it came from Florida? That doesn't make sense. There are plenty of toxic plants here in Rhode Island. Everywhere has some variety of poisonous plant."

"Not like this."

Her scrutiny bore into me. "What could be so powerful that its potency could last on such a long trip?"

"You truly don't know? You were in Florida."

"I'm not a botanist. I'm not even an ornithologist. I'm merely a proponent for our nation's birds. That's what took me to Florida, although I made several other stops on the way down and back. I wasn't in one place long enough to learn much about the environment, save the obvious."

It was my turn to study her. Was she telling the truth?

I picked up my handbag from the table and started to stand. She reached again for my hand.

"Emma, please. You've got to believe me. I didn't hurt anyone. I certainly wouldn't have murdered a woman who had become my friend."

I pasted on a smile. "I promise, Jennie. I'm doing everything I can."

Which didn't answer her plea that I believe her. The best I could do for Jennie Pierpont was discover the identity of the murderer, whether it be her or one of the others.

At home, I didn't rush upstairs to rummage through my guests' belongings, knowing they would soon return to their bedroom to prepare for dinner. Instead, I joined them outside. They seemed to never tire of being out-of-doors.

For once, Zinnia hadn't set up her easel. She and Amity were down at the waterline, standing on one of the large boulders and tossing breadcrumbs. Seagulls by the dozen swooped to catch each flying scrap in midair. Patch had accompanied them, and he leapt with enthusiasm whenever one of the gulls flew close. The combination of squawks, barks, and the ladies' laughter mingled with the churning of the waves.

"Hello, you two," I called out. "Making some new friends?"

Patch came running. The ladies turned to regard me, Zinnia holding her hat down against the wind. Amity leaped down off the boulder, proving to be a fit woman for her age. "How was your day?"

"Fine, thank you." With Patch trotting by my side, I breathed in a draft of salty breeze. "What have you been doing to entertain yourselves today?"

"A little of the same as every other day." Miss Carter's binoculars hung around her neck. I believed she could spend every day with her eyes on the sky and never utter a complaint.

To Zinnia, I said, "Not painting tonight," more an observation than a question.

Zinnia stepped down from the boulders more carefully than her aunt had done. "I worked on one of my canvases-in-process earlier. One must limit oneself and finish what one has started."

"Did you go anywhere particularly fascinating today?" I ducked as a gull darted above my head.

"I mostly walked the shoreline with these." Amity tapped the binoculars.

"I went inland a bit," Zinnia said. "Exploring colors and light. I took some notes, made a few drawings in my book."

"I see. Which route did you take?" Had she been down Carroll Avenue? It would be a good walk to the Van Horns' lodging house, but not an impossible one.

She shrugged. "I couldn't say. I didn't look at the street signs. I just went where my feet took me."

"And yet you managed to find your way back," I noted with genuine surprise. Our winding lanes typically bewildered most newcomers.

"She has an unerring sense of direction," her aunt informed me eagerly. "That memory of hers, you know. It never fails her."

"Yes, of course. So you don't necessarily spend your days together," I went on casually, as if it were of no account.

"If we spent every minute of every day in each other's company," the aunt said, "I fear we would soon be at each other's throats."

"Don't exaggerate, Aunt." Zinnia laughed and swatted a hand in the air. "I enjoy every moment of your company, as I hope you do mine, but we do have different purposes in exploring your island, Emma. And neither Aunt Amity nor I are so helpless that we cannot venture off on our own for an hour or so."

"I understand perfectly." That much was true. As much as I adored my husband, I had my own pursuits to attend to, as did he. It made our time together that much more fulfilling, and more precious.

But I couldn't help wondering if one or the other of my guests required time alone to pursue matters other than the ones they openly subscribed to. I thought about the timing of the deliveries that killed Lottie Robinson and the arrival of the tainted letters through the mail. It had begun the day after the Audubon luncheon. The ladies from Florida hadn't been staying with me yet; they had been rooming in town, giving either of them ample opportunity to hire Harry Walsh, poison the petit fours and the letters, and return them to him for delivery the next day. The mail had naturally taken longer and hadn't begun to arrive along Bellevue Avenue until the following day—the day after Lottie Robinson fell ill.

Yes, it was possible that either Amity Carter or Zinnia Lewis had committed the deed. As possible as it could have been for Jennie Pierpont or Anna Rose Van Horn. As for Mina Wallingford, I didn't yet know if she had recently been to Florida. Still, at present that made five suspects.

What drove a person to murder? Greed, revenge, jealousy, the need to silence someone.

Revenge had been foremost on my mind with each of our suspects. Jennie, punishing society women for their frippery; Mina Wallingford, getting even for being barred from the church committees; and Anna Rose Van Horn, having been shunned by her society peers because of her husband's crimes.

And Amity Carter and Zinnia Lewis? As we all three turned our attention back to enticing the seagulls with bits of stale bread, I sighed inwardly. With them, I could see opportunity but little motive. They were visitors, their home a world away, the society they kept vastly different from ours here in Newport.

My thoughts veered back to Anna Rose. Greed—perhaps not exactly that, but surely she and her daughter were lacking in funds. Revenge—yes, to those friends who proved less than dependable. Jealousy—because the man who should have married Sybil married Lottie Robinson's daughter instead. The need to silence someone—her own daughter, because perhaps Sybil realized the truth and threatened to tell the authorities.

I sighed again, out loud this time. Zinnia noticed and turned to me.

"Is anything wrong?"

"It's been a long day, that's all."

Zinnia linked her arm through mine. "Let's walk a bit. I always find that walking eases a disquieted mind."

We strolled along the oceanfront, following the unevenness of the land, the dips and rises, while skirting the boulders and leaping over gaps in our path. Patch, too enticed with his game with the seagulls, had opted to stay with Amity. Thus, nothing but the frothing of the waves and their slapping against the shore broke the quiet. Zinnia had been correct. My tensions eased, and along with them, my suspicions of these two women.

"I shall be sorry to leave here," Zinnia said, as we paused to gaze out over a rocky peninsula jutting into the ocean.

"Will you? I would imagine it will be good to see home again, though."

Zinnia slid her arm free of mine and bent down to gather some pebbles. When she straightened, she began tossing them into the water. "I'm still learning how to skip rocks. Sometimes I can do it, but mostly they plop right in."

"You need flatter rocks, for one thing." I gathered up a few of my own, looking for slivers of shale. "Here, do it this way." I angled my hand sideways, holding the rock edgewise between my thumb and forefinger. "And give your wrist a good flick."

She tried again, this time achieving two skips before the rock submerged. "I see! That was better, wasn't it?"

"Much better. You'll get the hang of it." Had she purposely avoided my comment about returning home to Florida? As if reading my mind, she met my gaze and smiled pensively.

"We have lots of shells and washed-up coral on our beaches at home, but we don't have flat stones like this." She breathed out, a sound filled with melancholy. "We don't have a lot of things in Florida."

"I thought you were happy there."

"I am, I suppose. It's just that . . ." She paused, looking reluctant to say more.

"Whatever it is will remain between us." I placed a hand on her shoulder.

She tilted her head. "I had very few prospects at home. My family isn't wealthy, and there was no dowry for me. When Aunt Amity asked me to come live with her, it seemed the perfect solution to everyone's worries. Even my own. But . . ." Another sigh. "It's lonely sometimes. Aunt Amity is good company, but often she is my only company.

Mr. Flagler invites us to many of his parties, but Aunt Amity doesn't always like to attend, and truth be told, neither do I. I don't fit in with those people. And Florida itself . . . It lacks—"

Her arms stretched wide as if to embrace the rocky ocean view before us. "This! All of this variety, the surprises, the excitement of how changeable both the land and the weather can be." She turned again to face me. "Do you know we can have the same weather for months at a time? Hot, hot, hot, all summer long, with a drenching rain for half an hour every afternoon."

"That does sound a bit monotonous." I gave a small laugh. "I'm sure the winters are heavenly, though. But is this about the weather, Zinnia, or something else?"

She hung her head. "I feel as though I'm betraying Aunt Amity for even bringing it up. She has done so much for me, truly. It's just that . . . she doesn't understand—doesn't re-member what it was like to be our age." She scrutinized my face. "I believe you and I are close in age. Anyway, perhaps Aunt Amity was never truly young. I don't think she ever longed for any other company than her books and birds and fellow naturalists. She is perfectly happy with her life. In the meantime, I go where she wants, when she wants, with very little say in matters."

"Does she not ask you about your preferences?"

"Rarely. I think she assumes I don't have any, other than finding views to paint."

This wasn't at all what she had implied when we discussed the subject with her aunt that first night they stayed at Gull Manor. Which proved to me she couldn't freely express her-self in front of her aunt. What else did Zinnia feel unable to do in front of Amity Carter? "Have you considered return-ing home to your family?"

"They wouldn't want me back. And that's not the answer

I'm looking for. I just wish for something . . . exciting . . . to happen to me. Perhaps in New York . . ."

"Your art," I said, having previously guessed that she might wish to be an artist in earnest, one who showed and even sold her work. Not easy for a woman, but not impossible. Perhaps my parents, with their art-world connections, could help her. "Have you spoken to your aunt about these things?"

"I couldn't possibly." She shook her head slowly. "As I said, she's done so much for me, giving me a home and security and every material thing I could ask for. I . . . couldn't hurt her feelings that way."

"But perhaps it wouldn't hurt her feelings. She might be more understanding than you realize. As you said, she may never have wanted the life you wish for, and perhaps that has blinded her to your desires. Bringing them to her attention might—"

"No." She spoke so abruptly I flinched.

After a brief silence filled only by the ebb and flow of the waves, I said, "Would you like me to help broach the subject with her?"

"No," she repeated, more gently this time. "Thank you, but please don't say anything. It could cause a rift, and I can't afford to have that happen. I could end up with less than I have now."

"As you wish. I'll mind my business. But don't give up entirely on the idea of talking to her sometime. You feel you owe her a lot, but you owe it to yourself as well."

She gave a dismissive shrug. Turning her back to the ocean, she gazed at the land Derrick and I could almost call ours. "The sale should be complete soon," she said. "I hadn't known about this tie to the north until Aunt Amity announced that we were coming here. I don't begrudge your buying it, mind you, but part of me . . . Well, never mind."

Did she wish she might inherit this land someday? And is that what she feared most about the idea of being honest with her aunt? That she might be disinherited, and the independence she could one day enjoy, perhaps was counting on, would be whisked away?

Would Amity Carter be so cruel to her niece and companion? Or . . .

Could Zinnia be at fault, perhaps only motivated to remain with her aunt because of an eventual payoff?

I couldn't fathom it either way, yet I felt convinced something more lay behind the seemingly congenial pairing of these two ladies. Obviously, the aunt held dominion over the niece, at least for now. Well-meaning? Perhaps. I didn't know them well enough, nor had I witnessed enough of their interactions with each other to know for sure. I only knew that, based on our conversation, I pitied Zinnia Lewis and wished I could do something for her. The thought of inviting her to remain at Gull Manor indefinitely dashed through my mind, but I discarded the idea. Zinnia had made it perfectly clear she wouldn't welcome my intervention. I would therefore hold my tongue and allow them to settle matters between them.

Despite my resolve to stay out of their personal lives, my suspicions concerning my houseguests refused to lie quiet. Later, while the others lingered in the parlor, I excused myself and hurried upstairs on the pretext of needing to outline an article I planned to write in the morning.

I didn't hesitate at the top of the stairs, but went directly to their room, quieting my footsteps as I went. The door stood open, almost an invitation for me to wander in.

The armoire beckoned. With a glance over my shoulder

and a prick of my ears to ensure no one was coming up the stairs, I opened its doors. Several dresses hung from the rack, with a small space between them in the middle, separating, I surmised, Amity's clothing from Zinnia's. The sizes of the dresses confirmed this, with the elder woman's gowns cut larger. As I expected, each woman had traveled with one black dress. Nothing fancy, just simple, lightweight muslin. The skirt of Zinnia's had three tiers with satin piping on each; Amity's dress possessed a plainer skirt, but with the billowing, leg-o'-mutton sleeves that had been popular a few years ago.

Either dress could have been worn for mourning, but not necessarily. They also made good traveling clothes, since they wouldn't show the dirt as lighter colors would. Besides, without a description from Harry Walsh, who could re-member no details about the woman's dress other than the color—black—I had nothing to go on.

So be it. My gaze next traveled to the shelf above the rack, which held two neat stacks of folded items. I reached up and pulled one down.

Using the foot of the bed to sort through them, I discov-ered two shawls, two lace collars, a silk sash, and several lightweight scarves, none of which were black. After replac-ing the stack, I took down the other, only to find similar items, but no mourning veils.

Once again, I paused to listen. The sounds of laughter drifted up the stairs, but I heard no footsteps. I had already searched through the bureau and their empty traveling cases the last time I'd been in the room. Although I had found nothing sinister that time, I returned to the wooden tea box that still occupied a corner of the dressing table. Both women, and particularly Amity, drank tea throughout the day.

My hand stilled on the lid as I hesitated. I took a deep breath, flicked it open, and peered inside. The dried leaves were still there, occupying their various compartments. Then I noticed something I hadn't detected before: the compartments were not built into the box itself, but were part of a removable tray. It took some maneuvering that nearly resulted in my catching a splinter in my index finger, but I soon pried the tray free and peered beneath.

A single, unsealed envelope met my gaze. My eyes darted into the corridor, and I listened again. Detecting no threat of imminent discovery, I opened the flap and slid the paper out. There were several pages. I scanned the topmost . . .

And felt ashamed. It appeared to be a contract for a book, yet unwritten, from a New York publishing house. Another in her series about Florida wildlife and birds.

Quickly, I slipped the contract back into its envelope, returned the envelope to the box, and settled the tray of teas back in place. My errand completed, I erased all traces that I had been there and skulked my way down the hall to my own room. There, I stood with my arms around my middle, regarding the tips of my house shoes and feeling dreadful for having suspected my new friends.

Perhaps Derrick was right, and I should leave investigating to Jesse and the police. I had come to suspect where no cause for suspicion existed. What did that say about the person I had become? Cynical, mistrusting, sneaky. In that moment, I didn't like myself very much.

Yet, after a fitful night's sleep during which I dreamed of being caught red-handed by my houseguests as I rummaged through their belongings—oh, the dismay and reproach on their faces—I awoke, not determined to stop investigating, but to finish what I'd started.

Chapter 16

Upon arriving at the *Messenger*, I telephoned over to the police station to find out whether Anna Rose Van Horn had been found. She had not. I inquired after Jennie and was told she had stopped speaking, except to insist she was innocent.

With Anna Rose still missing, my search of my guests' room yielding nothing incriminating, and Jennie already being held, my thoughts returned to Mina Wallingford. When I had called upon her, I hadn't yet learned of a possible Florida connection to the incidents. Had she ever been to the state? For all I knew, she traveled there each year, as more and more people were beginning to do now that Mr. Flagler had built his hotels. I decided it might be worth visiting her again, especially since, as yet, she had no idea she was being considered as a suspect.

I hadn't been lying the previous evening when I'd told my guests I had an article to outline for today's writeup. I spent the next hour going over everything we knew about Lottie Robinson's and Sybil Van Horn's deaths and documenting the straight facts without revealing the identities of the suspects or what I knew about them.

That done, I attended to a few other matters before pinning my hat in place. Derrick and Stanley Sheppard had their heads together when I reached the front office. They were deep in conversation over something or other to do with the running of the paper and must not have heard me. I slipped by, and by the time the jangle of the bell above the door captured their attention, I was halfway out.

I offered a quick wave over my shoulder. "Just stepping out. Back soon."

My patience with Derrick's objections to my being involved in police matters had begun to wear thin. We both knew he didn't mean them, but nonetheless felt obliged as my husband to issue such cautions. They weren't necessary, especially in this case. What harm could come to me at Mina Wallingford's home in the middle of the morning, with a housekeeper present and who knew how many other servants about?

Those were not the only people I discovered at the cantankerous woman's house. When I knocked, the housekeeper led me through the house to a set of open French doors leading out to the garden. To my great surprise, Mina Wallingford stood beside a fountain in the center of a cluster of rose bushes bordered by pretty rock walls. At least a dozen other ladies stood around her.

And they were chatting and laughing, as women do.

Was this the same Mina Wallingford whose arrogance had gotten her banned from church committees? Who had been ignored when she attempted to join in anyway? And who had shown me not the least hospitality when I called on her the other day?

She glanced over at where I stood beside the housekeeper

on the small brick terrace. There, too, roses in pots bloomed alongside peonies, begonias, and, stretching along a pergola above me, vines of wisteria. Bees buzzed happily in the blossoms, whose warm fragrance rose up to envelop me.

Mrs. Wallingford's brow puckered ominously, then smoothed. She said some words to her company and strolled toward me, several long-stemmed roses clutched in her hand. The housekeeper slipped back inside, leaving me to face the curmudgeon alone.

"Mrs. Andrews, you're back." Her gaze flicked up and down my length, coming to rest on my face. "I'm not entirely sorry."

Not entirely? A strange way to greet someone. The entire scene confused me and left me at a loss for words. Her lips curled in something approaching a smile. "As you can see, I have guests. I took your suggestion to heart and have started a gardening club with some of my neighbors. A couple of them are even on the Trinity Church committees, but it seems they have pardoned me for my sins. It could have to do with my cook being famous for making some of the best macarons to be found in Newport."

"A gardening club . . ." I repeated, still completely baffled.

"Yes, and I have you to thank. You told me I should pursue other interests, take up a hobby, or some such thing. I don't remember exactly what you said, but here I am, and there they are, and in a little while, we shall enjoy refreshments together, including some of those macarons, and continue our discussions on the best times to plant which garden flowers, and the most beneficial and ornamental ways of laying out our beds."

"I'm glad to hear it, Mrs. Wallingford."

"Come, join us. Oh, and here." She handed one of her roses to me, its coral blossom, with shades of pink and amber, identifying it as a newly developed variety called a Soleil d'Or. My Aunt Alice had some growing in her garden as well. Mrs. Wallingford about-faced and marched back to the ladies, leaving me to either follow or take my leave.

Thus, I spent the next hour and a quarter in their company, learning about plantings, cuttings, perennials versus annuals and which to plant where, and otherwise experiencing a very different Mrs. Wallingford than the one I had previously met. Though still brisk in her manner, her prickly edges had somehow softened with an approachability that hadn't been evident before. I cannot say it didn't do my heart good.

But I hadn't come here to check on the woman's well-being or witness the renewal of her social life. I'd come to ask her a very specific question. Her guests, I realized, smoothed the way for me to make my inquiry in a way that might have been awkward at best and accusatory at worst had Mrs. Wallingford and I been alone.

At a signal from her housekeeper, we filed across the yard and through another set of French doors into the dining room, furnished in golden-hued woods offset by scarlet upholsteries and drapes. Afternoon tea had been laid out, complete with tiny sandwiches, petit fours, fruit tarts, and the promised macarons in a rainbow of color. The petit fours gave me pause, but I shook off my reservations.

We took our places, and soon the conversation flowed as it had outside. I waited for a lull and then asked, "Is anyone traveling this autumn, or perhaps next winter, to escape the frigid temperatures?"

A few of the women spoke of their travel plans in the coming months. A lively discussion of destinations and means of travel kept them busy while I bided my time. I had learned my lesson with Mrs. Wallingford. It didn't do to be overly direct; these women required a subtle approach.

Finally, I broached the subject that had brought me there. "Have any of you been to Florida?"

"Florida?" Several of the ladies scrunched their noses.

"In the winter, of course," I clarified. "I understand that, thanks to Mr. Flagler and his hotels, polite society has found a wintertime haven in Palm Beach. Some other areas as well." I widened my eyes in innocence. "Has no one been? My husband and I are considering a visit ourselves, perhaps as soon as next winter."

Mrs. Wallingford emitted a "Bah," from her end of the table. "Why on earth would anyone go to a wilderness like Florida?"

"Because it is no longer a wilderness, Mrs. Wallingford," I calmly explained. "I presently have two houseguests who make their year-round home in Florida. It's become quite civilized."

"Florida is for heathens and scallywags," she said with finality. Around the table, the ladies tittered with mirth.

"Really, Mrs. Wallingford," one of them ventured, "it can't be as bad as all that or Henry Flagler wouldn't have wasted his time there."

"My guests are anything but scallywags," I added, pretending to be amused by Mrs. Wallingford's pronouncement when, in reality, her indirect insult concerning Amity and Zinnia raised my ire. It seemed her true colors were showing again. "They're refined ladies of high intelligence. In fact, Mr. Henry Flagler—"

"Is a scallywag," she burst in. "Like all railroad men." She stopped and compressed her lips. Then, with a slight show of humility, she said, "Forgive me, Mrs. Andrews. I forgot your own relatives made their fortunes in the railroads industry. But even you must admit such men are a pack of scoundrels and ruffians. Why, railwaymen might as well be highwaymen. No, if Henry Flagler and others of his ilk are what I'll find in Florida, I shall never set foot there."

I showed her a weak smile. "Then you've never been?"

"Of course, I haven't been. But I've heard enough about it to know of what I speak." She signaled to her housekeeper, lingering discreetly near an art nouveau screen that undoubtedly camouflaged the door into the pantry, waiting to pour more tea. "And I would dissuade anyone else from going. Malaria, alligators, hurricanes . . . the place is downright deadly."

Did she protest too much? One could never be entirely sure. Perhaps she feared being connected to the toxin. Yet as she had made her assertion, she hadn't blinked or blushed or exhibited any other sign that she might be lying.

At home, the evening passed pleasantly and with interesting conversation. As had become our habit, after dinner the group of us, Nanny included, adjourned outside to appreciate the night sky and the reflected silver lights dancing on the blackened waves.

It surprised me, therefore, when Amity came to my side and murmured for my ears alone, "Might I have a word, Emma? Inside?"

Apprehension rose up. Had she suddenly changed her mind about selling her property? My stomach clenched as I nodded at her request and walked with her into the house. When we reached the hall, I started to turn into the parlor, but Amity surprised me by continuing up the stairs. I followed her. "I hope nothing is wrong."

She paused on the steps, one hand on the banister as she turned to regard me over her shoulder. Her lips were compressed, holding back words I could only guess would be difficult to speak, based on her grim expression. A certainty filled me that Derrick and I would never own the property next door. In my mind's eye, I watched our anticipated school sink into a morass, never to be raised again.

Finally, she unclenched her lips. "Please," was all she said as she continued leading the way to the bedroom she shared with Zinnia. That word held none of its usual politeness, but sounded like a command. Once in the room, she lit the kerosene lamp on the bureau and whirled to face me. "Someone has gone through this room. Somehow, I don't believe it was Katie looking to steal from us. Was it you?"

"I . . . um . . ." Flames rose to scorch my cheeks, quite visible, I was sure, even in the flickering glow of the lamp. With no choice but to admit to what I had done, I sucked in a breath. "Yes, it was me."

"Why?" Her voice rose on that single syllable, not in a shout, but a kind of wail of disbelief and hurt. "How could you? We trusted you and everyone in this house. We believed ourselves to be surrounded by honest, amiable people. While all along . . ."

"Not all along. I understand why you're angry, truly I do, but you must understand, I am involved in helping to discover who is behind the poisonings."

"And you think it was Zinnia and I?" Her hand pressed her bosom.

"I had to be certain it wasn't."

"By sneaking about and rummaging through our things." Not a question, an accusation. She made a sound of disgust in her throat and shook her head indignantly. "Did you truly think I wouldn't notice?"

No, I hadn't. I had taken care to replace things exactly as I had found them, or so I had believed.

"How could you, Emma? How dare you?"

Her vehemence had the opposite effect she intended, for rather than cower, my back stiffened and my shoulders squared. "The truth isn't always easy to come by, but it's worth any effort that must be made. I'm sorry to have intruded upon your privacy, but there were reasons, sound ones, why I did what I did."

Her nose flared. "Such as what?"

"Such as you and Zinnia being lately of Florida."

"What has that got to do with anything?" she demanded after a moment's hesitation.

"There is a connection between these crimes and your home state. I cannot say more."

"Tell me then, what did you find?" Without waiting for my answer, she strode to the dressing table and opened the wooden box that held her varieties of tea. "Dangerous, aren't they? You've already sampled one—the dried passionflower blossoms I gave Mrs. O'Neal to mix with her regular blend. I believe you rather enjoyed it."

That explained the unfamiliar, earthy tea I had sampled one night shortly after our guests joined us here. She was right, I had enjoyed it. I had meant to ask Nanny about it, but had forgotten.

Amity wasn't finished admonishing me. "Or what about the contract from my publisher underneath? As nefarious as it may have seemed, I only put it there for safekeeping. You realize, travel desks are sometimes stolen by people on trains hoping to find cash. I thought the contract would be safer with my tea collection. Apparently not."

"Amity, I'm sorry . . ."

"I'm surprised you didn't cut through the lining of my traveling bag to see what I might have secreted inside."

For a hair's-breadth of a moment, I berated myself that I hadn't thought to do just that. "I'm sorry," I repeated. "The damage is done, I suppose. What will you do now?"

"What I should do is pack our belongings and take Zinnia away from here this very night." With a huff she turned away, went to the window, tugged the curtain aside, and peered out. Then she whisked back around. "She has no notion of any of this. Think how hurt she would be if she knew you suspected us." Her simmering gaze met mine. "She is fragile, my niece. Her self-worth is easily undermined, especially by cruelty. I have dedicated my days to protecting her from the unkindness of others. She considers you her friend, and I believe she looks up to you for your accomplishments. This would break her heart."

"It was not my intention to hurt either one of you."

"Unless one or both of us turned out to be a murderess."

I inclined my head, unable to deny the truth of that.

Then, something in her gaze changed, the anger obscured by a shrewd gleam. "Tell me, does your husband know about this?"

A lie formed in an instant, as I saw no reason to implicate Derrick in what had been my idea, and mine alone. No, it was more than that—and less noble of me. I wished to maintain Derrick's honor in her eyes, as it might prove convenient later on. "No. He has no idea."

"I see." Her lips rolled between her teeth, and she nodded slowly as she stared into my face. One haughty brow arched. "For now, then, he needn't. Zinnia and I shall stay on until the sale of the property is finalized. But should I suspect another such intrusion, I promise you I will go straight to your husband and tell him everything."

"I understand."

"I hope you do." She raised her chin in a show of disdain. I guarded my thoughts carefully to prevent them from showing on my face. Little did she know that I myself would go straight to Derrick at the first private moment we shared.

"It must have been horribly awkward," he said, putting his arms around me after I'd described the confrontation. We were in the kitchen; everyone else had gone up to bed.

Together we took out mugs and everything we needed to make tea, and I retrieved the cookie tin from the pantry. Molasses cookies nestled inside.

"It was, and it took me quite by surprise. I thought I'd been so careful to replace everything the way I'd found it."

"Did she realize you had been in there twice?"

"If she did, she didn't mention it." The kettle began to boil, so I eased from Derrick's embrace and went to the stove. As I poured the water into the pot and stirred the leaves, I thought of Amity's collection of tea. Innocent enough. Yet, had she been too angry with me? Too unable to understand? Two women had died, while others had been injured. Surely, under such circumstances, she should have been able to see past her indignation. "I wonder . . ."

We brought mugs, plates, and cookies to the table and took seats beside each other. Derrick's hand covered mine. "What do you wonder?"

"Whether she's hiding something."

"Her anger didn't ring true?" He released me, chose a cookie, and took a large bite.

"Oh, it did. Perhaps too much so. It was more than a recrimination, it felt like . . . a warning." I took a bracing sip of tea and reached for a cookie. "I hadn't thought of it that way until just now, but yes, she had been warning me away not only from going through their things again, but suspecting them at all."

"Which makes you suspect them all the more."

I nodded at his insight. "I don't want to, though."

"Whom do you wish to suspect?"

"No one," I said, as he had known I would. "Especially not any of the present suspects. Except perhaps Mina Wallingford. That woman is so disagreeable." We nibbled our cookies and sipped our tea. "I do wish I had thought to check the lining of their travel cases."

"Emma . . ." His voice held a warning. "If Jesse believes there is good cause to suspect our guests, let him come with a warrant. I think you've done enough."

"I know, but the police can't see beyond Mrs. Van Horn and Jennie Pierpont as suspects right now."

"The evidence is stacked against them both." He handed me a second cookie, seeing that I had finished my first. I dunked the edge into my tea and savored a warm, soggy bite.

"I hope Mrs. Van Horn turns up soon. You don't think . . ." I paused to consider the idea that had popped into my head, not liking it one bit.

"Think what?"

"That Anna Rose Van Horn met with a similar fate as her daughter?"

Our gazes locked. I could see his mind working it over, until he shook his head. "Jesse said she was seen on the mainland. No, I think she's on the run. Or she might have some other reason entirely, a perfectly legitimate one, for leaving Newport and still doesn't know what happened to her daughter."

"But it would be in the mainland newspapers by now. I can't believe she hasn't heard a word about her daughter."

"I'll admit it's odd, but it doesn't mean she's fallen victim to foul play."

"No, you're probably right." I sipped my tea. "She and Sybil did seem to be hiding something when Jesse and I spoke to them. A pointed look certainly passed between them."

"But it might have nothing to do with the toxin. It could have concerned Mr. Van Horn's crimes, and they didn't wish to discuss it."

"Perhaps, but what if it did have to do with Lottie Robinson being poisoned? What if they knew something but were afraid to tell us because they feared retribution? And what if that retribution has come to pass? There is no saying Anna Rose wasn't followed off the island and murdered somewhere on the mainland."

"We have to hope she's found soon," he concluded, "and that when she is, we'll have our answers."

Chapter 17

Another day passed with no word of Anna Rose Van Horn. More than with any other investigation, I felt I had failed the victims, all of them. Aunt Sadie had been a friend to every woman in need who crossed her path. She had opened Gull Manor to any woman seeking shelter. I had pledged to continue her legacy, but so far I had made little difference to the women of Newport who had been targeted. Was Anna Rose among them? I prayed not.

That afternoon, as Derrick and I prepared to leave the *Messenger* for the day, I received a missive from the police department. Jennie Pierpont wished to see me. Derrick dropped me off and continued to our flat on the Point, where we occasionally stayed when work at the *Messenger* demanded more of our time.

Once again, an officer brought Jennie to me in the interrogation room. I was glad—glad I didn't have to see a woman like Jennie, ordinarily so spirited and full of energy, locked in a cell. I was sitting at the table when she came in. She took the seat opposite mine and reached across for my hands. But she waited in silence until the door closed and we were alone.

Then she said, "I'm told Anna Rose Van Horn hasn't yet been found."

Her bluntness took me aback, and it was a moment before I replied. "Yes, that's right. I'm surprised the police are telling you anything."

"I asked your friend, Detective Whyte. He's a good man."

Though the direction of the conversation puzzled me, I nodded. "Most definitely."

"I've remembered something," she said after a pause.

I gave a little gasp. "What is it?"

"The books."

"What books?"

Jennie's eyes lit with excitement. "They kept a stack of them on the dresser. French texts of some kind. I don't speak French—not well, anyway. I asked Sybil about them once and she said they were attempting to maintain their skills in the event they were able to travel to France again in the future." She gave a sad, fleeting smile. "All that ended for them when Mr. Van Horn was arrested. Anyway, I remember them being gone the night I visited Sybil. Her mother must have taken them with her."

"Why would Mrs. Van Horn take French books with her to the mainland?" I wondered aloud. Then, a thought struck me. "To sell, perhaps? They needed money and might have already gone through most of their valuables. But then, what's taking her so long to return?"

"Maybe she thought she had a buyer for them, who turned out not to want them after all," Jennie theorized. "The poor woman might be traveling from town to town, hoping to find an obliging bookseller. But don't you see? It means she couldn't have murdered Sybil. Not if the books were already gone when I arrived at the house. Mrs. Van Horn had already left."

I leaned closer to her. "Jennie, while this might help exonerate Mrs. Van Horn, I'm afraid the information won't help your case. If you're right about Mrs. Van Horn leaving to sell off some books on the mainland, it perhaps crosses her off the list of suspects." I nearly mentioned the woman wearing a mourning veil seen on the ferry leaving Newport that evening, but thought better of it.

"I know it won't, not directly." For a moment, I thought she might cry, but she compressed her lips and drew herself up. "But doesn't my telling you this suggest that I have nothing to hide? That I'm more concerned about Mrs. Van Horn's fate than my own, and that I'm willing to help exonerate an innocent woman because I'm not guilty either?" Before I could comment, she carried on in a rush. "I'm terribly worried about her. What if the killer knew where she was going and followed?"

"I'll admit I've entertained the same thought. But we have no evidence that any harm has befallen her, and the police are doing their best to find her."

"The police." Jennie dismissed them with a flick of her hand. "I believe you could find her if you set your mind to it."

"Jennie, if she's left the island, which is what we believe, I won't be any more effective than the police. Less so, in fact." The entreaty in her eyes made the rest of my protest die on my lips. I changed tack. "Why did you send for me rather than speak with the police directly? Why not tell Detective Whyte when he informed you they hadn't found Mrs. Van Horn yet?"

"Because of exactly what you said a moment ago. I feared they'd condemn me as their only remaining suspect."

"You're not the only remaining suspect." I might be treading where I had no right to, but this young woman's future hung in the balance, and she deserved the most thorough investigation possible. "Do you know a woman named Mina Wallingford?"

"No, I don't believe so. Was she at the luncheon?"

"She was not. But think, Jennie. Did either of the Van Horns ever mention her? Even in passing?"

Her gaze absently traveled the room as her attention turned inward. Then, "No, I don't remember Sybil ever mentioning such a woman. As for Mrs. Van Horn, she and I never had much occasion to speak other than the day we went bird-watching at Hanging Rock. And even then, I spoke to Sybil much more. Why? Who is this Mrs. Wallingford?"

"Someone with reason to resent many ladies of the Four Hundred. At least, she did," I added, remembering her garden party and how it had seemed to lend her an entirely new aspect—a much more congenial one.

Yet, were her new friends safe?

Jennie broke into my thoughts. "Do you think she might be responsible for not only Sybil, but the others as well?"

"There is no evidence linking her to them," I admitted. "Only a possible motive. Are you sure Sybil never mentioned her? Or anyone, for that matter, in a disparaging way? Someone who treated her and her mother badly because of their troubles."

"No, no one specifically. I would remember." Her eyes narrowed on me. "You suspected them both, mother and daughter, because of how society treated them."

I didn't attempt to deny it. "Again, possible motive."

"Like me."

I nodded, my gaze sliding away from hers. Even now, I couldn't wholly discount her any more than the police could. It was and had always been my greatest struggle: not wanting to believe the worst of someone I esteemed. There had been times when it worked to my benefit and the benefit of the individual concerned. Take my brother, for instance. Once he, too, had been accused of a crime, and despite his many faults at the time, I had refused to believe the boy I'd grown up with could do anything so monstrous. But there had been other incidents when my trust had led me wrong, at least temporarily.

Two faces filled my mind's eye: Amity's and Zinnia's. I had nothing on which to base my doubts about them, other than the coincidence of their living in Florida and the possibility that the toxin had in fact been a product of the manchineel tree. Then again, Jennie had been to Florida as well, as had Mrs. Van Horn.

After a quick inner debate, I asked, "What impression do you have of my guests?"

"Amity and Zinnia?" When I nodded, she angled her chin at me. "What are you getting at? That one of them is guilty? For what reason?"

"None that I know of."

"And opportunity? Haven't they been staying with you?"

"They have, but they have all day to entertain themselves—Amity with her binoculars and notebook, Zinnia with her paints." As I said it, the possibility that either of my new friends could be a murderess seemed absurd.

"Emma, have you considered that it could be someone no one suspects at all? Not you, and not the police?" She gave a bitter laugh. "They're too happy with their present culprit to look farther afield."

In truth, I hadn't considered others. The connections between the women who were targeted and those who obviously bore grudges against society had been too compelling to ignore. What if I'd been wrong about that? "If you have any ideas, Jennie, please share them."

"I'm not from here, nor a member of the Four Hundred," she reminded me.

"You are related to the Morgans," I pointed out. "And they're most certainly of the Four Hundred."

"Perhaps, but I don't mix with them. My interest in coming to Newport lay in establishing a Rhode Island Audubon Society. I did not come hoping to be adopted into any wealthy circles, at least not in any social sense."

No, she had come to win over society to her cause and persuade them to open their pocketbooks. That some of them hadn't, which had angered Jennie, couldn't be ignored either.

Chapter 18

By the time I left Jennie, Derrick was back at the station, speaking with Jesse and waiting for me. As I approached Jesse's desk, both men stood, and a disorienting sensation ran through me, as if the world tilted slightly off-kilter. A buzzing filled my ears, and dark spots swarmed before my eyes. I nearly stumbled. Shooting out a hand, I clutched the back of a chair.

"Emma!" Derrick leaped to my side and encircled my waist with a protective arm. "Are you all right?"

It was a couple of seconds before I found my voice. "I am . . . I'm sorry, I just lost my balance for a moment." It had been more than that, but I didn't wish to make a fuss. "Clumsy of me."

"Are you sure that's all it was?" His worried countenance filled my vision, making me feel unsteady all over again.

"Of course." I lifted my hems an inch or two and lifted each foot to glance at the heels, as if one of my boots had caused my sudden ungainliness.

"Come and sit." He took my arm to draw me to Jesse's desk.

"I'm fine, really. It's time we were on our way home."

Jesse forestalled us with a question. "What did Jennie have to say for herself?"

"Oh, yes . . . Jennie." How could I have forgotten her revelation about the French texts? Instead of protesting further, I gave in to Derrick's nudging and sank into the chair across from Jesse. Derrick drew up another beside me. After taking a steadying breath, I launched into a description of the books Jennie insisted were missing.

"French books?" Jesse rubbed his palm up and down the side of his face. "What on earth would Mrs. Van Horn have taken them for?"

"Jennie and I decided she might be attempting to sell them on the mainland. The Van Horns needed the cash," I reminded him. My stomach twinged, and an ache thumped behind my left eye. I did my best to conceal my discomfort.

"Emma, you're not all right."

Drat. Derrick had become far too perceptive when it came to me.

"I'm fine, I tell you," I replied irritably. "Please don't be like Nanny."

Nonetheless, he continued scrutinizing me, as did Jesse. Their blatant examination made me want to squirm — or stand up and stride away.

"How long were you in there with Jennie?" Derrick asked, his voice low and serious.

I shrugged. "I went in as soon as we arrived, and I just left her now. Why?"

Instead of answering me, he homed in on Jesse with hawk-like fierceness. "Is it possible Jennie Pierpont smuggled something in with her?"

"Such as what?" The words had barely left his lips when Jesse went pale. "You don't mean? Transferred by touch?"

Derrick nodded grimly, but I only grew more annoyed. "What are you two going on about?" And then it struck me, too. For a long moment, I was too stunned, too frightened, and too queasy to speak. Then the word slipped out. "Manchineel."

"I told you, I'm already feeling much better."

My protests fell on deaf ears—Derrick's and my good friend Hannah's. Hannah Hanson worked as a nurse at Newport Hospital, and when we had arrived at the cottage that had once been a private home on Friendship Street in the north end of town, she had dropped what she had been doing and met us in the first-floor examining room.

With the efficiency of an experienced nurse, Hannah tossed my hat and handbag aside, removed the tie at the collar of my shirtwaist, and unbuttoned the top two buttons. She also brought ice for my head, despite my insistence that the ache had subsided. She then ordered me to recline with my feet up. Some fifteen minutes later, our family physician, Dr. Kennison, came in.

"Emma," he addressed me, as he had known me all my life, "what seems to be the trouble?"

"Nothing. I had a bit of a dizzy moment and a slight headache, but as I keep telling everyone, I'm fine now."

Dr. Kennison chuckled at that. He removed the stethoscope from around his neck, inserted the earpieces into his ears, and placed the diaphragm against my chest. He listened, moved it, listened again. Then he sat me up, placed the instrument against my back, and instructed me to breathe. Next, he donned his head mirror and examined my eyes, mouth, and throat. "Nothing alarming so far . . ."

"We think she might have been poisoned," Derrick said, "possibly through touch."

I shook my head. "The more I think about it, the more I realize it would have been impossible. Yes, Jennie and I held hands—we women do that when we're comforting each other—but there are no burns on my palms." I held them out. "And if there had been, Jennie would have suffered the same injury. It simply doesn't make sense."

Dr. Kennison took in this exchange with a puzzled expression. "We could keep Emma overnight as a precaution . . ."

"Yes," Derrick said eagerly.

"No." I was adamant. "I am going home. It's not as though we live on the other side of the island. If I should feel unwell again, I'll come back."

Derrick pressed a palm to my cheek. "Emma, please."

"A compromise," Hannah declared as Doctor Kennison draped his stethoscope around his neck and removed his head mirror. He gave the impression of not wishing to insert himself in the debate between Derrick and myself. But Hannah seemed to have no such qualms. "Emma, stay a while longer so we can observe you and see how you're feeling. If nothing more happens to concern us, you can go home."

I opened my mouth to decline even this reasonable course of action, but the hopeful gleam in Derrick's expression silenced me.

As did the sudden wave that coursed through my stomach. Not enough to make me ill; it was subtle, not much more than a traveling twinge, but there nonetheless. I bit down until it passed and attempted to keep my features even.

"Is it happening again?" Derrick leaned in closer, his hand moving to my brow.

Blasted man.

"I'm glad you're feeling better, Emma." Dr. Kennison hovered near the doorway, obviously ready to go attend more serious cases. "It could have been a bit of dyspepsia. Have you eaten anything odd lately? Anything out of the ordinary?"

"Not that I can think of . . ." I went silent again. Amity's tea. I had tasted its distinct flavor again that morning. Nanny had especially liked it, and Amity had made her a gift of a portion of it. But everyone had drunk from the same pot, including Amity and Derrick.

"Well, then. Someone will let me know if you need me again." With that, Dr. Kennison hurried on to his next patient.

"I have things I need to do as well," Hannah said, with a note of apology. "But I'll check on you every little while until we're confident you can leave." She came to the side of the examining table and gave me a quick hug. "Let's visit soon."

I agreed to that wholeheartedly. Then Derrick and I were alone.

"You were thinking of something when the doctor asked if you'd eaten anything unusual, weren't you?" he asked.

"Not eaten, drank. Amity's tea, the one she dried from the plant called passionflower." I shook my head quickly. "But we all had some this morning. You, too. How have you been feeling?"

"Perfectly fine."

"There, then. This was nothing. No reason to be alarmed."

"With two women dead and others suffering toxic burns, I'd say there is every reason to be alarmed." He hopped up beside me on the examining table and drew me close. "I wish you didn't insist on being so stubborn. Even if it's only to humor me. Let yourself be taken care of when it's needed."

I laughed at that. "All right, but this time it wasn't needed. Truly."

On the way back to Gull Manor, I began to entertain doubts again as Derrick steered the carriage along Bellevue Avenue away from town. As a journalist, I had read countless stories about people being poisoned through gradual means. Arsenic, for example, could be administered over time, making it look as though an illness had come on slowly, building up steadily until the victim finally expired. A clever coroner would detect the accumulation of the poison in a person's system, but autopsies weren't typically performed after a malady, especially if the victim died at home and no one suspected foul play.

No one else at home had been taken ill recently. I stole a glance at Derrick's profile beside me. His skin glowed with its customary healthy hue, and his hands were steady, yet relaxed on the reins. Nanny and Katie, too, had exhibited their usual hardy constitutions, even if Nanny had begun to slow down in recent years. It was nature at work, not malice.

But I also typically enjoyed the vigor of a farmhand. Aunt Alice used to bemoan my insistence on keeping up with my male cousins, eschewing playing with dolls and jumping rope with Gertrude in favor of rough-and-tumble games with Neily and Alfred. My robust constitution had also enhanced my abilities as a reporter, allowing me to tirelessly follow stories around town.

Until recently. Until Amity and Zinnia had come to stay with us.

"You're lost in thought." Derrick's comment startled me back to the present. We had reached the sharp turn at the southernmost end of Bellevue Avenue, turned onto Cogge-shall, and then again onto Ocean Avenue. A bracing ocean breeze rolled off the expanse of Bailey's Beach, dotted with canopies and people sitting on blankets on the sand. A few late-day bathers bobbed in the waves. "What are you con-templating now?"

The question oozed with the suspicion that I might be scheming some ill-advised plan.

Before I could answer, he followed up with an equally ap-prehensive, "Are you feeling unwell again?"

Actually, I was, a little. I almost admitted as much to him, but I feared he would turn the carriage around and take me right back to the hospital. Yet I didn't want to lie either, not completely. Instead, I deflected with, "What you said back at the hospital, implying I might have been poisoned. It's got me thinking."

"You pooh-poohed it then."

"Yes, because we were speaking of Jennie and the possi-bility that she had smuggled some of the toxin into the jail. That still seems impossible. But what if I've ingested some-thing other than manchineel? Something like arsenic. It's available everywhere. Rat poison, insecticide. We have some at home, I'm certain. It can bring on sudden nausea and dizziness."

He slowed the carriage and, with one hand, grasped my chin and turned my face toward him. Without releasing me, he allowed his gaze to travel over my features. His jaw jut-ted, and his brow drew tight. He brought the carriage to a full halt and began turning my face this way and that, an-gling it toward the sun.

I attempted, in vain, to pull free. "What are you doing?"

"Nausea and dizziness aren't the only symptoms of ar-senic poisoning. I'm checking for patches of redness or darkened skin. Bloodshot eyes. Do you have any abdominal pain?"

"No, there's no pain. Just a bit of queasiness. But not now," I added quickly.

He released my chin and gathered up my hands, searching, I surmised, for any roughened patches of skin or those telltale white lines on my fingernails that also signify arsenic poisoning. After what seemed an eternity, I felt his hands relax. "I should take you back to Friendship Street."

"Don't be silly."

I realized my mistake as soon as the words had been snatched away on the salty breeze. A storm flashed in his eyes. "Silly to take precautions with your life? To make certain nothing happens to you?"

"No." I leaned into him, nestling my cheek against his coat front, tipping my hat askew. "Of course not. But I'm not fragile, and you needn't worry so."

His arms went around me. A sigh gusted from deep inside him. "Yes, you're right. I can't help myself sometimes." We straightened, and I looked deeply into his dark eyes. His worries hadn't fled, they had simply, at my insistence, quieted themselves. "Let's look at this logically," he said. "If someone has been slipping you some kind of poison, it would have to be one or both of our . . ."

"Houseguests," I finished. "Amity was so angry with me."

"Understandably."

"Yes and no. As I thought at the time, given what had been happening to women all over Newport, she might have been a bit more understanding of my motives. But I saw a side to her I hadn't expected." I paused to try to put my finger on it, and then concluded, "A cold, almost vindictive side. What if there was more to her reaction to my snooping than mere anger at the intrusion?"

"You mean that she's hiding something. Physically hiding something, I mean, and she fears you're getting close to discovering it. But she wouldn't dare use manchineel against you. That would exonerate Jennie and widen the investigation again."

"Perhaps Amity resents me for a reason unrelated to the poisonings. What if she overheard some of my conversations with Zinnia and is afraid she'll lose her niece because of my influence?"

"Could she have overheard you?"

"Not the time Zinnia and I took a walk off the property, but it could be as subtle as her noticing a change in Zinnia. A boldness that hadn't been there before. Perhaps Zinnia has been speaking up for herself." I thought back to our first meeting at Vinland. Zinnia had barely spoken two words. I'd been surprised a day later at how chatty she could be, and how intelligent.

And I recalled how despondent Zinnia had been when speaking of her loneliness. Yet she was adamant that I not intervene. Did she fear her aunt?

Should I fear her aunt?

After we had changed our clothes for more comfortable, at-home attire, I found Nanny upstairs in the sewing room, altering a dress for Katie. She saw me and stilled her foot on the treadle of her new Singer machine.

Despite the sudden silence as Nanny fixed her attention on me, I didn't immediately speak, but walked farther into the room and moved a stack of waiting garments from the only other chair besides the one Nanny occupied. She looked puzzled but waited patiently for me to begin.

"How often are our guests in the kitchen?"

This clearly wasn't what she had been expecting. "I don't suppose I've given it a thought. Not in this house."

I understood what she meant. Unlike my relatives or, indeed, any members of the Four Hundred, we ran an informal household—shockingly so, by the standards of others. With Katie, our maid-of-all-work, always welcome in the front rooms, guests were equally welcome in the kitchen or, for that matter, the kitchen garden and even the laundry yard.

I set my hand on my knees and leaned forward toward her. "Think about it now. Are they there while you and Katie fix meals?"

"Why, yes, I suppose they are. Is that a problem?"

"I'm not sure. Do they help with the cooking? Or the serving?"

"Now that you mention it, a little of both. Only the small things. Fetching things I need and occasionally sprinkling in an ingredient at my request while I'm busy doing something else. Why?"

"Nanny, I want you to keep a close eye on them."

She removed her half-moon spectacles and set them aside. "What is this about?"

"It's about two dead women and the others who have been hurt," I said in a flat voice that sounded nearly as desolate as I felt. There it was again—my stubborn reluctance to want to suspect anyone I had developed a regard for. Even with Amity's anger, hearing myself say out loud that I suspected her of murder—or Zinnia, for that matter—threatened to call back my earlier malaise.

After wiping her glasses with the hem of her apron, Nanny rose and shut the door to the hallway. She moved her chair closer to mine, set her spectacles back on her nose, and spoke quietly. "What's happened?"

How transparent I must be that anyone who cared for me—in this case, first Derrick and now Nanny—could read me so easily. "I felt ill this afternoon. Suddenly dizzy and nauseated."

"It's not the first time."

I looked away as she studied my features, then the rest of me. "It's the first time I felt this ill."

"You've been tired and pale lately. And you think . . ." She reached out suddenly, grasping my forearms. "The toxin?"

"No, Nanny." I shook my head firmly. "Not the manchineel. This isn't anything so blatant as that."

"But something else, and you think one or both of them might have slipped something into your food."

"Or tea. Or something." I shook my head again. "I don't know. It's just . . . quite a coincidence. Too much so to ignore."

"Neither of them will step foot in my kitchen again."

"No, Nanny, let them. Only watch every move they make." The next thought had my heart pounding in my throat. "How have you been feeling? And Katie?"

"I can assure you we've both been fit as fiddles."

"Are you sure? You promise?"

She put up her hand as if swearing an oath. "The honest truth."

I relaxed.

"Why would they do this to you? Never mind. I know why. It's because you're always searching for answers. You put yourself in danger, Emma."

"I don't know that they've done anything. I could be off on a wrong trail. I hope so, I truly do. We just need to be careful."

Her faded blue eyes took on a new spark behind the lenses of her spectacles. "You needn't tell me twice. They won't so much as sneeze without my knowing about it from here on in."

"Good. Derrick has pledged not to take his eyes off them either."

Chapter 19

As Nanny and Katie served dinner, Nanny assured me in a whisper that she had shooed our guests out of the kitchen with assurances that everything was going smoothly. "Don't worry, they don't suspect a thing."

"Don't let on that I've been ill," I whispered back.

She put a finger to her lips to indicate they were sealed. Once we were seated around the table, I asked Zinnia and Amity about their day.

"We walked up to Bailey's Beach." Zinnia sliced into the layers of shepherd's pie Nanny had made. "And stopped along Hazard's Beach along the way as well. Lovely, both of them. We were asked if we belonged and used your name. I hope that was all right?"

"Of course it was," Derrick replied. "And if the two of you would like to play a round of golf, you can use our names at the Country Club as well."

I smiled indulgently. It had been for Derrick that I had agreed to join some of the more exclusive recreational establishments in Newport. Before our marriage, the boardwalk and crowded sands of Easton's Beach had been just fine for me. And I wasn't much for golf. But these places allowed Derrick to socialize with business associates and investors and stay current on industry and financial trends.

"I'm afraid you don't want me swinging clubs around other people," Zinnia said with a laugh. "Except with a paintbrush, I'm not terribly coordinated."

"Nonsense, Zinnia," her aunt burst out. "You're far more competent than you give yourself credit for. Why, you hike and swim and play croquet and badminton . . ."

"Badly, Aunt." Zinnia grinned broadly. "I play croquet and badminton deplorably."

"Ah, well. The point is, we have been keeping happily busy." Amity addressed this, along with a smile nearly as bright as Zinnia's, to everyone around the table, myself included. Had she forgiven me for my transgression? And had I let my imagination take flight with my suspicions? Perhaps, as Dr. Kennison had suggested, I'd experienced a rare bout of dyspepsia along with a bit of fatigue, and there had been no foul play at Gull Manor.

Following dinner, I sent Nanny and Katie outside with the others to watch the last wisps of daylight dissolve into the ocean, while I stayed inside to finish tidying up. I had just put the stack of dinner dishes in the china cabinet and turned back to the dining room table to begin transferring the clean wine goblets onto their shelf, when I stopped with a gasp. Amity was standing only a few feet away, watching me. How long she had been there, I couldn't say.

I set a hand on my heart. "You startled me!"

"I'm sorry, I didn't mean to." She stood calmly, with her hands clasped at her waist.

If she hadn't meant to, why had she entered the room without a sound? I swiped a stray wisp of hair back from my face. "Is there something you need?"

"No, except to apologize for the other day."

"Oh . . . no. It was my fault . . ."

"I overreacted." She said something more, but I had spoken over her in my haste to defuse matters between us. We both laughed. I remained silent as I waited for her to continue. She swallowed and said, "It's just that I'm so terribly protective of Zinnia. Perhaps too much so, but she means the world to me."

"I understand." But to myself I acknowledged that she had been angry for herself as well.

"I hope, then, that you no longer suspect us of anything nefarious?" A small chuckle accompanied the question, abruptly cut off when I hesitated a fraction too long in replying. She quirked an eyebrow in query.

"I needed to be certain," I said.

"And now you are?"

I smiled. I also crossed my fingers at my side. "I am."

"I'm glad." She turned toward the table and picked up a wine goblet in each hand. Stepping around me, she placed them on their shelf in the cabinet. "At any rate, we won't be in your hair much longer. The paperwork on the sale should be finalized by tomorrow or the day after."

This surprised me. "Have you heard something from the land agent? Has your brother-in-law finally decided to cooperate with the process?"

"Ezra? Yes, I suppose he's finally realized that being the executor doesn't give him the right to deny me my due. We received a letter today from our attorney. I'm surprised you haven't heard from yours as well."

"I'm sure we will, then. He's based in Providence, and I suspect his letter has been delayed." I pondered what seemed like the sudden end to Amity and Zinnia's stay. Would they leave Rhode Island immediately? Or would they linger a while longer? Either way, it sounded as though they intended to quit Gull Manor.

Would a murderer slip through our fingers?

No, Amity, I'm still not certain of anything.

From the rear of the house, the kitchen door slammed. Derrick called to me as his footsteps thudded along the corridor. I called in reply, and before he reached us, Patch trotted into the dining room. He circled each of us and sniffed at our hands, hoping for a petting. I bent down and obliged him. I was just straightening when Derrick turned into the room.

He looked us up and down. "Everything all right in here?"

"Indeed, yes," Amity said. "We were just discussing the finalizing of the property sale. Another couple of days and it will be yours. Then Zinnia and I can return to Florida with our future that much more assured."

I noticed she said *future*, and not *futures*, as if they were one and the same, with Zinnia continuing to be at Amity's beck and call indefinitely. My heart once more went out to the young woman, but I said nothing. I merely smiled, put away the remaining dinnerware, and joined Derrick and the others outside until it was time to retire.

The following day passed with no word from our attorney. Amity jokingly asked if we were having doubts about whether we still wanted the property or not.

"Perhaps you've asked your attorney to stall, while you search your hearts?"

"Not at all, Amity," I replied. She and Zinnia and I sat together in the parlor, having tea. Nanny had prepared the tray, once again shooing our guests out of the kitchen when they attempted to be helpful. I had experienced no further unpleasantness, but we were taking no chances.

"Nothing has changed," I told the ladies. "The property is

perfect for our plans, and Derrick and I still wish to go ahead with the purchase."

"Good. Perhaps, then, we should make a trip to the bank and prearrange the transfer of funds? After all, Zinnia and I won't wish to travel with a check made out for such a large amount. I would much prefer to wire the money directly into our bank account in Florida."

I saw no problem with that and told her so. In the morning, then, Amity accompanied Derrick and me into town. He went directly to the *Messenger*, while Amity and I continued on to Washington Square, to the brick and columned building that housed the Savings Bank of Newport.

The Corinthian columns lining the front of the building continued inside, a double row spanning the large room from back to front, supporting a vaulted ceiling marked by plaster medallions and two grand chandeliers. Thick brass trim lined the teller windows, with two impenetrable vaults standing tall behind them.

From one of several desks beneath tall, arched windows, a man saw us and rose. He tugged his suit coat into place as he approached us with a smile. "Mrs. Andrews, how lovely to see you today."

"Hello, Mr. Lawton." We shook hands. Thomas Lawton, a man of middle age with distinguished graying hair, a clean-shaven face, and a gentlemanly air, held the position of vice president of the bank and personally attended only their most valued customers. It still surprised me that I was now one of them. "This is Miss Amity Carter, of Florida."

They greeted each other, and Mr. Lawton led us to his desk. Once Amity and I had settled in comfortable chairs across from him, he leaned over his desk and tented his hands. "Tell me, ladies, what may we do for you today?"

We explained about the property, whereupon he asked a secretary, a young man barely out of his teens who seemed overeager to please, to retrieve the proper documents. He jumped up from his desk and rummaged through a filing cabinet. Within minutes, he returned with a packet of papers.

"Here we are." Mr. Lawton set a pair of spectacles on his nose and perused the pages in his hands. "Yes, yes, this is what we need. Now, I'll need Miss Carter to fill out her portion. Mrs. Andrews, we can fill in your information for you, it's all on file. Except for the sale amount, of course. We'll let you and your husband fill in those figures. Will Mr. Andrews be available to come in and do that?"

"Of course," I said. "The account is joint, and I understand you'll need both our signatures."

He cleared his throat. "In any case, I'll need your husband's."

"And mine," I pressed. I angled a glance at Amity; she appeared as taken aback as I.

"Mr. Andrews's signature will be sufficient." Mr. Lawton smiled in a way that made me feel all of six years old.

I gritted my teeth and let my gaze bore into him for a full ten seconds. Oh, I realized this was standard procedure at any bank—the husband took precedence even when the accounts were held jointly—but that didn't mean it didn't chafe. Badly. Amity was a middle-aged single woman, and as such could handle her own affairs. Had she been my age, they would have insisted a male member of her family vouch for her.

With the paperwork in order and my having indicated that Derrick would be by to oversee whatever they needed him to oversee—and yes, I allowed a certain amount of sarcasm to enter my voice—we took our leave. Rather than my driving Amity all the way back to Ocean Avenue, she had planned to do some shopping along Bellevue Avenue, where Zinnia would join her by lunchtime, arriving in one of Aunt

Alice's coaches, which she graciously continued to lend my guests.

That evening, the conversation turned to my experience with Mr. Lawton. Amity tsked as she ran a finger along the rim of her sherry glass. She sat on the parlor sofa at my side. Zinnia sat to my right. "It was galling, pure and simple. I'm so sorry you were subjected to that, Emma."

"I agree." Derrick raised the sherry bottle in an unspoken question as to whether anyone wanted a refill. Our two guests and I shook our heads no. Nanny and Katie were still preparing dinner. "However, I suppose we'll have to play along if we want this sale to go through."

"Which we do," Amity agreed, and Zinnia nodded.

"It's nothing new, and I shouldn't have expected anything less." With a sigh, I stared down into velvety brown liquid in the small stem glass I held. Its flavor, ordinarily rich and nutty on my pallet, tonight tasted overly sweet, cloying. I'd been fine all day, though, with nary a twinge of illness. "But having never been in such a position before, it still took me by surprise. I've never engaged in such a large transaction, and any banking I did previously was in my own name."

Derrick, facing us in one of the armchairs, smiled apologetically. "Times are changing, and rules like that will change as well."

"Perhaps, but it's a slow road," I observed.

"Very slow." Amity chuckled wryly. "Men don't like to share their power. I believe you are a rarity, Mr. Andrews, to be so evolved in your thinking."

"Please, it's Derrick," he said with a wave of his hand, "and I'd like to think younger men these days are more enlightened."

"We'll see." Amity sounded unconvinced.

I stole a glance at Zinnia. She had a faraway look in her eyes, as though she barely registered the conversation and had little interest in taking part in it. What thoughts held her attention? Was she longing to be back at her easel? Or to be wandering the coastline in search of inspiration to take back with her to Florida?

"Well, enough of that," I said with a light clap of my hands. "What are your plans for tomorrow?"

"We haven't anything in particular planned," Amity replied. Zinnia looked around me at her aunt, started to say something, but compressed her lips. I frowned, wondering what the silent encounter meant. Did they have plans they didn't want me to know about?

Then again, if they did, would it necessarily mean anything out of the ordinary? Perhaps they merely wanted one of their remaining days in Newport to themselves.

"I'm taking you back to the hospital." Derrick stood beside our bed, his arms crossed and his feet planted firmly on the floor like a sentinel. I groaned, then attempted to cover the sound with a cough. He wasn't fooled. "I'll bring the carriage around, and then I'm going to carry you downstairs."

"You'll do no such thing." Leveraging myself upright into a sitting position, I made an effort to appear normal. After scrubbing a hand across my eyes, I surveyed his workaday attire, a subtly pinstriped sack suit with padded shoulders and loose-fitting trousers. A hunter-green silk necktie secured the high, stiff collar of his shirt. "Why are you ready so early?"

"It's nearly seven-thirty."

"What?" I swung my legs over the side of the bed. "Why did you let me sleep so late?"

"I nudged you as usual. You were sleeping too deeply to stir. Which only proves my point."

"It's just a slight headache." I pressed my palms to my temples, which were throbbing lightly. "Nothing alarming."

"It is alarming. Emma, you're never unwell. What if—"

"I'm not being poisoned," I whispered, not wanting to be heard outside our door. I tossed my sleep-tousled braid over my shoulder. "We know that for certain now. Nanny hasn't let them near the kitchen in the past two days, and they haven't been left alone anytime there has been food or drink being served. As Dr. Kennison said, it's merely a bout of dyspepsia."

"We've taken precautions, yes, but that doesn't mean one of them couldn't—"

"Get past Nanny? Hardly. Besides, I was completely fine all day yesterday and all night. I just need to take my time this morning. You go on ahead, and I'll join you at the *Messenger* later."

"No, I'll wait for you here."

"Don't you have meetings this morning with potential advertisers? The Glenwood Furnace Company, A. C. Titus Furniture and Carpets, Cozzens Carpets and Wallpapers . . . Those would be valuable accounts for us. And I know there are others."

He held up a hand to stop me. "Yes, all right. I have meetings. They can wait."

"No, they can't." I shoved my feet into my house shoes. "I'm fine. I'm just a little slow getting started this morning." I wasn't lying, I realized. Already my headache had begun to subside. I stretched my arms over my head and yawned. "Don't wait for me. Go on ahead, and I'll follow in a bit. I'll borrow another of Aunt Alice's carriages."

"Or don't."

"Don't borrow a carriage?"

"Don't come in. Work from home today. Or don't work at all. You deserve a day off." When I started to argue, he sat down beside me and snatched my hands. "Emma, for once, don't argue. The *Messenger* will not fall apart if you're not there for a day. Ethan can fill in for you, and for that matter, so can I." He leaned closer, his shoulder lodging warmly against mine, tempting me to lean my cheek against the lightweight serge. "You see, it takes two of us mere mortals to accomplish what you do on your own."

"I'll take the morning off and come later."

With a groan of impatience, he released me, his fingers curling as if they itched to wrap themselves around my neck. "I give up."

"Good."

He deposited a kiss on my cheek and pressed to his feet. "I'll see you later."

As he left, Patch came streaming in through the open door, his nails clicking on the hardwood floor until he reached the rug that stretched beneath the bed. He stood on his hind legs and placed his paws on my lap.

"See if you have any better luck with her, boy."

I hadn't noticed Derrick still standing there, just over the threshold. He showed me one of his lopsided grins and then was gone. My fingers combed through Patch's fur, alternating in large patches of brown and white—hence his name. "You understand, don't you, boy?" I crooned down at him. He regarded me with liquid brown eyes that seemed to comprehend. At the very least, he seemed willing to listen. "Have you eaten yet?"

He let out a *ruff*. "Well, I haven't. Shall we go down?"

"You'll stay right where you are, Miss Emma." Katie came through the doorway, holding a tray with a teapot and a covered platter. "Mrs. O'Neal sent me up with your breakfast."

"My husband's influence?"

"When you weren't up with him earlier, we all guessed you might not be feeling well again."

"Honestly, this family worries far too much. Can't a person have a late morning once in a while?"

At my use of the word *family*, Katie's rosy lips curved in a smile. I knew it meant a lot to her to be included as one of the people I held dear. She set the tray on the desk in front of the rear-facing window. "Of course, you can, and you are." She indicated the desk. "Is this all right?"

"It's fine, Katie, but I would have been equally fine coming downstairs." I rose and crossed the room, then lifted the cover from the platter. The sight of fluffy, golden scrambled eggs, two sausages, and two thick slices of Nanny's bread, toasted, made my stomach rumble. A good sign. I pulled out the desk chair and sat. "I promise I'll be good and eat every bite. What are our guests doing?"

"They were down for breakfast, then returned to their room for a while, and now they're back downstairs in the parlor writing letters."

"Good. I'll come down and check on them soon."

She pointed to a bowl on the tray that held a cloth. "That's soaked in feverfew tincture and water for your headache."

That stopped me short. "How did you know . . . ?" I sighed. Nanny knew everything. She had a sixth sense when it came to me. "Oh, never mind."

"Would you like help getting dressed?"

"I'll manage, thank you, Katie." My usual summer attire of skirt and shirtwaist, with light petticoats beneath and a corset that hooked easily from the front, granted me autonomy in getting ready in the mornings. Likewise, a simple chignon allowed me to fix my own hair, although Nanny always gave me a once-over and made any necessary adjustments.

When I finally descended the stairs, it was to find the house unusually quiet. Nanny and Katie's voices drifted from somewhere outside. I followed the sound through the kitchen and out into the rear garden. I found them in the laundry yard, hanging linens to dry.

"Finished the wash early today," I commented as I walked

around the concealing greenery until I came to the opening cut into the hedge. Sheets, pillowcases, and towels undulated in a gentle breeze.

"It's not all that early," Nanny called back.

"Yes, yes, I've been errant, lying abed half the morning," I joked.

Nanny slipped a final clothespin onto a corner of a sheet and came toward me. "How are you feeling?" When she reached me, she pressed her palm to my forehead. Despite a temptation to pull away, I endured her ministrations as she also pinched my cheeks, then held my chin and turned my face from side to side.

"As you can see, I'm quite well, thank you. Where are our guests?"

"They left only minutes ago." Katie had pulled a damp sofa antimacassar out of a basket and draped it over the line.

"Left? For where?"

"Vinland," Katie answered. "Mrs. Twombly sent a carriage for them. They're to have brunch and spend the day there. Miss Carter said Mrs. Twombly arranged it as a treat especially for them."

"Oh . . ." I hadn't been invited, it seemed. As if sensing my thoughts, Nanny tsked.

"Rather rude of her not to invite you, Emma. They're your guests, after all."

"Perhaps Mrs. Twombly wished to visit with Amity quietly. They knew each other at Miss Porter's. Now that Amity is an author, Mrs. Twombly must be especially interested in renewing the acquaintance."

"That's exactly what Miss Carter said." Nanny pressed her hands to her back and stretched. "She said Mrs. Twombly meant to have them over sooner, but with all that happened and Mrs. Robinson's daughter being there, well . . . But now that the daughter has returned home, Mrs. Twombly felt free to extend the invitation."

"That makes sense," I said.

Nanny scowled. "Still seems impolite."

I smiled. Nanny was my greatest champion, besides Derrick, of course.

Although I had planned to arrange for a carriage to take me into town as soon as I'd breakfasted, I found myself lingering at home. The headache had left me, and I had no other complaint, yet I found myself enjoying Katie and Nanny's company too much to want to leave. I settled in for a while longer, sifting flour for tonight's loaf of bread, scrubbing some potatoes, trimming the rosemary for the stew Nanny planned to make.

While we worked, they related all the Newport news gleaned from trips to the market, the occasional evening spent with other servants at Forty Steps, and talking to the deliverymen. They always knew who was ill, who had just had a baby, who had spent the night in a holding cell due to drunkenness. I sometimes thought they were better reporters than I was. I enjoyed listening to their banter amid the warm, savory scents of the kitchen; it brought me a sense of peace and wrapped me in companionship.

The jarring sound of our telephone, summoning me to the alcove beneath the stairs, startled us all. I hopped up from my seat at the table and hurried down the corridor.

I yanked the ebony earpiece from its cradle on the side of the mounted wooden box and spoke loudly into the mouthpiece, because the lines typically buzzed and crackled. "Gull Manor. Mrs. Andrews speaking."

"Emma, it's me," my husband's voice said in a rush.

"I told you, I'm fine—"

"I'm glad to hear it, but that's not why I'm calling. A telegram arrived only minutes ago, from Providence."

My hand went immediately to press my heart. Derrick's parents lived in Providence. "Goodness, no one is ill, are they?" Or worse, I thought.

"No, it's nothing like that. It's from Robert Harwood."

"Our attorney?"

"Yes. There's a problem with the property sale."

At that moment, I wished for a chair. Somehow, I'd known our purchase of Amity's property was too good to be true, but until now I'd remained hopeful. "What's wrong? Has she backed out?"

"No. He indicated a letter would follow with more details. All I know at this point is that Amity Carter doesn't own that property. Not outright, at any rate, and she has no right to sell it."

Chapter 20

I felt my stomach drop to my feet. It took me several moments before I could breathe, much less speak. Finally, I managed to stutter, "Wh-what do you mean?"

"Seems she has a male cousin who was also mentioned in the will."

I held my forehead in my free hand. "And this cousin doesn't wish to sell?"

"We don't yet know. The only certainty at this point is that Amity doesn't own the property free and clear and can't authorize a sale on her own."

"Why would she lie?"

He hesitated. "She might not have intended to. It's possible she didn't understand the terms of the will."

"An intelligent woman like Amity, who puts so much stock into being self-reliant? If nothing else, she would have had one of Mr. Flagler's lawyers look over the documents for her." I remembered something else. "She said she received a letter from the land agent saying the paperwork should be finalized by today. He couldn't possibly have told her that, not with things as they are."

"That does seem odd. But again, perhaps she didn't understand."

I shook my head, even though he couldn't see me. Suddenly, I remembered that our conversation might not be completely private, that sometimes, whether intentionally or not, the telephone operator could be listening in. I was tempted to call Gayla Preston's name into the line. She was Newport's main daytime operator and had been for several years now. She was also a renowned gossip, however much her intentions never seemed to be malicious. If she were listening, she had already heard an earful, but that didn't mean we needed to add more fuel to her fire.

"Let's talk more about this later," I said.

"Yes, but for now, I wouldn't mention anything to Amity. Let's wait for the letter."

"Good idea. Perhaps it will clear matters up. Perhaps the misunderstanding is at Mr. Harwood's end." There, that should temper any impressions Gayla might have concerning our business with Amity.

"Perhaps."

We ended the call. Deep in thought, I made my way slowly back to the kitchen. Halfway down the corridor, I turned around and went to the hall table where we kept the post tray. Nothing sat on it. I had been hoping the invitation from Mrs. Twombly might be there. After a moment's thought, I hurried up the stairs to their room. I checked the tops of all the cupboards and tables. No invitation revealed itself to me. Perhaps Amity had taken it with them.

I retraced my steps and returned to the kitchen. As soon as Nanny looked up, she could see something was wrong. "You're feeling ill again, aren't you?"

"Yes, but no, not really." I sank into a kitchen chair. "You mustn't say anything, but that was Derrick. He was notified by our attorney that Amity doesn't fully own the land next door."

"What?" Nanny and Katie exclaimed at once, and then Nanny said, "Then why on earth did she agree to sell it?"

"Sounds like a flimflam to me," Katie said, whisking loose coppery hairs away from her face.

"I don't know..." A small wooden bowl of fragrant, fresh-picked parsley sat in front of me. I gently fingered the tiny leaves. Why would Amity intentionally lie about being sole owner of the property? She would have to know she'd eventually be caught out. Had this been an attempt to speed matters along, so that Derrick and I would hand over the money and be none the wiser?

I gave a sudden gasp. "The bank." That caught Nanny's and Katie's attention. When they both stopped what they were doing and waited expectantly, I added, "It had been Amity's idea to go to the bank. She wanted to prearrange the transfer of funds so that she wouldn't have to travel with a check for such a large amount of money."

Nanny sat in the seat beside me. "On the face of it, a transfer makes sense. But it's also much harder to cancel, once it's done."

"Whereas a check can be canceled until it's been cashed." I came to my feet in such a flurry that Nanny flinched back in her chair. "I'm going to Vinland."

"Why?" Nanny pressed to her feet as well. "What can you accomplish there during brunch, to which, I might add, Mrs. Twombly didn't invite you?"

"Did you see the invitation? Either of you?"

"No." Nanny shrugged. "I took their word for it."

"I did, too," Katie said. "Didn't see any reason not to believe them."

"Perhaps they didn't want me there. Perhaps Amity didn't,"

I clarified. "And if she's trying to flimflam Derrick and me, to use Katie's word, what's to say she isn't trying to do the same to my relative? They have a history, Mrs. Twombly and Amity, and Amity might try to play on Mrs. Twombly's sympathies."

I headed for the doorway, but Nanny stopped me. "And if you're wrong about this?"

"Then I'll be an uninvited guest. Florence Twombly already thinks little of me, so I fail to see how this could hurt matters."

"Shall I go with you, Miss Emma?"

"No, Katie, I'll be all right. What can happen in a house full of servants in the middle of the day?" Those words tugged at my memory and prickled my nape. I ignored the sensation. "But please call over to The Breakers' carriage house and see if they have a vehicle available." Nanny reluctantly stepped out of my way. Upstairs, I gathered my hat, gloves, and handbag.

I wondered how many carriages Aunt Alice actually had at her disposal these days. They had indeed once been numerous, but with Uncle Cornelius gone and Neily, Gertrude, and Alfred all married, she might well have sold several of them off. Nonetheless, a small, enclosed brougham, polished to a high sheen, complete with a driver in tails and top hat, waited for me on the driveway. Was it Aunt Alice's personal vehicle? The gilded crest with the initials AVG, the V larger than the two letters flanking it, suggested it was. I didn't doubt that if she believed I needed it, she would go without for a day.

When we arrived at Vinland, I released the driver. I could return home with Amity and Zinnia, or I could telephone Derrick in town. I went to the front door and knocked. The footman who admitted me appeared puzzled, even when I reminded him who I was.

"Mrs. Twombly and her guests aren't here at the moment, ma'am."

I'd pushed my way past him and was about to cross the hall into the drawing room. That stopped me in my tracks. "Where are they?"

"Outside."

I peered through the drawing room and through the French doors leading outside. I glimpsed no one on the terrace, lawn, or gardens. "Outside where?"

"I'm sure I don't know, ma'am. They've already finished brunch and decided to take some air. Perhaps if you leave your card . . ."

This last he called to my retreating back as I hurried through the drawing room and let myself out onto the terrace. Another sweep of the lawns, this time with nothing blocking my way, revealed no trace of Mrs. Twombly, Amity, or Zinnia. The Cliff Walk, perhaps?

I started to turn back into the house, only to discover the same footman had followed me onto the terrace. "Does Mrs. Twombly walk along the Cliff Walk?" I asked him. Most ladies of the Four Hundred didn't, preferring to view the ocean from their upper verandas, where they ran no risk of either tumbling over the side or encountering undesirables out for a stroll.

"Occasionally." He shaded his eyes with a gloved hand and stared past me. "However, I don't see her there at the moment. She rarely ever walks beyond the boundaries of the property."

"Did they go out in the carriage?" I practically snapped the question at him.

He backed up a step. "I—I don't know, ma'am. I'll go ask."

"Please," I said, lightening my tone. "But do hurry."

"Is there an emergency?" As the footman retraced his steps, the housekeeper took his place in the doorway.

"I . . . don't know." She eyed me askance, and I realized how I must have sounded. What was I worrying about—whether Amity planned to con my relative out of a sum of money . . . or whether she was responsible for Lottie Robinson, Sybil Van Horn, and the others?

"Did Mrs. Twombly tell you where she and her guests were going when they went out?"

"Mrs. Twombly isn't obligated to inform me of her every move." Her expression became stern. "Perhaps if you hadn't been unforgivably late to brunch, you yourself would know where they've gone."

"I was invited?"

"Well, of course you were invited. I should know. I planned the menu for four, didn't I?"

I turned back around to face the cliffs, several acres away from where we stood. "Where would they have gone," I mused aloud.

"Ma'am?" The footman had returned. "Mrs. Twombly has not gone out in her carriage."

My heart began to race, and the return of that morning's headache pulsed in my temples. I spun around and said to the housekeeper, "Call the police. Ask for Detective Whyte and tell him Mrs. Twombly is missing. If he isn't there, ask for Officer Binsford."

"I'll do no such thing." The woman drew herself up. "We have no reason to believe any harm has befallen Mrs. Twombly or her guests."

I gripped her forearm, sending her eyebrows surging above the saucers her eyes had become. "Do you know what has been happening in Newport? Mrs. Twombly's own guest, Mrs. Robinson, died because someone has been poisoning women. Another woman was bludgeoned to death in her own bedroom. Now, go and telephone the police and tell them they need to send someone out here immediately."

"Yes, yes, all right." She turned and scurried into the house.

My gaze shifted to the footman. "Find some of your fellow servants and spread out over the property. We must find Mrs. Twombly and her guests."

"Yes, ma'am." He didn't dither for an instant before disappearing inside.

I didn't wait for his return with whatever force he might gather in the house. With my questions pulsing through my mind—is Amity Carter a con woman, or a murderer?—I gathered up my skirts and took off at a run toward the Cliff Walk. At this moment, that precarious footpath posed the greatest danger, if indeed that was where Mrs. Twombly had gone with her guests.

As I neared the cliffs, the ocean wind played havoc with my hat, trying to tear it from the pin that held it in place. The result was that I stumbled along, barely able to keep my balance. To prevent myself from teetering—possibly right over the precarious edge—I plucked the pin out and let the breezes do as they would. My hat took flight among the gulls and cormorants flying in dizzying circles overhead.

Without a hat brim, the sunlight pinched my eyes. I blinked as I reached the path and came to a halt. Directly before me, the cliff dropped off in a sheer, nearly vertical incline bordered by a low hedge, rather than the gradual, rocky slopes found elsewhere. I inched as far forward as I dared and peeked over, half dreading what I might find. Far below me, the waves slapped against the cliff face, giving up a spray that caught the sun in rainbows of light.

With one hand shading my eyes, I looked first north, in the direction of Ochre Court, and then south, toward The Breakers. From here, I could just make out their rooflines if I angled my sights inland. But I detected no one walking, no movement at all along the Cliff Walk, other than the occasional bird coming to rest. There weren't even the usual tourists.

That brought me a measure of comfort. I turned around again to view the house and lawn. Seeing no sign yet of a search party, I chose a direction at random. Which way would Florence Twombly have gone, if indeed she had come this way? I ruled out Ochre Court. Depending on how far they walked, that route would lead to Forty Steps. Mrs. Twombly detested the steep wooden staircase that led down from the Cliff Walk to the sea-swept boulders at the bottom. It was where the servants often gathered in the evenings, after work, for an hour or so of merriment before curfew. Florence Twombly considered such places trouble in the making.

I headed toward The Breakers. I'd only gone a few yards when something up ahead moved, disengaging itself from the tree and plant-strewn hill upon which it had perched. I might have noticed it sooner had it not been completely still for some minutes. Now, the figure of a woman stood and straightened, skirts billowing as she propped a hand at her waist and stretched her back. I recognized the shape of a simple, straw sun hat.

"Zinnia!" I cried out and hurried along as fast as I safely could.

"Emma!" She showed me a surprised smile as she descended the hill at a gravity-induced trot. She had tied her hat beneath her chin with a bright yellow scarf that encompassed the crown and held the brim against the sides of her head. In her left hand she held her sketchbook, in her right a charcoal pencil. "What are you doing here? Does Mrs. Twombly know you've arrived?"

"Not yet. Where are they? Where are Mrs. Twombly and your aunt?"

"I'm not quite sure." She looked this way and that, even out over the ocean. I looked too, half expecting them to come sailing by. They did not. The only vessels on the water were farther out—several yachts and, beyond them, freighters and fishing trawlers negotiating the currents as they entered the mouth of Narragansett Bay.

I turned back to Zinnia. "Think, please. Where would they have gone?"

Her expression turned serious. "Why? Has something happened? Has there been another . . . ?"

I knew she was asking if there had been another murder. "No. But there could be danger. Did they come out here with you?"

"Let me think." She let out a breath. "I become so involved when I'm painting or sketching. I'm afraid I barely paid attention to where they went." Once again, she glanced right and left. "I believe they were walking toward your other relatives' house."

"The Breakers?"

"Yes, that's the one."

"How long ago?"

"Hmm . . . I've quite lost track of time. But I'm sure that's where they went. Come." After setting her sketchbook and pencil on the grass beside the path, she linked her arm with mine. "I'll go with you. We'll find them."

We skirted the remainder of Vinland's sweeping lawn, reaching a copse of copper beech trees that formed the property line along Sheppard Avenue and blocked our view of both houses. I could, however, see along the Cliff Walk and detected no sign of either Mrs. Twombly or Amity. "Perhaps they've gone up to the house? Or to see the gardens?"

"Perhaps, although I don't believe that was their intention. There were plants along the cliffs Mrs. Twombly wished to show Aunt Amity."

"The rugosa roses?" How odd if that had been Mrs. Twombly's aim. I couldn't envision her taking particular notice of what amounted to weeds along the cliffs.

"Hmm . . . Yes, I believe that's what she said."

Something in Zinnia's answer—in all her answers—tugged at a wary sensation inside me. Suddenly, it hit me so starkly I came to a halt. With our arms linked, I brought Zinnia to an abrupt standstill as well.

She looked surprised, then guarded. "Is something wrong?"

I studied her plain features, shaded here and sun-dappled there by the loosely woven brim of her hat. Before I could think better of it, I blurted out, "You don't forget. Amity said you have a perfect memory. Yet you keep saying, 'I believe' and 'I think.' You know where they are. You have to."

"Oh, Emma, don't be a goose. I have a good memory, yes, but no one has a perfect memory. As I told you, I was so focused on my sketching that I didn't pay attention to where they were going."

I narrowed my eyes at her, only half listening. Not Jennie Pierpont—she hadn't committed murder. Not Anna Rose Van Horn. Not Mina Wallingford. Not even Amity.

Zinnia.

It hadn't made sense that someone not from Newport had committed the attacks. How could Zinnia know who these women were and where they lived? And what could she possibly have against them?

But, again, Zinnia remembered everything. She could have drifted among the tables before and after Mrs. Twombly's luncheon, reading name placards, then enlisting Harry Walsh to deliver her handiwork. But what happened at the luncheon that could have caused Zinnia to take such drastic action? She hadn't been a speaker. Why would the ladies' rudeness have mattered to her?

And why Grace, who hadn't been at the luncheon? How

did she know Grace resided at Beaulieu? Or had she? Perhaps she had merely addressed as many letters to the women of Bellevue Avenue as she could. Their places of residence were certainly no secret.

But again—why? What motive . . . ?

"Flagler's wardens," I murmured, the words tumbling unbidden from my memory, and then from my lips.

Zinnia slid her arm free of mine and grabbed hold of my wrist. "Why do you say that?" When I hesitated to answer, she gave my arm a twist that brought tears to my eyes. "What do you mean by that?"

I became aware of how close we stood to the edge of the cliff, so close that if I attempted to yank free of her hold, we both might go over. We were hidden from view of anyone in either The Breakers or Vinland, and Sheppard Avenue ended a good dozen yards in from the Cliff Walk, shielded from view by a thick holly hedge. As for boats on the water, they were far out of reach, even if they did notice two women struggling . . .

"He wasn't your father," I said, remembering the details of the drawing I had seen in her sketchbook. "Nor an uncle . . ."

"Who wasn't?" She tugged again and shoved her face close to mine. A tide of anger swept her features, raising a hot, angry flush. "You went through my sketchbook again."

"Was he one of Flagler's wardens, the man you drew? Who was he? Were you . . ." *In love with him?* I didn't need her to answer. He may have been a good deal older than Zinnia, but she wouldn't be the first young woman to fall in love with a man many years her senior. I saw the truth in every line of her face, in every spark of hatred flashing in her eyes. "He was murdered," I went on, remembering what I had learned about the Florida wildlife wardens that morning at Hanging Rock.

"By poachers . . . greedy men reaping fortunes killing off Florida's birds for these women . . ." She spat the last word. "These useless, vain, haughty wives and daughters of the Four Hundred. I hate them. I hate them all. I wanted them to suffer for what they've done. I only regret that most of them haven't suffered enough."

"Lottie Robinson did, permanently," I reminded her. Meanwhile, I strained my ears, praying for someone to come along. I saw and heard no one. Again, I considered shoving Zinnia away and attempting to run, but we were too near the edge. And I wanted the truth. I wanted to hear it from her. "Sybil, too. Zinnia, why Sybil?"

"Because she guessed. That day at Hanging Rock, I confided too much about George—" She broke off and half turned away, blinking. I tried to seize the moment of distraction, but she was too quick to return her attention to me. Her fingers dug into my wrist, the nails piercing my flesh. "I told her too much about George and Florida. She knew of only one substance that could produce the effects the women had exhibited. She had learned about manchineel when she and her mother were in Florida. And now you know, too. Did you think I didn't realize you'd gone through our things? I even saw you, peeking through the curtains in our room. I knew then I had better tread carefully around you. Still, I didn't think you'd put it together."

I hadn't; I had believed it to be Amity. But I didn't tell Zinnia that. I remembered the feather clutched in Sybil's lifeless hand. It had been a clue, one that pointed to Zinnia, enraged that her wildlife warden had been murdered for the price of exotic feathers.

"It's over now," I said. "The police know about the manchineel. It must have been Sybil, and not Anna Rose, who sketched the manchineel tree and hid it away. She must have suspected it had to do with the attacks. Did her mother suspect, too? Where is she, Zinnia? Did you do something to Mrs. Van Horn?"

"I don't know what you're talking about," she snapped back. Then she seized both my arms and pushed me toward the edge. I tried to dig my feet into the rocky soil of the Cliff Walk, tried to grab onto the long weeds growing beside it. But she had taken me by surprise, upended my balance, and suddenly, I felt myself sliding, staggering, tumbling over the brink . . .

Chapter 21

In a shower of dirt, I slid several feet straight down, clutching at the air until my left hand found purchase around a cluster of thick stems arching outward from between the rocks. The cliff face here, though sharp and rocky, was more of a slope than a sheer drop, and as I halted my momentum, I wedged the toe of my right boot into a crevice. With my left arm shaking from the strain of holding on, I reached out with my right and wrapped my fingers around a jagged outcropping.

Above me, Zinnia laughed. "You can't hold out for long. You'll tire soon enough."

I let out a yell for help. The result was a torrent of sand and pebbles kicked down on me by Zinnia. Grit entered my mouth and stung my eyes, and I lamented the loss of my hat. Instead, I ducked my head as another round of debris cascaded down.

"Goodbye, Emma. I'm going back now. Don't worry, I'll raise the alarm that you've fallen over the edge. I'll be ever so distraught. Except I might just take my time about getting back."

I didn't bother responding. Releasing my slippery hold on the weeds, I stretched my arm as far as I could above my head and wrapped my sweating fingers around the base of a sapling. I tugged to test it. It held. Lifting first one foot, finding a toehold, and then doing the same with the other, I inched toward the summit.

"Oh, no you don't." More sand and rocks rained down. They struck my head and shoulders, pinging like hailstones. I ducked my head, shut my eyes, and did my best to ignore their sting. In the next lull, I pulled myself higher, shimmying like a lizard along the cliff face. Soon I was but inches from the top. My entire body trembled, and the muscles in my arms screamed from the effort.

"Troublesome woman. I see I'll have to help you along."

She sat down on the edge, her legs dangling over. With the heel of her boot, she kicked at my hands, first one, then the other. My grip, slick with sweat, slipped from the crevice I'd found. I felt my body sliding, my strength waning. With a painful effort, I reached higher and, this time, managed to grip . . . something far too smooth to be a rock or plant life. I braved a glance upward and realized I had clutched Zinnia's booted ankle. At the same time, cries echoed from along the Cliff Walk, from the direction of Vinland. The footmen, the police—someone had arrived.

I was not about to plummet to my death with help so close within reach. With Zinnia distracted, I seized the opportunity to hoist myself higher—forgetting that the purchase I had found was Zinnia's ankle. As I scooted upward, she lost her balance, slid forward, and slipped over the side . . .

A harrowing scream echoed against the rocks and out over the waves. I grappled one-handedly for her even as I, too, slid downward. Within seconds she had fallen past me, somehow missing me but hitting the boulders jutting from the cliff face, bouncing from one to another, with none of them enough to break her fall. Somehow, I managed to cling to the rocks, shaking, tears streaming from my eyes, my forehead pressed painfully into the jagged surface.

And then hands wrapped themselves under my arms, and I felt myself being tugged upward. Slowly, painstakingly, someone above me—I dared not look—dragged me higher and higher until several pairs of hands gripped various parts of myself and my clothing and hauled me over the edge. Never in my life had I been so happy to lie facedown in the dirt.

The next minutes were a blur, until I found myself in Mrs. Twombly's drawing room, surrounded by her, Amity, Derrick, and Jesse. The latter had telephoned the Life Saving Service, who would be scouring the area in their boats to recover Zinnia's body. After examining the cliff where she fell, Jesse's partner had taken several officers to Gull Manor to pore over Zinnia's possessions for evidence of manchineel. I didn't think they'd find any. I believed Zinnia had used the last of her supply or disposed of it days ago. She would have been foolish not to, to leave any trace behind to link her to the attacks.

I sat on one of the sofas wrapped in a satin quilt, pillows at my back, a cup of strong tea laced with one of Mrs. Twombly's analgesic powders in hand. Derrick's arm spanned my shoulders, holding me close. Amity sat on a smaller love seat across from me. She had just given her statement to Jesse, who had taken down every word and now reread the pages he had recorded.

Zinnia's death—her final scream—and my near fall had left me shaken and nearly mute. I had certainly been incoherent in those first moments after being pried from the cliff face. The tea sent heartening warmth through me, and gradually I regained my equilibrium. My entire body stung and throbbed, but the powder dulled the worst of it. My fingertips had been scraped raw, my knees were bruised, and my forehead scratched. The toes of my leather boots had been shredded by the rocks, and my dress was ready for the rag heap.

But I was alive. As the silence in the room grew, I settled my gaze on Amity, who pointedly avoided it. "When did you know?" I asked her bluntly. It was the one question Jesse hadn't asked her yet. I half suspected he had left it for me, knowing I would want to confront my erstwhile guest.

Amity's head dipped between her shoulders. Her voice sounded muffled. "I didn't. I swear I didn't."

"Then when did you suspect, for I know you must have."

Beside me, Derrick tensed in what I could only identify as anger and outrage. But then, the rigidity of his limbs had yet to ease from that first embrace he'd wrapped me in when he had arrived, frantic, at Vinland.

"Emma," my relative said with a gasp, "leave the questions to the detective."

Amity lifted her face to me. She sat framed by the geometric Viking designs carved into the wide doorway behind her. The retribution of those warriors would have been swift and harsh. Did she fear the same now? Her gaze briefly slid to Jesse, then ventured back to me. "I knew she had changed, that she had become . . . angry. She denied it, but last winter she retreated into herself, shying away even from me, and I could do nothing to draw her out."

"George," I said, remembering the name Zinnia had uttered in response to my questions about the man she had sketched. Amity showed me a baffled frown. "He was a wildlife warden hired by Henry Flagler," I said, "charged with protecting native species, especially birds, from poachers."

She nodded. "Yes, I know about them. But why would Zinnia—"

"Because she was in love with him." All eyes turned to me now; Jesse stopped checking over his notes, and Derrick pulled slightly away to look down into my face. Even Mrs. Twombly waited anxiously, sliding practically to the edge of her seat. "They were in love, and he was murdered by poachers. And that created in Zinnia an intolerable bitterness toward the society women who sport feathers for fashion. You didn't know about the two of them?"

"No." The word scraped from her throat. "She was painting more last autumn and into the winter, walking out on the beach and along the dunes near our property. Or so she said."

"She was most likely meeting him." The pain in the older woman's eyes triggered in me a stab of pity. "I believe their intentions were honorable. I believe they wished to marry." At least, I believed this to be true in Zinnia's case. As for her beau, who knew?

"How could I not have known this?" Amity pressed trembling fingers to her lips. "Why had she not told me?"

Mrs. Twombly rose from her chair, resettled beside Amity, and took her hand. "Perhaps she meant to, but there hadn't been time. You know how young people are. They like their secrets when something is new—it makes it more special."

"But then he died," I reminded them, "and Zinnia . . ." I drew a deep breath.

"Was never the same," Amity finished for me. "I thought this trip would do her good, bring her out of whatever melancholy had gripped her."

"It appears she planned everything from the moment she learned she would be coming north," Derrick said. "She brought this substance from the manchineel trees with her."

"The sap. It's deadly." Amity shut her eyes tight. "How on earth had she extracted it with without burning herself?"

Derrick held up his hands. "Gloves, protective clothing, an apple press . . ."

"You haven't answered my question." I ignored another disapproving look from my relative. Amity Carter might be her childhood friend, but two women lay dead—no, three. Zinnia had lost her life as well. "When did you begin to suspect your niece might have been responsible for the poisonings?"

Mrs. Twombly gasped but said nothing. The fingers of Amity's free hand curled into a fist. "After Sybil Van Horn died. No, was murdered," she corrected herself, saying the word as though it physically hurt to utter it. "Zinnia went out that morning, right after you left for Vinland, Emma . . . but how was I to know . . . ?"

"Jennie Pierpont was accused of Sybil's murder," I said, the anger in my voice unmistakable. "You let her sit in that jail cell all this time."

Amity snatched her other hand free of Mrs. Twombly's and whisked both to her eyes. Her shoulders shook as sobs burst from her lips. "How could I have fostered such a monster?"

Jesse caught my gaze and shook his head, a gesture for me to pause in my questioning. I pursed my lips. I wanted answers, one of them being how far Amity had been willing to go to protect her niece. He waited until her weeping subsided, and then asked, "Were you aware of your niece owning a black veil?"

"Yes, she did. I thought she had packed one, but I never saw it once we arrived, so I thought I must have been mistaken. When the poisonings occurred, I remembered it. I searched for it and was relieved when I didn't find it."

"She kept it hidden," I said. Derrick's shoulder came up against mine again, warm and steadying, even through the quilt. Nevertheless, a chill shimmied through me, and I tightened the cloudlike satin around me.

"Yes, she must have hidden it," Amity replied. She sniffled and drew in a breath. "Along with the manchineel sap, which must have been among her painting chemicals. This is my fault, isn't it? If I had been more vigilant, more willing to see anything but the best in my niece. But how could I have known she would turn into a cold-blooded killer?" She appealed to each of us for an answer—one we couldn't supply. Except . . .

A smidgeon of compassion, buried deeply by the rocks and sand Zinnia had thrown on me, somehow made its way to the surface. "She didn't mean to kill. Not at first."

"What can you mean?" This came from Mrs. Twombly, who appeared genuinely taken aback that I would reach such a conclusion.

"Ada Norris didn't die from the petit fours she ate." I leaned forward eagerly as I explained the theory I had formed. "She tasted the manchineel soon enough that it made her spit out most of what she had in her mouth. The effects were painful but not deadly. I believe Zinnia intended just that. Only Lottie Robinson died, and it was because she put several in her mouth at once, not giving her enough time to realize the sweetness would turn to acid. Zinnia meant to punish, not kill."

"But Sybil," Amity whispered.

"Yes. Sybil realized about the manchineel. She and her mother had also been to Florida, and she must have let on to Zinnia that she had grown suspicious. That made Zinnia desperate." I leaned back, finding myself cradled against Derrick's side. For an instant, I thought I felt his lips in my hair, but the sensation was so fleeting I thought perhaps I'd imagined it, or merely wished for it.

He reached for my hand, enwrapping it with his own. "There is another matter, though it seems trivial now."

Jesse looked over at him. "What is that?"

"The property," I said. "It doesn't belong to you, Amity. Not outright."

This drew the astonished gazes of the others to Derrick and me.

"That can't be," Amity protested. "My uncle left it to me in his will."

Derrick leaned closer to me, making me feel as though we had formed a battalion of two. "You have a cousin," he said.

"Rodney?" Amity spoke the word like it was a ghost from her past. "But . . . he disappeared out west years ago. No one has heard from him in ever so long."

"Are you certain of that?" I challenged her. Did I believe her show of innocence, or was it just that—a sham?

"I'm quite certain. I've long assumed he died."

"Well, he's very much alive and was mentioned in your uncle's will. I'm surprised you didn't know this." Derrick crossed one leg over the other, smoothing a palm along the crease of his trousers. "You can't sell the property without his agreement. And yet you wished to hurry the transaction by arranging a transfer of funds to your bank in Florida."

"That's standard procedure," Mrs. Twombly said with a note of indignation. "You can't blame her for that. I'd have done the same thing."

"But it would have been much harder for us to retrieve our money should we have failed to finalize the sale," I said. I hadn't bothered to smooth the accusation from my voice.

"Please, you must believe me." Amity appealed to Jesse. "I understand why you no longer trust me, but I surely didn't mean to deceive anyone. I believed the property to be mine, free and clear."

"We'll be looking into it, ma'am," he replied and made a note in his book. "A lot will depend on our finding your cousin."

"But how will you do that? I have no idea where he might be." Amity sat back, a scowl crossing her face. "This must be Ezra's doing. My brother-in-law. He's been stalling in order to track Rodney down. Well, I won't believe he's alive until I see him with my own eyes."

"I have people working to track him down," Derrick told her, and I imagined he had just that morning entreated a young man or two at his family's newspaper, the *Providence Sun*, to see what they could find out. "It's likely he doesn't know about the inheritance. But as I said, it's now a trivial matter."

Yes, I silently agreed. The prospect of starting a new school hadn't lost its importance for me, but the details, and the convenience of locating it beside my own home, no longer seemed vital. Gull Manor would eventually become our school, and we would find a suitable property elsewhere, perhaps farther along Ocean Avenue. In the meantime, it was more important to help the women of Newport, those who had survived the attacks launched by Zinnia Lewis, to heal.

"What about Mrs. Van Horn?" I looked to Jesse, hoping he might have an answer by now. After today's events, I began to believe the woman had fallen prey to Zinnia's madness, and that her body lay somewhere on the island or would wash up along the shore.

Jesse shook his head. "Though we had a witness who believed she saw a woman matching Anna Rose Van Horn's description on the mainland, the trail has gone utterly cold."

"No, it hasn't."

At the sound of the familiar voice coming from the hall, we all turned and then sprang to our feet.

Anna Rose Van Horn, buttoned to the chin in a dove-gray traveling outfit more suitable to autumn weather, stood in the doorway. Though she had removed her hat and gloves, a short, fitted jacket covered all but the high collar of what should have been a crisp white shirtwaist. But everything about her looked rumpled and tousled. Wisps of hair had fallen from her coif to tease her sagging shoulders, while fatigue cradled her eyes in deep shadows.

"Mrs. Van Horn," I cried out. The coverlet had pooled on the floor at my feet, so great was my shock.

Derrick took a step forward. "How long . . ." He trailed off, as dumbfounded as I.

"Since this morning," she said, her voice carrying but a thready suggestion of its usual timbre. "Since I arrived at our boardinghouse to find everything locked up, the landlady apparently gone. A neighbor told me she'd needed to leave Newport. She didn't tell me why. So I came here."

"Do you know . . ." I began, but Mrs. Twombly took over for me.

"I told her. She's been upstairs ever since."

"Yes. My Sybil is gone." Mrs. Van Horn's voice broke. "My darling girl." She swayed, prompting Derrick and Jesse to hurry over to her. They flanked her sides, each cupping a hand to her elbow, and guided her to the sofa on which Derrick and I had been sitting. I grabbed up the quilt and draped it over her lap.

Mrs. Twombly swept to the liquor cart in the corner and quickly returned with a glass half full of sherry or brandy, I didn't know which. She helped Mrs. Van Horn take a sip. Then she sat beside her friend, just as she had with Amity.

"Let's all slow down and stay calm," she said in a voice that brooked no argument. A bulwark, Mrs. Twombly was, and few would dare to breach her defenses.

It was to her that Jesse addressed his question. "Did you know we have been looking for Mrs. Van Horn?"

"Yes, I knew," Mrs. Twombly replied, with a cavalier shrug of her shoulder. "And I told no one she was here, not even Amity and her niece when they arrived a couple of hours later. When Anna Rose learned her daughter's fate, her well-being took precedence over all else, including the needs of your investigation, Detective. It delayed matters a few hours. Surely no harm has been done. Especially since . . ." She stole a glance at Amity, still hovering on her feet.

"Since we know it was my niece doing these dreadful things." Amity gazed across at Mrs. Van Horn, her eyes beseeching, her breath coming in heaves. I sensed she wished to ask for forgiveness but hadn't yet found the courage.

"Zinnia?" Mrs. Van Horn's gaze traveled the room. "Where is she?"

Jesse crouched in front of her. "We'll get to that. First, where have you been, Mrs. Van Horn? We've been scouring the island and the mainland looking for you. Ever since . . ."

"Did you think I'd done it?" she asked in a whisper. "Murdered my own daughter?"

Jesse didn't vacillate. "We didn't know. But please, answer my question. Why did you seem to leave with such secrecy?"

She inhaled and blew out a long breath. "Because I didn't want anyone to know where I went. You see . . . I've taken a tutoring position. I teach French to the children of a family in Westerly."

"The French books!" I exclaimed. "That's why you took them."

She looked at me as if I'd gone daft. "Of course."

"I don't understand." Jesse searched her face. "Why the secrecy?"

"Because of who I am, how I grew up. Women of my social circle do not work, Detective. We desperately needed the money, but have you any inkling what it would have done to Sybil's reputation, to her marriage prospects?" The indignation faded; her face crumpled, and tears spilled over. Against Mrs. Twombly's shoulder came the heartbreaking words, "Not that any of that matters now. Nothing matters anymore."

A week later, I came out of my bedroom in the morning to find my newest houseguests already up and heading downstairs for breakfast. "How did you both sleep?"

"Well, thank you, Mrs. Andrews." The pallor of Anna Rose Van Horn's complexion, especially against the black of her mourning gown, belied that claim, but one couldn't expect her to recover from her daughter's death so quickly. I had noticed less of a tremor in her hands yesterday, which gave me hope that she might soon regain her strength and her determination to persevere.

"I'm glad. And please, call me Emma," I turned my attention to the younger woman beside her. "And you, Jennie?"

"Good gracious, I'm positively in heaven after sleeping in that jail cell all those days—or not sleeping, I should say." Jennie Pierpont had been released later the very same day the truth had come out. She had immediately resumed her Audubon fundraising activities, pooh-poohing any suggestion that she should spend time at her parents' home to recuperate. "Rest is not for the unwavering, and I am certain of that when it comes to the Audubon Society's vital work," she had stubbornly declared.

I understood. After my near death at Zinnia's hands, everyone within earshot had urged me to spend the next days and even weeks off my feet, quietly relaxing and regaining my full health. Yes, I had felt drained afterward, but Derrick and I had a newspaper to run. There were stories to be written and edited, and I used column space to help Jennie's cause as well. I also resumed planning for our eventual school. So far, this Rodney Briarton, Amity's cousin, had not been found, but I held out hope of acquiring Amity's property. She had left Newport. After Zinnia's broken body had been found floating half a mile south of where she had fallen, Amity had found it too painful to remain. But she had gone only as far as Providence as we waited for news of her cousin.

Despite Jennie's insistence that she needed no cosseting, she had accepted Derrick's and my offer to stay with us at Gull Manor for a time. I had no doubt that Nanny's cooking would restore the bloom on both women's faces.

"Shall we?" I gestured for them to precede me down the stairs, and we made our way to the morning room.

Breakfast had been laid out on the sideboard, the usual fare of eggs, sausages, potatoes, cooked apples, and toast. I noticed one plate had already been filled—nearly to brimming—and set on the table at the very place where I usually sat. I stared down at it in puzzlement. Nanny had never chosen my breakfast for me before. Did I say *chosen*? No, she had simply piled on helpings of everything. Beside the plate sat a glass of milk.

"Nanny," I called into the kitchen. "What is all this?"

She came shuffling in, coffeepot in hand. As she set it on the table, she said quite matter-of-factly, "That's for you."

"Yes, I gathered that. Why?"

"Because you'll need it."

"Emma will need what?" Derrick sauntered in, smelling of ocean air. He'd apparently already been outside.

"A hearty breakfast." Nanny grinned at him.

Derrick and I traded sideways glances. I said, "I never eat this much in the morning."

"You will from now on." She patted my cheek. "The baby will need it."

"What?" Derrick and I exclaimed as one. Then I continued more sedately, "Nanny, don't be such a goose. Even if I were expecting, this would be far too soon for any of us to know. And don't you think I might have noticed something?"

"You've been tired, pale, and queasy. Why else do you think I've been after you to rest more and wear a shawl to keep the chill off your shoulders?" Her eyes glittered with both tears and glee. One grizzled eyebrow arced above the other. Though her next words issued a challenge, her voice plunged to a murmur, one no doubt heard by everyone in the room. "And when, exactly, did your last courses come?"

Having this conversation in front of a rapt audience brought a rush of heat to my cheeks, but I remained steadfast. I counted off the weeks on my fingers. "When they should have. About a month ago."

"Are you sure?" Her half-moon spectacles flashed as they caught the sunlight from the window.

Beside me, Derrick let go a gusty sigh. He looked as though someone had knocked the wind out of him. "A month ago, Emma, we were embroiled in chasing down another killer. And now that I consider it, I don't think you . . . that is . . ." He shook his head. "I don't remember you having . . ."

"Oh, my goodness." I pressed my fingertips to my lips as the room around me swayed slightly. I thought of Grace and how, with each of her two pregnancies, she had lost her energy and her fondness for certain foods, even some of her favorites. And I recalled that time a month ago, when, as Derrick had said, we had been consumed with finding a murderer, with little thought for anything else. As attuned as we had been to clues and motives and opportunity, when it came to myself, I had been utterly blind. "Now who's the goose?" I whispered.

"Unless I've lost my powers of deduction," Nanny declared with a self-satisfied expression, "I'd say you're nearly two months gone with child."

Jennie and Anna Rose cried out their congratulations, but I barely heard them as I was swept up in Derrick's arms, right off my feet. He spun me around, once, twice, hugged me until I couldn't breathe, and then set me down. In the next instant feminine arms engulfed me—Nanny's, Jennie's, Anna Rose's, and Katie's, who had come running in from the kitchen, Patch trotting in behind her to see what all the fuss was about. I felt their embraces, heard their joyous voices and Patch's curious yips, but I saw only Derrick, standing a few feet away, his gaze locked on mine, his dark eyes brimming with love and excitement and tears. Although the panic of ensuing motherhood would sneak up on me later, at that moment I felt only a great sense of joy and a certainty that whatever came, with these people—my family—I would always prevail.

Author's Note

Catharine Lorillard Wolfe was an heiress who inherited a fortune made in real estate development from her father, and tobacco money from her mother. Her siblings predeceased her at young ages, leaving her sole heir, and she never married. Wolfe owned properties in New York and in Newport. Her original Newport house overlooked Touro Park, where, in the summer months, Wolfe's view included Newport Tower, or the Old Stone Mill, as it's often called, reputed by some to have been built by the Rhode Island's first governor, Benedict Arnold (not the Revolutionary War traitor) or by Vikings who supposedly came to Aquidneck Island a millennium earlier. Wolfe apparently subscribed to the latter theory and was so inspired by Newport's "Viking heritage" that when she had her "cottage" built by Peabody and Sterns out on Ochre Point in 1882, she had Norse-inspired elements incorporated into the design. She didn't have long to enjoy the house, however; she died in 1887.

In 1896, Vinland was purchased by Hamilton and Florence Twombly, of New York and New Jersey. His fortune was made in railroads, and she was the sister of Cornelius Vanderbilt II. Beginning in 1907, the Twomblys began a renovation that included expanding the property. Rather than simply adding on, they had the two main wings of the house pulled apart and added a ballroom in the space that opened up. Unlike the Twomblys' erstwhile sister-in-law, Alva Vanderbilt Belmont, Florence Twombly abhorred publicity and conspicuous ostentation, her lifestyle being more in keeping with the older, blue-blooded Knickerbocker families, such as the Astors. She and Hamilton owned an extensive farm in New Jersey called Florham (a combination of their first names), where everything they needed to stock their various properties, from meat and produce to delicacies to flowers and more, were grown and produced. In 1955, the Twombly's daughter, Florence, donated the estate to Salve Regina University. Known now as McAuley Hall, it is not open to the public.

The Audubon Society was established in 1886 by George Bird Grinnell. By the late 1890s and early 1900s, Audubon Societies were being established on a state-to-state basis. Harriet Hemenway founded the Massachusetts Society in 1896. The Florida Audubon Society was established in 1900. I did take literary license with the founding of the Rhode Island Audubon Society, which came into being in 1897 and became active in 1900. The character of Jennie Pierpont is entirely fictional. Edith Roosevelt, wife of Teddy Roosevelt, was the Second Lady of the United States at the time of the story and would become, only a month later, First Lady following the assassination of President William McKinley. Her involvement in any Audubon Society is my own invention, based on her husband's dedication to conserving natural resources and establishing laws that protected wilderness and wildlife.

I took license again with the use of manchineel. While it is possible to extract the poison from various parts of the tree, and a small amount is enough to cause serious burns and/or kill, using it on correspondence, as I portray in the story, would probably affect its potency.

Trinity Church, the favored house of worship among the Four Hundred summering in Newport, stands on Spring Street between Mill and Church Streets, and overlooks beautiful Queen Anne's Square, a park bordered by picturesque eighteenth-century homes. The Square, however, did not exist until the 1970s, when the Newport Restoration Society, headed by Doris Duke, took on the project to redesign the space. Until then, a crowded hodgepodge of stores and businesses surrounded the church and mostly obscured it from view from Thames Street and the harbor. This is how it would have been in 1901 as well. Carr Rice House, which is currently used as Trinity Church's vestry, was another 1970s addition. I assigned a fictional structure to act as the vestry in the story.

The natural areas mentioned in the story—Hanging Rock, which is now part of the Norman Bird Sanctuary (established in 1949), and Sachuest Point—are both located in Middletown near Sachuest (Second) Beach. These unspoiled examples of New England coastline offer educational activities, hiking trails, and panoramic views without the crowds.